The Zigzag Effect

WITHDRAWN

Lili
WILKINSON

ALLEN&UNWIN
SYDNEY · MELBOURNE · AUCKLAND · LONDON

First published in 2013

Allen & Unwin
83 Alexander Street
Crows Nest NSW 2065
Australia
Phone: (61 2) 8425 0100
Email: info@allenandunwin.com
Web: www.allenandunwin.com

A Cataloguing-in-Publication entry is available from
the National Library of Australia – www.trove.nla.gov.au

ISBN 978 1 74331 303 9

Cover design by Kirby Armstrong
Cover photos by Shutterstock: aragami1 (girl with rabbit), italianestro (hand), PashOK (roses), Phase4Photography (marquee lights), dencg (curtain)
Text design by Lisa White and Kirby Armstrong
Set in 12/18 Adobe Garamond
Printed in Australia by McPherson's Printing Group

10 9 8 7 6 5 4 3 2 1

MIX
Paper from
responsible sources
FSC® C001695

The paper in this book is FSC® certified.
FSC® promotes environmentally responsible,
socially beneficial and economically viable
management of the world's forests.

For my peeps

1. Production: in which something appears, seemingly from thin air.

'Before you go,' boomed the magician, 'I want to show you something a little different. A little … dangerous.'

Sage felt Zacky lean forward slightly in his seat.

The magician raised his hand in a dramatic gesture, and his assistant swept onstage, graceful despite her towering strappy heels. The gold sequins on her bodice glittered under the theatre lights. Perfect teeth were revealed in a smile that didn't quite reach her eyes. Sage wondered how she came to be a magician's assistant.

A young man in black wheeled a tall, narrow wooden cabinet onto the stage, then melted back into the wings. The cabinet looked like polished mahogany. Sage realised it was about the same size as a coffin, and felt the skin on the back of her neck prickle.

The magician opened the door of the cabinet, revealing a wooden chair tucked inside. The assistant stepped in and sat down, and the magician closed the door behind her. The stagehand came back on, dragging a heavy trunk, which the magician opened, producing a long, glinting sword. He threw a red silk scarf into the air and swept the sword through it, slicing the cloth in half to prove how sharp the blade was. The two silk halves fluttered to the ground and rested there like pools of blood.

Zacky leaned over and whispered hotly in Sage's ear, 'Don't worry, he isn't a real wizard. They're just tricks.'

Sage nodded. 'Thanks for letting me know,' she whispered back.

Her little brother was obsessed with magic and wizards. When Dad had produced two tickets to *Spellbinding Sorcery with The Great Armand*, he'd galloped around the kitchen like a wild creature, jumping and twisting in the air. Sage had laughed, then noticed the expression on her mother's face.

'Can we really afford this?' Mum had murmured to Dad.

'A client gave them to me,' he'd said with a reassuring smile.

Zacky had stopped galloping for a moment, his eyes still wide with excitement. 'Do you think the magician will have a magic wand?' he'd asked breathlessly. 'Will he have a pointy hat and a cape? Will he know *expelliarmus*? Will he have a pet owl or a toad or a cat? Do you think he can teach me magic?'

Sage hoped Zacky wasn't disappointed by The Great Armand. He was no Dumbledore, after all. He looked exactly as Sage had expected he would: black tails and top hat, a pointed beard and curling moustache. His accent sounded vaguely European. He was the epitome of 'magician': mysterious, arrogant and just a little camp. His dark eyes glittered as he ran through the standard collection of magic tricks: producing a sleepy rabbit from a hat and silk scarves from his assistant's mouth, guessing which card an audience member had chosen from a shuffled deck. It all seemed a bit...tacky. Sage had seen this kind of performance before on TV, and she knew it wasn't really magic. She didn't know exactly *how* each trick was achieved, but she did know that that's all they were, tricks. She decided she'd rather be back at home playing magicians with Zacky. His imagination could produce things far more impressive than rabbits out of top hats.

On the other hand, the theatre had excellent heating.

The Great Armand plunged the first sword into the side of the cabinet. Zacky drew a sharp breath, and there were murmurs from the audience as Armand proceeded to insert sword after sword into the cabinet, from the front, the back, and at different angles, so the swords presumably crossed over each other inside. There was no way the assistant could have ducked around them.

Although Sage knew it was a trick, and that the girl had probably already escaped from the box through a false panel, she still felt slightly squeamish. Images of swords slicing into the assistant's bare arms, legs and stomach kept appearing in her mind. She imagined the assistant crouched in the box, in the dark, wooden sides pressing up against her, and the swords pushing deep into her flesh. She shuddered.

Sage's family had moved to Melbourne a fortnight ago. The house was still full of unpacked boxes and screwed-up newspaper used to wrap plates and glasses. Sage's dad was at his new job in the city most of the time, and he came home brimming with excitement and stories. He'd promised Sage he'd take her into town so she could photograph the old laneways, and explore the galleries, but when the weekend came around, he and Sage's mum spent it talking in quiet, angry voices and looking worriedly at spreadsheets full of numbers. There was no more Saturday-night Japanese takeaway, and although Sage's mum hadn't said anything, she'd switched to buying no-name-brand groceries: coffee that tasted like dirt and biscuits that didn't taste like much at all. Whenever Mum spoke to Sage or Zacky, she wore this tight, making-the-most-of-it smile, a smile that fell off whenever she looked at the unpacked boxes, and when she spent hours clicking around employment websites. Sage tried to help with housework and unpacking, but more often than not she found herself slinking off to her room and tinkering with filters in Photoshop, dreaming about the photography course with Yoshi Lear that her parents had promised she could attend.

Of course, Zacky was blissfully unaware of any tension in the family. He loved the draughty old terrace house that was their new home. He loved the weird gargoyles carved into the banister, the overgrown, tangled backyard, and the secret attic, accessed by a pull-down ladder. Zacky thought it was a house of magic. Sage tried to match Zacky's enthusiasm – the house *was* beautiful and old in a crumbly, worn sort of way. She'd taken some great photos. But despite endless games of make-believe and hide-and-seek, Sage couldn't help seeing the house through her mum's eyes: a house of rising damp, rusted pipes and peeling wallpaper.

And the cold. Back home in Queensland, Sage had owned barely any clothes with sleeves. She was used to warm days and balmy evenings. But Melbourne was *freezing*. The house had no heating, just ancient cast-iron fireplaces and chimneys full of birds' nests. The cold seeped into everything, and the woolliest of socks couldn't keep Sage warm. The only time she wasn't cold was when she was in the shower, but as soon as she stepped onto the icy tiles on the bathroom floor, the heat from the water was sucked out of her. Her shoulder muscles ached from hunching over, and even though she slept in pyjamas, socks, a heavy knitted cardigan and *two* doonas, Sage's dreams were filled with bitter winds and bleak, swirling fog.

Then there was the calendar. Sage's friends from her old school had given it to her for Christmas, marking in their birthdays in sparkly glitter-pen. Each month featured photos of them together – at the pool, on Year Nine camp, in pyjamas at a sleepover. July was a picture of them all together at the beach: Nina and Eleanor wearing giant floppy hats, and Parama buried under the sand, with only her head poking out. Sage had taken the photo, of course. It used to make her smile, but now she couldn't even see it. All she could see was the giant red circle around July 16. The first day at her new school. The family had arrived in Melbourne three weeks before school holidays started, and it had been decided that it would be less disruptive if Sage and Zacky waited to start school at the beginning of third term.

It felt like the giant red circle was around Sage's neck, squeezing. Who moved schools halfway through Year Ten? Everyone would already have established friendship groups. How would Sage ever fit in? She'd always be the New Kid, all the way to the end of Year Twelve.

The Great Armand pushed the last sword straight through

the front of the cabinet to where the assistant's head had been. He paused dramatically, then threw the door of the cabinet wide open. To Sage's relief, the assistant was gone, the swords criss-crossing each other in the dark, empty space.

'Of course I would never let the lovely Bianca come to harm,' said Armand grandly. 'I have whisked her away to safety – to somewhere where she can't be hurt.'

He stood back and raised his arms. A blue stage light came on, illuminating the dark space above the cabinet to reveal the assistant, still sitting on the wooden chair, floating about a metre above the cabinet. As the audience gasped and whispered to one another, Armand waved his wand, and the assistant vanished in a shower of what looked like rose petals. The chair fell to the stage as if the strings holding it had been cut. The dull wooden *thunk* made Sage start.

Armand pulled the swords from the cabinet, one by one, and finally opened the cabinet door to reveal the smiling assistant, the white rabbit cradled in her arms. The Great Armand took a bow.

Sage looked around. Everyone was applauding wildly. She clapped too, because that was what you were supposed to do, but she didn't really feel impressed. She could see the assistant right there, without a scratch on her. It had just been a trick. But it had felt ... icky.

Armand and his assistant left the stage, and the house

lights came up. Sage felt oddly relieved to see the theatre's worn carpet, peeling plaster and threadbare red velvet curtains. Zacky was frowning as they shuffled up the aisle. 'Are you okay?' asked Sage, still feeling uneasy. 'I thought you were enjoying the show.'

'Oh, I liked it,' said Zacky. 'He was very clever, doing all those tricks. But I think...' He shook his head, letting his shaggy brown hair fall into his eyes. 'I think maybe that last trick – not the thing with the box and the swords, but that very last bit where he made her float above the stage and then disappear? I think that was *real* magic.'

Sage took his hand. 'I think so too,' she said, pushing images of dark boxes and swords from her mind.

They stepped out onto the street, and Sage paused to look up at the theatre's façade. It had definitely seen better days. The theatre was on the threshold of the city, in a shabby, forgotten area consisting largely of industrial buildings and boarded-up shopfronts. The parade of flashing lights on the theatre's awning only had about six working globes left – someone had installed a few energy-efficient fluorescent bulbs which refused to flash on and off, and just glowed with a cold, bluish stubbornness. Sage shivered and tugged Zacky down the street, hunching against the cold.

They got as far as the bus stop before Zacky realised he'd left his wand in the theatre.

'It was poking into my tummy,' he said. 'So I put it on the floor.'

The bus pulled up with a hiss of hydraulic brakes. Sage pulled her phone out of her bag to check the time. It was Sunday, so there probably wouldn't be another bus for an hour. She took a deep breath. There was no point in yelling at him. 'Okay,' she said. 'Let's go back.'

The theatre foyer was totally empty when they returned, but the doors to the auditorium weren't locked. Sage could hear voices coming from inside. 'Wait here,' she said to Zacky. 'I'll be right back.'

She slipped into the theatre. Two people were searching the seats and floor for rubbish, which they were angrily stuffing into garbage bags as they yelled at each other. The girl was tall and thin, with her blonde hair hanging in loose curls past her shoulders. She wore a long cotton dress with a paisley print, and several strings of beads and jewels that clinked as she moved. The guy looked younger, maybe a year or two older than Sage. He had slightly-too-long dark hair that curled around his ears, and wore black jeans, a black T-shirt and a brown tweed blazer that looked like it had come from an op shop. His brows were angled down in a scowl over brown eyes. He was in the middle of delivering a patronising lecture to the girl.

'All I'm saying is that if you clomp around backstage, it

makes it very hard for the audience to believe that you're still in the sword cabinet.'

'I'm not *clomping*,' the girl said, her voice cold. 'The floorboards squeak. It's a crappy old theatre, and it's hard to tiptoe around in six-inch stilettos. If you want the chair reset with ninja stealth, then I suggest you do it.'

The guy shoved an empty popcorn bucket into his bag with vicious force. 'You know I can't. I have to be at the back of the auditorium, ready to open the doors and let all the nice people go home. That's why we need to hire someone to help.'

The girl's lips tightened. 'There's barely any money coming in anyway,' she said. 'We don't need to waste what little there is on unnecessary new staff.'

'Armand said we could hire someone to usher and do the bookings. Unless *you* want to volunteer for those jobs?'

The girl's expression grew even more frosty. 'You think I don't already have enough to do? I work harder than you *and* Armand!'

'You work hard *onstage*,' said the guy. 'After the show you slack off.'

'I do not slack off!'

'I'm just saying, there's a lot of cleaning up after each show, and you disappear off to your dressing-room every time.'

The tall girl tossed her head and the blonde curls bounced

around her shoulders. 'Would you rather I came out here in my glittery leotard?' she asked, then looked disgusted. 'No, wait. Don't answer that.'

Sage realised that the blonde girl was The Great Armand's beautiful assistant. She looked different in her floaty dress and loose hair, with no makeup on. Even more beautiful, because now it was effortless instead of spangled glamour. Sage looked again at the guy, and recognised him as the stagehand who'd wheeled the box onstage for the final illusion.

'Excuse me?' Sage raised her voice to be heard across the theatre.

The two theatre employees turned to look at her. Sage explained about Zacky's magic wand, and after a few minutes of hunting, it was produced.

'Thanks,' she said. 'And, um … we have squeaky floorboards in our new house. I mean, our old house. It's new to us, but it's ancient. If you sprinkle talcum powder on them and then walk over it to get it into the cracks, it lubricates the boards and they don't squeak anymore.'

'Thank you,' said the guy, and elbowed the blonde girl in the ribs.

'Ow!' she said. 'What was that for?'

'We should ask *her*,' said the guy in a whisper that Sage could hear perfectly well.

'Ask her what?'

The guy rolled his eyes and jerked his head towards Sage. 'About the *thing*.'

The girl glanced at Sage, confused. Then her forehead crinkled in a frown. 'Are you crazy?' she whispered back. 'We don't even know her.'

'So? She's smart and she knows about floorboards. I bet she knows about computers too.'

'I know a bit,' said Sage, trying to be modest.

The pair started and looked guiltily over at her, as if they hadn't realised she'd been able to hear their whole conversation.

'I just don't think we should rush into anything,' hissed the girl.

The guy adopted a long-suffering expression. 'Maybe she was *sent* here,' he said, with heavy irony. 'Maybe it's *fate*.'

The girl's frown faltered, and she looked unsure. 'I–I don't know,' she said.

The guy groaned. 'Do you believe in fate?' he asked, turning to Sage.

Sage blinked. She had no idea how to answer that question. Did she? It was a nice idea, that everything happened for a reason. It meant that maybe moving to Melbourne wouldn't be the worst thing that had ever happened to her. Maybe her workshop with Yoshi Lear would transform her into an award-winning photographer.

The guy was still staring at her, awaiting an answer. Somehow, Sage wanted him to like her.

'No,' she said, surprised at how certain she sounded. 'I believe we each make our own fate.'

'Great,' said the guy, looking oddly relieved. 'Do you want a job?'

The blonde girl whipped her head around to him, her expression outraged.

Sage blinked. 'I'm sorry?'

'A job. Helping set up and clean up and sell tickets and stuff. It's not very interesting, but you'd get paid. Just think about it, okay? We're here for about a month.' The guy smiled at her, a wide, unexpected, goofy smile that made his rather aloof expression collapse into something slightly adorable.

The girl kicked him in the shin. 'You didn't think we should *discuss* this first?' she said between clenched teeth.

The guy ignored her.

'Um,' said Sage, not sure how to reply. 'Thanks. I'll think about it. Er. Thanks for ...' She waved Zacky's wand around vaguely. 'Bye.'

A little dazed, she returned to the foyer and handed the wand to Zacky, who was sitting in a red velvet armchair.

'Can I keep this?' He thrust a flyer advertising THE GREAT ARMAND at her.

'Sure,' said Sage, still feeling odd. 'Let's get out of here.'

Zacky was still chattering away about the magic show when they walked in the front door. He didn't notice Mum's tight-lipped smile, or the way she looked down at her hands when she said that Dad was going to be working late again. He told Mum all about Armand and his beautiful assistant as they ate their spaghetti bolognese, while Sage noticed that there was no garlic bread, and that the salad had boring iceberg lettuce instead of the fancy gourmet stuff, and that Mum was drinking water instead of her usual glass of red wine.

As soon as Zacky had finished, he galloped upstairs to rid his bedroom of evil trolls. Sage started to stack the plates. The house didn't have a dishwasher, so she and Mum were taking it in turns to do the dishes. Sage hated the clammy, damp feeling of the rubber gloves, and the way the detergent made her sneeze.

'Darling,' said Mum. 'Can you sit down for a moment?'

This had to be serious. Mum wasn't even pretending not to look upset anymore. Sage sat.

Her mother explained to her that money was tight, that the move had cost them more than they'd budgeted for, and that it was taking her longer than she'd expected to find a job. Sage tried to feel grown-up and pleased that her mum was confiding in her, but mostly she just wished that she could be happy and oblivious, like Zacky. In Zacky's world, problems could be solved with a wave of a magic wand, and treasure was buried around every corner. Sage missed thinking like that.

'It's all just temporary,' said Mum. 'As soon as I get some work and your father's back-pay comes through, everything will be fine. We can get this place fixed up a bit' – she glanced at the dark splotches on the ceiling, where water damage had ruined the plaster – 'and everything will be fine. I'm sure we'll love living here.'

Sage nodded. She wasn't so sure. She missed her friends. She didn't want to start at a new school.

'But, honey.' Mum put her hand on Sage's knee. 'Just for now, for the next couple of months, I'm afraid we can't afford your photography classes.'

It had been part of the pitch her parents had concocted to convince Sage that moving to Melbourne would be the best thing that had ever happened to them. Dad had found an art college in the city that ran evening photography classes. It had a brand-new, state-of-the-art developing studio, and the next course was being taught by one of Sage's photography heroes: Yoshi Lear, whose work hung in galleries all over the world. Sage had sent in her folio and, to her surprise and delight, she had been accepted into the course. Dad had promised her a new camera as a thankyou for helping out with Zacky during the move. Sage had already picked out the one she wanted, the same manual SLR that Yoshi Lear used. She'd never used film before – she'd always had a digital camera – but Yoshi Lear was a photography purist, and Sage was looking forward to learning how to process and develop her own film. She had spent long evenings reading online reviews of the camera, and poring over her Yoshi Lear photography books, looking at the way he used light and shadow.

It had given her something to do other than mope around after Daniel had dumped her. It was the one thing she'd been looking forward to, the one thing that made the red circle on her calendar a teeny bit less terrifying. Even if school was terrible, even if she didn't make a single friend, at least she'd still have her classes with Yoshi Lear.

Not anymore.

'I'm sorry, darling,' said Mum. 'I know you were looking forward to it. But I promise by September everything'll be fine, and you can go then.'

Sage nodded and tried to look brave. She knew full well that Yoshi Lear's ten-week course would be over by then. She told her mother that it was okay, that she didn't mind, and then carried the dirty dishes into the kitchen and cried silently into the soapy water.

2. Palm: in which an object is concealed in the hand.

The house was unusually quiet when Sage woke up the next morning, just after nine. Usually Zacky bounded into her room at around seven-thirty, hollering at her to get up and play with him, but today everything was silent. She pulled on an extra pair of socks and a scarf, and went down to make herself some toast. Still quiet. It felt slightly eerie, as if some kind of apocalypse had happened and taken everyone away. She got quite a fright when her mum came into the kitchen to put on the kettle.

'Where's Zacky?' Sage asked.

'At some exhibition on computer games,' said Mum with a broad smile. 'The family next door just got back from a big overseas trip. They have a little boy – Roman – who is exactly Zacky's age! I took Zacky over to say hi, and they got on like a house on fire. Roman's mum looked pretty pleased about it too – he looks like a handful. She's taken them into the city for the day.'

'Oh,' said Sage, feeling oddly jealous. Why couldn't next door have a teenage girl as well? Or ... even a teenage boy would be all right. If he was the *right* teenage boy. Sage sighed and remembered the stagehand guy's goofy smile.

'I thought you'd be pleased to have him out from under your feet,' said Mum. 'You've been so good with him with the move and everything, and I'm very grateful, but you need to have a life too. You should do something with the rest of your holidays. I'm sorry you can't do your photography course, but I'm sure there are plenty of free classes you could take. You could try the local community centre, or the State Library.'

'Sure,' said Sage, feeling the squeeze of the red texta circle around her neck.

'I can drop you in the city if you like,' said Mum. 'I have a job interview at eleven.'

'No thanks,' said Sage. 'I can take the train.'

With Mum gone, the house was even more creepy. It was grey and windy outside, and a tree branch scrabbled at the living-room windowpane. Sage mooched from room to room, peering into unopened boxes full of books and knick-knacks. She considered unpacking a few, but it just felt like too much effort. She sat down at her computer and opened Photoshop, but didn't have the energy to process any of the shots she'd taken over the last few weeks. The gloomy, moody photos she'd taken around the house just reminded her of how gloomy and moody everything had felt since they'd left Queensland.

She wandered into Zacky's room. It was its usual explosion of toys and books and dirty socks, just as it had been at home. How come little kids adjusted so quickly? Sage noticed the flyer for *THE GREAT ARMAND* wonkily blu-tacked to the wall, next to a Harry Potter poster and a self-drawn portrait of Zacky riding a broomstick. She remembered what the guy at the theatre had said. He had asked if she wanted a job. Jobs paid money. With money, she could afford to take Yoshi Lear's photography class. She might not get the manual film camera she wanted, but she still had her digital one. That would do, wouldn't it? Or maybe there was one she could borrow at the art college. Then she could learn to develop the photos herself at the college's studio, soak each print in chemicals and then hang it from a clothesline and watch the picture appear. She'd always wanted to do that. Film was vintage and romantic, like vinyl records and rotary dial telephones.

But did she want a job? Really? Did she want to spend the last three weeks before school started selling tickets and scooping up spilled popcorn? Back in her own room, she pulled open her bedside drawer and yanked out a stack of photos. She'd taken them last year, during the winter holidays. She'd spent nearly every day hanging around the Strand with her friends, laughing and soaking up sunshine. In one, Nina was swinging around a lamppost. Another featured Eleanor and Parama arm-wrestling at a beachfront café.

Sage lingered over the next photo. It was Daniel, standing on the jetty at sunset, looking out to sea. The orange and purple rays reflected off the water, making it look like Daniel was surrounded by coloured flames. That evening, he'd fastened a silver chain around her neck with a tiny silver camera charm hanging from it, and told her that he loved her.

Sage scowled at the photo, and considered ripping it in half, but the composition, light and colour was so good that she couldn't bear to. Instead she shoved the stack of photos back into her drawer and slammed it shut.

Sage texted Nina to see if she could IM, but got no reply. She tried to read a book, but the red circle around July 16 seemed to be throbbing on the calendar page. Last summer's Sage laughed at her from the photo. There were twenty-one days between her and that red texta circle. Twenty-one long, lonely, pointless days.

Before she could change her mind, Sage marched back into Zacky's room and snatched the flyer from the wall.

Surely working for a magician had to be better than reality.

∿∿∿

There were no performances on Mondays or Tuesdays, but Armand's blonde assistant and the stagehand were in the auditorium. The assistant sat on the edge of the stage, her legs swinging. She looked effortlessly beautiful in a long purple skirt and white peasant top. The stagehand sprawled across two chairs in the third row, a notebook in his lap. He seemed to be wearing the exact same black T-shirt and tweed blazer as the previous day.

'So what if we just swap it around?' the assistant was saying. 'I can ditch the old card and load the fake at the same time.'

'No, you can't,' said the guy, scribbling in his notepad. 'Not with the same hand.'

'I can!'

'Bianca,' said the guy with an exasperated sigh. 'You're an excellent assistant, but it's impossible to ditch and load with one hand in this trick, because of the Swami gimmick. Even Armand can't do it, and he's wearing a specially tailored suit. You're wearing a leotard – where exactly do you plan to store the cards? Now let's try to focus on a *practical* solution.'

The assistant noticed Sage and frowned. She eyed the

stagehand and jerked her head towards Sage. The guy turned, and his face broadened in a wide grin.

'You came back!' he said. 'Excellent, excellent.'

He sprang to his feet and made his way directly across the auditorium to Sage, climbing over seats instead of coming up the aisle. 'Welcome,' he said, grasping her hand. 'We really need some help around here. We do six shows a week – evenings Wednesday, Thursday, Friday, two shows on Saturday, and matinee only on Sunday – plus we'll pay you an extra two hours per day for administrative stuff. There's a small amount of filing and handling of invoices, that sort of thing. Nothing to worry about. There's some paperwork in the office to get you started.'

He spoke in a rush, still beaming, his hand still holding hers. Sage felt amused, overwhelmed and a little squirmy, all at the same time. This guy was strange. Cute, but strange.

The blonde girl slid off the stage and walked up the aisle, so graceful that Sage wondered if her feet ever touched the carpet at all.

'I'm Bianca,' she said, once she reached Sage. Up close, her beauty was all the more overwhelming, because Sage could see that it wasn't achieved with lighting or makeup. Bianca's skin was flawless, her features perfectly proportioned. But there was something else, an unexpected sadness in Bianca's eyes that made her look fragile and delicate.

Shyly, Sage introduced herself, and Bianca's sad eyes suddenly crinkled with a genuine smile.

'Your name is *Sage*?' she said.

Sage nodded. Was her name really that weird? The guy closed his eyes in what looked like anticipated pain.

Bianca let out a tinkle of laughter. 'This will be fun.'

Sage frowned. 'What's so funny about my name?'

Bianca pointed at her. 'Sage,' she said, and then pointed at the guy. 'Herb.'

The guy sighed. 'Thanks,' he said to Bianca with a sarcastic tilt of his head.

'Your name is Herb?' asked Sage.

'It was my grandfather's name,' said Herb, rolling his eyes. 'Herbert Jackson. It's a dumb name. I'd go with Bert, except I don't want everyone to always be asking me about my bottle-cap collection.'

'I think it's cool,' said Sage. 'Retro.'

Bianca poked him in the ribs. 'I hope you'll call your firstborn *Garnish.*'

The guy blushed bright red, and shot a resentful look at Bianca.

'Well,' said Bianca to Sage. 'Welcome to the Lyric Theatre. I hope there'll be enough for you to do.' This comment appeared to be directed towards Herb. Sage shifted uncomfortably – Bianca clearly didn't think she was necessary.

'There'll be *plenty* for her to do,' said Herb.

Bianca shrugged, and started to glide back down the aisle towards the stage. 'Oh,' she said vaguely over her shoulder. 'Don't worry if you hear weird noises in here. The theatre's haunted.'

Sage blinked, and Bianca disappeared backstage.

Herb let out a heartfelt sigh. 'Did I mention?' he said to Sage. 'Bianca believes in ghosts. And auras. And horoscopes. And the Easter Bunny, for all I know. It's very annoying.'

Sage shivered and looked around. Did *she* believe in ghosts? And if there *was* a ghost in the Lyric Theatre, how awesome would it be to get a photo of it?

᭜᭜᭜

Herb showed Sage around backstage. Behind the wings was a short corridor leading to three cramped rooms: Bianca's and Armand's dressing-rooms, and a third room which Sage would share with Herb as an office. There was also a store-room at the end of the corridor, and a stage door to the alley that ran alongside the theatre.

The office contained a rusty filing cabinet and two desks. One desk was littered with screwed-up pieces of paper, magazines with names like *Genii* and *Magicseen*, and a plaster bust of Harry Houdini. Most of the other desk was taken up by an ancient computer that Sage suspected might be older than her, and an in-tray overflowing with what looked like overdue invoices, magazines and unopened mail.

'We really need someone to overhaul our existing system,' explained Herb.

Sage looked dubiously at the teetering pile of paper. 'What *is* the existing system?'

'We put everything in the in-tray.'

Sage waited for the next step.

'That's it.' At least Herb had the decency to look a little ashamed. 'We're not very good at the ... organisey stuff.'

Sage nodded, and pulled out a chair from the desk so she could sit down, but discovered a white rabbit had beaten her to it. She squeaked. The rabbit blinked sleepily.

'This is Warren,' said Herb, lifting it up and waving one of its paws at Sage. 'Say hello, Warren.'

'Hello, Warren,' said Sage, touching the rabbit's soft ears. 'Shouldn't you be in a hat somewhere?'

Warren hung limply from Herb's hands. 'Are you sure he's alive?' asked Sage.

'He's just lazy,' said Herb. 'Lazy but clever. He does this stunt where Armand puts him in a frying pan and turns him into Welsh rarebit. Which isn't rabbit, you know. It's just a grilled cheese sandwich.'

Herb deposited Warren in the middle of the desk, where the rabbit yawned and immediately fell asleep.

'Any other tenants I should know about?' asked Sage, gingerly sitting down on the chair.

'We did have three white mice,' said Herb. 'But they're currently on recreation leave.'

Sage raised her eyebrows.

'They ran away. You'll spot them every now and then backstage. I'm sure they'll come back when they're ready. Oh, and there was a dove, too.' He shot a guilty look at the filing cabinet. 'Best not to ask what happened to it.'

'I take it you don't always see eye-to-eye with Bianca,' said Sage.

'Very rarely,' Herb replied. 'But what specifically were you referring to?'

'The theatre being haunted.'

Herb snorted. '*If* there was a shred of scientific evidence to suggest that ghosts exist, I still can't imagine why any spectre would bother to haunt this dump.'

Sage didn't say anything.

'Please don't tell me you believe in ghosts,' said Herb, his voice pained.

'I–I don't know what I believe,' said Sage. 'But if there *is* a ghost, I'm going to get a photo of it.'

Herb winced, as if Sage had done something terrible to injure him. 'Good luck.'

Sage blew dust off the computer's keyboard and booted

it up. The startup chime made Herb cock his head.

'Huh,' he said. 'I didn't know it was even plugged in.'

'You don't use the computer? Ever?'

Herb raised one shoulder. 'Bianca is scared of technology,' he said. 'And I ... just don't really care.'

'So ... what exactly do you do here?' asked Sage, as the computer started to whirr.

'I help set up the show,' said Herb. 'And help Armand refine his effects. There are one or two that I designed myself.' He attempted a modest look, but failed miserably and shot Sage his goofy smile.

She smiled back. 'So you do magic too?'

He nodded. 'I'm pretty good,' he said, clearly having abandoned modesty. 'I'm working on some new material – big stuff, which I'll use when I eventually go solo.'

The desktop finally appeared on the computer, and Sage clicked around. 'Do you have a booking system?' she asked.

'We have an answering machine. People just leave a message if they want to book.'

'But where do you record that booking? On a spreadsheet or something?'

'We just write it down on a post-it.'

Sage narrowed her eyes. 'You're kidding, right?'

Herb blinked and looked apologetic. 'Um,' he said. 'No. I don't really *do* computers. I know about Wikipedia. And

27

YouTube. And there are a few magician's forums I post on at home. Otherwise … not so much.'

Sage peered around the back of the computer. 'Um,' she said. 'I don't suppose there's an internet connection?'

Herb spread his hands helplessly.

Sage sighed. 'Okay,' she said. 'Is there any kind of budget for upgrading the system? Can I order a broadband connection? Then I could set up an online booking system.'

'I'm not sure what any of that means, but it sounds very impressive. I'll talk to Armand.'

Sage shook her head in disbelief. 'What century are you guys from?'

'I'm *really* good at designing magic effects,' said Herb. 'I've won competitions and stuff.'

'Did you design that last trick?' Sage asked, hoping Herb would say he hadn't. The image of the swords penetrating Bianca's flesh still made her feel uncomfortable.

'Nah,' said Herb. 'That's an old one. Although I did add the bit at the end with the floating chair and the petal explosion. I actually wanted to rework the whole thing, and do it with a cardboard box instead of a wooden one, and umbrellas instead of swords. But Armand says it looks too cheap. I told him it would work better, because with the fancy wood cabinet, everyone just figures it's specially built with a trick bottom for the assistant to slip into.'

'Isn't it?'

'Well,' said Herb, looking slightly put out. 'But that's the great thing about the cardboard box – the whole illusion changes. This German magician, Hans Moretti, does it with a cardboard box, and I watched it about a million times on YouTube before I finally figured it out. It took a whole week, of just watching it over and over again. I don't think I showered or slept. But it's an awesome trick. You see, the cardboard box…' He stopped, and rubbed his hand over the top of his head. 'I can't tell you,' he said, with an apologetic smile. 'Magician's Code.'

'Magician's what?'

He shrugged. 'There's a code. I'm a member of the Magician's League, and I swore an oath that I wouldn't give away any magic secrets to non-members.'

Sage snorted. 'You swore an oath? Did you put your hand on your heart and everything?'

Herb didn't seem to notice her sarcastic tone. 'Yes,' he said, and put his hand on his heart. '*As a magician I promise never to reveal the secret of an illusion to a non-magician, unless they take the Magician's Oath in turn. I promise never to perform any illusion without first practising the effect until I can maintain the illusion of magic.*'

'Fine,' said Sage, feeling a little put out. 'Show me a trick, then. You're allowed to do that, right?'

As if he'd been waiting for her to ask, Herb lifted a metal bucket from a milk crate in the corner and put it on the desk with a clank. Warren started, and looked accusingly at the bucket.

'Sorry, Warren,' said Herb. 'Didn't mean to wake you. Here.' He pulled a carrot and a handful of lettuce leaves from the bucket, and placed them near the edge of the desk. Warren loped across and began happily munching.

'That wasn't the trick.' Herb pulled the milk crate over and sat on it. 'The carrot was already in the bucket. The bucket is now empty.' He showed it to Sage.

She nodded. The bucket *was* empty.

'Now,' said Herb. 'Do you have a dollar?'

Sage produced one from her purse. Herb took it, and dropped it into the bucket with a metallic clang. 'This is how our wages get paid,' he explained. 'It's a magic bucket that fills up with coins.'

'I get paid with my own dollar?' asked Sage, laughing. 'That's it, I'm joining a union.'

'No, no, no,' said Herb. 'It's more like an investment account. You need to put a dollar in there to start things rolling. Like a seed. Then, hopefully, more money will just appear—' he pulled a coin from the air and dropped it into the bucket, '—out of nowhere.' He pulled another coin from the air, then one from Sage's ear, and one from his own ear, then one from Warren's ear. Each coin clanged as it was dropped into the bucket. Herb spat a handful of coins from his mouth into the bucket, then turned Warren's carrot into another handful, much to Warren's indignant disgust. He produced a handkerchief and sneezed into it, then shook it out over the bucket, producing another shower of coins.

'Can you move your hand?' he asked.

Sage lifted her hand from where it rested on the desk, and there was another dollar underneath it. Herb's movements were so smooth and in control, it was like watching a ballet. He lifted up Warren, revealing another handful of coins. Warren was not impressed, but Sage was.

Coin after coin clattered into the bucket. Finally Herb peered inside.

'That looks like a decent wage,' he said. 'But coins are annoying, right?' He picked the bucket up, struggling with its weight. Sage could hear the coins clinking together inside. Then Herb turned the bucket upside down. Sage flinched, expecting hundreds of coins to come spilling out. But instead just one small rectangle of plastic tumbled out and fell onto the desk in front of her.

'So I put the money in your bank account,' said Herb.

Sage picked up the plastic card. It was her bank card. She stared at it, open-mouthed. 'How did you get this?' she said, turning it over to check that it was real. 'Did you pick my pocket? Tell me how you did it! And the coins. Where did they all go?'

Herb's mouth twisted in just a hint of a smile. 'I can't tell you.'

Sage felt a little wounded. 'Not even a clue?'

'Nope.'

'Then do it again.'

'Absolutely not. A magician *never* repeats an effect.'

Sage scowled at him.

'How about instead I teach you a basic coin vanish?' Herb said. 'This one isn't really a secret. Here.' He handed back her dollar, and produced another from his pocket, showing her how to tuck it between the folds of her palm.

'This is the classic palm,' he explained. 'By just slightly bringing your thumb and little finger together, you can grip the coin in your palm, and still move your hand around like there's no coin there. You can also do a thumb palm,' he tucked the coin in the corner where his forefinger met his thumb, 'or a finger palm,' he placed the coin on the lower section of his fingers, curling them down a little to hold the coin in place. 'Now, get ready, because I'm about to tell you the most important secret of magic.'

'I thought you weren't allowed to.'

'This particular secret is a pretty well-known one,' said Herb with a grin. 'It's on Wikipedia, so I don't think they'll send the magic goons after me for telling you.'

'I'm all ears.'

'Misdirection,' said Herb. 'The number-one most important thing.'

He put his coin on the table and slid it towards him, curling his right fist around it. He seemed to transfer it to his left hand, which he also closed in a fist. 'Which hand?'

Sage thought about what he had said. 'That one.' She pointed to his right hand, feeling clever.

Herb blew on his fist and opened it, wiggling his fingers. It was empty.

'That one, then,' Sage said, pointing to his left hand.

Herb blew again, opening his left hand and wiggling the fingers. No coin.

'It's up your sleeve,' said Sage.

Herb rolled up his sleeves, and held his hands out to Sage for examination. She turned his palms over, looking for the coin. His hands were smooth and warm, with long, graceful fingers. Sage suspected that if he'd lived two hundred years ago, he would probably have enjoyed a career as a pickpocket.

'I give up,' she said, even though she was reluctant to let go of his hands. 'Where is it?'

Herb grinned. 'It's vanished,' he said, with a theatrical flourish. 'Magic.'

Sage stared at him. 'Okay,' she said. 'Now tell me how you do it.'

'There's a thing called the Sucker Effect,' said Herb. 'It's where you fool people by making them think they've figured it out, when really they're not even close. It's a kind of misdirection.'

'So where's the coin?'

Herb shrugged. 'You never pick up the coin,' he said. He dropped it back on the table, and using his fingers, slid it towards him. 'You just slide it off into your lap,' he said. 'And then pretend that you picked it up. Then when you've checked both my hands and sleeves, I pick it up from my lap, palm it, and pull it out of your ear.'

'So you were asking me to pick which hand,' said Sage. 'But it had never been in either hand.'

'Correct. That's the Sucker Effect. You do something, while making the audience *think* you did something else. So they're all busy feeling self-congratulatory that they figured it out, and it gives you all this awesome wriggle room to keep tricking them.'

Sage practised sliding the dollar across the table and making it look like she was picking it up. 'Zacky is going to love this.'

'Your boyfriend?'

'My brother,' said Sage, feeling weirdly pleased that the

mention of a potential boyfriend had wiped the smile from Herb's face.

'Ah,' said Herb, brightening. 'He of the misplaced wand. He likes magic?'

'He *loves* magic. He wants to be Harry Potter when he grows up. He sleeps with his wand under his pillow.'

Herb grinned. 'I admire a young man with ambition and dedication to his craft.'

Sage grinned back at him. Maybe moving to Melbourne hadn't been such a terrible thing after all.

3. Load: to secretly place an object in a location.

As she slipped in the front door, Sage heard voices in the living room. Dad was home before ten on a weeknight – perhaps it was a special occasion. Sage paused at the living-room door and listened.

'The thing is,' Dad was saying, 'splitting up a family always has big repercussions. It's not just the emotional impact on the kids. There's also a big financial impact. Expenses basically double.'

Sage froze, her hand on the doorknob. Splitting up a family? Whose family?

'I suppose sometimes it just can't be helped,' said Mum, her voice so soft that Sage could barely make out the words. 'Sometimes things just don't work out.'

A funny feeling started to seep into Sage as she listened. Who were they talking about? Before she could hear any more, the sound of pounding feet on stairs filled her ears, and Zacky came tearing into the hallway.

'Sage!' he bellowed. 'I went to see an exhibition in the city with my new friend Roman!'

Sage pushed aside the funny feeling and smiled at her brother. 'Really?' she asked. 'What kind of exhibition?'

'Computer games,' said Zacky, his eyes shining. 'There were MILLIONS of games there and me and Roman played ALL of them except for some that Roman's mum said we weren't allowed to because we're not old enough. But I played the Harry Potter game and one with an elf and one with a snake and one where I got to fly a plane...'

Sage nodded encouragingly and tuned him out. She knew from experience that Zacky's lists could go on for some time. Eventually he stopped, and Sage pushed open the living-room door.

Mum was curled up on the sofa, laptop on her knees. Dad sat opposite her in an armchair, leafing through a manila folder.

'Sage,' he said with a beaming grin. 'We were about to send out a search party.'

'You're home,' she said. 'On time.'

Dad put down his folder and held out his arms for a hug. Zacky pushed past Sage and launched himself into Dad's lap. Sage smiled and leaned over to hug them both, breathing in the familiar smell of Dad's aftershave.

'So what adventures have you been up to?' asked Dad. 'I've already heard all about Zacky's. In great detail.'

'Um,' said Sage. 'I got a job.'

Mum looked up from her laptop. 'You what?'

'Helping out with the magic show we went to see. Zacky forgot his wand and I went back into the theatre and they offered me a job.'

Zacky looked thunderstruck. 'You're going to work for The Great Armand?'

'Yep.'

'Are you going to learn how to do magic?'

'Probably not,' said Sage, thinking of Herb. 'Magicians are pretty secretive.'

'Well done, kiddo,' said Dad, his face splitting open in a grin. 'Your first job. Next stop – prime minister of Australia.'

Sage looked at Mum, who didn't look as pleased.

'Are you sure you can handle a job right now?' she asked, her brow creasing in a frown. 'I mean, we're still settling in here, and you've got school in a few weeks.'

'It's only until school starts,' said Sage. 'Plus it's mostly in the evenings, so if you get a job I'll still be at home during the day to look after Zacky.'

'If I'm not playing at Roman's house,' said Zacky.

'Of course,' said Sage.

'Great,' said Mum. 'It sounds great.' But she didn't really look as if she meant it.

'It means I can pay for the Yoshi Lear course,' said Sage. 'I rang them up and they said I can pay in instalments, and there's an old film camera at the studio I can borrow.'

'Fabulous,' said Dad. 'This calls for a celebration! What about pizza?'

Mum shot him a Look. 'Greg, I'm not sure we should be spending—'

'Pizza it is!' said Dad. 'Zacky, run and get the menu off the fridge while I change out of these work clothes.'

They both left the room. Sage looked at her mother, who was staring at the laptop again. 'Mum? Are you all right?'

'I'm fine,' said Mum with a faint smile. 'Just tired. I'm sorry for not being more excited about your job. I think it's great, I really do. I only wish we'd been able to pay for your photography classes. I feel bad.'

'Don't,' said Sage, plonking herself down on the couch next to Mum. 'This is a good thing. I think I'm going to enjoy working at the theatre. There are a couple of other young people there, and I'm getting to know the city a bit better.'

She rested her head on Mum's shoulder.

'Mum?'

'Yes, sweetheart?'

'What were you and Dad talking about? Before Zacky and I came in?'

There was a long pause. 'Just a case that your father is working on.'

'Right,' said Sage, and wondered why she didn't feel more relieved.

〰〰〰

Sage's duties at the Lyric Theatre were pretty straightforward. She would arrive mid-afternoon on Wednesdays, Thursdays and Fridays, and mid-morning on Saturdays and Sundays for the matinees. She would help Herb set up the stage, then retire to their poky little office and work on the outstanding invoices. Apparently Armand had approved the broadband connection, as Herb had produced a company credit card from Sage's ear and told her to proceed. After two days, she'd worked through most of the in-tray, throwing out the junk mail and dealing with the unpaid invoices. Her job next week was to sort out the bookings system. Sage had grand plans for an online database, although before she tackled that she had to clean out the filing cabinet, which was a daunting task.

The show's matinees were always full of excited kids, but the evening performances were a little more subdued. People looked unnerved to be in such a forgotten part of the city, and eyebrows were raised at the theatre's threadbare carpets and flaky ceilings. Sage ripped tickets and made sure everyone found a seat. Once the show started, she hung around at the back of the auditorium, watching the performance and opening the door for anyone who needed to duck out to the toilet or answer a phone call. Herb was backstage, making sure the right props were set in the right places and that the curtains opened and closed, as well as operating the sound and lights from a little console.

Once the show was over, she and Herb tidied up the theatre and reset the stage for the next night's show, while Bianca got changed and Armand did … whatever it was that he did in his dressing-room.

Disappointingly, there'd been no signs of any ghostly activity. Sage had her phone in her pocket everywhere she went, ready to take a photo if she heard or felt something spooky. She even took it out and took regular, random snaps that she could analyse later to see if anything showed up. She'd done some reading at home, and knew that to be a true paranormal investigator, she'd need a lot more equipment: thermal imaging devices, an electromagnetic field detector, digital audio recorders as well as a video camera. But she still hoped to have some success with an ordinary photo.

'I'm going out to the bins,' said Herb, hefting his black garbage bag full of empty cups and popcorn boxes. 'Oh,' he said, as he passed Bianca coming in. 'Decided to grace us with your presence, did you?'

'I had a splinter,' said Bianca, holding up a bandaged finger. 'From the vanishing cabinet.'

'Poor baby.'

Bianca pulled a chair onto the stage, and sat down, pulling out a needle and thread, a box of sequins, and her sparkly costume.

'So nice you could come out here and join us,' said Herb. 'What a picture of domesticity.'

She delivered a flat look at Herb. 'The light isn't strong enough in my room.'

He rolled his eyes, and disappeared backstage with the garbage bag.

'Are you okay?' asked Sage. 'With the splinter?'

Bianca looked up, seemingly surprised that Sage was there. 'I'm fine,' she said, and went back to her sewing.

Sage grabbed a broom and began to sweep the stage. She wasn't sure what she'd done, but it was clear that Bianca didn't like her. Apart from giggling at Sage's name, she had barely acknowledged her presence, except to occasionally tell her how to correctly set a prop. She reminded Sage of the Snow Queen, fragile and brittle and unimaginably beautiful. Sage wondered what it would take to melt her frozen heart.

She heard footsteps and turned, expecting Herb, but saw The Great Armand instead. He didn't look nearly as grand up close. He was older, for one thing, with yellowed teeth, and grey pouches under his eyes. A stale mustiness emanated from his clothes.

'Armand,' said Bianca, 'this is Sage. Remember how Herb asked if he could hire someone to look after the books and tickets and stuff? Well, here she is. Apparently she's a genius with computers.' Bianca didn't sound particularly impressed.

'It's not that complex,' said Sage. 'It's just a basic booking system.'

Armand's eyes slid over Sage, as if she weren't quite interesting enough to focus on. 'Welcome,' he said vaguely, all trace of his mysterious and theatric European accent gone.

'Er,' said Sage. 'Thank you. I'm very happy to be here.'

Armand clearly wasn't listening – he was staring at Bianca. She was wearing a loose velvet dress, and with her head bent over her sewing, she looked like a princess from a fairytale. Sage noticed that Armand's eyes were not on Bianca's face, or her shining golden hair, or even on her sewing. They were firmly focused – with all the focus that he had failed to achieve with Sage – on Bianca's cleavage.

Sage's skin crawled. Didn't Armand get to stare at Bianca's boobs enough? She was practically naked through the whole show.

'Actually,' said Sage, 'there was something I wanted to talk to you about.'

'Hmm?' Armand's eyes didn't move.

'Um,' said Sage. 'I've just been going over the accounts, tidying up the financial records and things. I learnt how to do basic book-balancing at school. And there seem to be some discrepancies.'

Armand wrenched his gaze away from Bianca's boobs. 'Discrepancies?'

'I'm sure it's just an accounting error,' said Sage, 'but there seems to be some money missing. Not a lot, around nine hundred dollars. I was just wondering if there's some extra paperwork that I don't know about.'

Armand's face clouded over. 'It isn't really your job to be poking through my financial records,' he said shortly. 'When I want financial advice, I'll consult a professional.'

Sage felt her face go red. 'Oh,' she said. 'Okay. It's just that I thought—'

'You were slow in the sub-trunk routine yesterday,' said Armand, turning back to Bianca, who was sucking on her finger and glaring at her sewing needle.

'Sorry,' said Bianca, taking her finger from her mouth. 'The hinge on the box sticks. I'll get Herb to look at it.'

'The routine isn't working.'

Bianca put down her needle. 'Have you thought about

my suggestion?' she asked. 'Of me performing the switch from inside the box, instead of you doing it once I'm gone? I think the misdirection would be much cleaner.'

'Don't be stupid,' said Armand in a weary voice. 'If you're already in the box, there's nowhere to slide the dummy.'

Bianca shrugged, and nodded her head prettily. 'I guess it was a little optimistic.'

'When will you learn to *think* before you speak?' said Armand. 'I know we make it seem easy, but these effects are the results of years of planning and design, even before we get to rehearsals. It's all very easy to dream up a new solution, but translating it into something that's actually usable onstage is another matter entirely.'

'You're right,' Bianca said with a placatory smile. 'Sorry.'

'I'm adding a new routine at the midpoint,' said Armand. 'The Zigzag Effect.'

Sage saw Bianca's shoulders stiffen. 'Really?' she said, after a moment's pause. 'You don't think it's a bit close to the sword cabinet in the finale?'

'I do not,' said Armand. 'You know the routine. We'll run through it once before the show tomorrow. Make sure you're on time.'

He nodded sharply, then dragged his eyes away from Bianca's chest and wandered back in the direction of his dressing-room.

'I will,' Bianca said brightly. She waited until they heard Armand's dressing-room door close. 'As if I'm not always here three hours before he is,' she muttered.

'He seems ... kind of mean,' said Sage. 'And more than a little sleazy.'

Bianca shrugged. 'He's not that bad,' she said. 'You'll get used to him ogling you.'

Sage didn't bother to point out that Armand had barely noticed her, and that Bianca had been his sole ogling target. 'How long have you worked for him?' she asked instead.

Bianca counted on her fingers. 'Five years,' she said. 'Since I was seventeen.'

'Is he always this ... grumpy?'

Bianca snipped a thread with a little pair of scissors. 'He's especially grumpy today because he's just found out that Jason Jones, a rival magician, has booked a show at the Arts Centre in the city while we're still mouldering away here in this dump.'

This was by far the longest conversation Sage had ever had with Bianca. She felt like she was making progress, so she pressed on with a question she'd been dying to ask.

'You said the theatre was haunted?'

Bianca looked up from her sewing. Sage had finally got her attention. 'There are lots of stories about this place,' she said. 'And I've definitely felt things.'

'What kind of things?'

Bianca leaned forward with a conspiratorial air. 'Occasionally when I'm onstage, I walk into a really cold spot, even though the lighting coverage is totally even. Just one little spot is icy cold. And sometimes when I'm here late at night, I see little movements out of the corner of my eye, as if someone's there. But when I turn around, they're gone.'

Sage shivered.

'I've also heard weird noises,' said Bianca. 'Like someone muttering. And sometimes I come in and find the props have been moved around, or some of my makeup has been knocked over. That sort of thing.'

'Is there anywhere in particular where it happens?' asked Sage, wondering where she could centre her investigation.

'On the stage,' said Bianca. 'And in my dressing-room.'

Sage told Bianca about her mission to capture a photo of the ghost. 'I'd love to take some photos of you, too,' she said shyly. 'In your dressing-room or onstage. It's for a photography class I'm about to start.'

Bianca shrugged. 'Sure,' she said, and Sage thought she'd seen a hint of warmth beneath her emotionless exterior.

'What's the new trick?' asked Sage, not wanting their conversation to end. 'The Zigzag Effect?'

Bianca's cool expression faltered slightly. 'It's a classic,' she said. 'I get into a cabinet and then Armand splits it into four boxes and moves them around so it looks as if I've been cut into thirds, but I can still wiggle my toes and wave a handkerchief.'

Sage remembered her sick feeling when Bianca had been inside the box and Armand had pushed in the first sword.

'It sounds creepy,' said Sage. 'But it's safe, right? I mean, they're all just tricks. You're not really getting cut up.'

'Of course it's safe.'

'You've never been injured during a show?'

Bianca hesitated, then lifted the blonde hair from her forehead to reveal a two-inch scar. 'That was from the sword cabinet,' she said. 'And I have a burn on my stomach from the flaming torch effect. And I've always got bruises on my shins from the sub-trunk, and various other scrapes and bumps and splinters and things.' She took one of her bare feet in her hands and rubbed the sole. 'Not to mention how much my *feet* hurt after every show.'

Sage swallowed. 'What happened? With the swords.'

Bianca shrugged. 'That effect is all about timing. If Armand breaks his rhythm for some reason ...' She put her hand to her forehead. 'It bled all over the place. Luckily it was the last effect in the show, so we didn't have to stop halfway through. I went backstage and called myself an ambulance while Armand took his curtain call.'

'You called *yourself* an ambulance?'

'Who else would have done it?' Bianca asked. 'It was before Herb worked here. It was just me and Armand.'

She didn't say anything else, but there was a sad, lonely look on her face that made Sage itch to photograph her. How did she start working for a magician? And why did she stay? Bianca was beautiful and talented – why didn't she become an actor or a model or something that would pay better, without putting her in danger of being stabbed or burnt every night?

'You still do it,' she said. 'The swords in the box. Even though you got hurt.'

Bianca smiled. 'I was too scared to for a while,' she said. 'But then Herb came along and totally redesigned the effect. It's completely safe now – there's no way I could get hurt.'

'When was that?' Sage felt nosy asking so many questions, but she wanted to know how the strange group fitted together. Plus, Bianca seemed to be opening up a little.

'Two years ago,' said Bianca. 'He's a pain in the butt, but I guess he's useful for some things.'

'My ears are burning,' said Herb as he joined them, his arms full of lollies and chips from the vending machine. 'Say more nice things about me.'

Bianca raised an eyebrow. 'Sorry. That was all I had.'

Herb dumped the junk food on the table. 'I was hungry. Help yourselves.'

Bianca wrinkled her nose, but Sage opened a packet of jelly snakes and took out three green ones.

'Green?' said Herb. 'Really?'

'I like green. What's wrong with green?'

Herb shook his head. 'If you have to ask the question, then you don't deserve to know the answer.'

Sage hid a smile. Herb was definitely flirting with her.

'You realise this is all for your benefit, right?' said Bianca drily, turning to Sage. 'He's usually Mr Sourpuss Grumpypants after a show, can't wait to get out of here.'

'Bianca.' It was Armand again, his face blank and empty. 'Can I see you for a moment? In my dressing-room?'

Bianca nodded, and put away her needle and scissors.

'Wonder what that's about,' Herb said, chewing on his purple snake.

'Probably about the new trick Armand wants to add.'

Herb frowned. 'What new trick?'

'I think it's called the Zigzag?'

'Armand wants to add Zigzag?' Herb made a face. 'Isn't it too similar to the sword cabinet?'

'Apparently not.'

'I bet Bianca's thrilled.'

'It sounds awful,' said Sage. 'I hate those creepy lady-cutting-up tricks.'

She put her broom away, and she and Herb started to

set the props and effects for the next performance. Sage was learning where everything went, and realising how much preparation was involved in Armand's show. Certain objects had to be hidden in the black velvet bag behind the card table. Two wooden chairs needed to be positioned in a certain place in the wings. A backstage table held paper, black markers, a spare top hat, silk scarves, metal rings and other assorted items.

Sage picked up Armand's white-tipped black magic wand. 'It looks just like my brother's one,' she said.

'Ah,' said Herb, taking the wand from her. 'But can your brother do this?'

Herb's post-show sugar high was in full swing. He juggled the turnip, egg and orange from the cups-and-balls routine, and then caught the egg on the tip of Armand's magic wand and let it balance there. He leaned backwards as he tried and failed to balance the magic wand on the end of his nose. The wand clattered to the stage floor, and Sage lunged across the space between them to catch the egg before it splattered on the ground. To her surprise, she caught it, but her mad dash had thrown her off balance, and she stumbled backwards, stepping on the magic wand and snapping it in half.

Sage stared at the egg in her hand. It wasn't cool enough, and the weight was all wrong. 'It isn't real,' she said, disappointed.

'This is magic,' said Herb, taking the egg, bouncing it off the floor and catching it. 'None of it's real.'

'What have you done?' It was Bianca, standing in the wings, a strange expression on her face.

'Oops,' said Sage. 'Sorry.' She bent to pick up the broken wand.

'Don't touch it.' Bianca took a step forward. 'A broken wand on a magician's stage is a terrible omen.' She looked as if she was about to burst into tears.

'Oh brother,' said Herb. 'Bianca, cut the theatrics. Sage, it's not as if it's Harry Potter's wand. It's a piece of wooden dowel painted black and white. The reason it looks the same as your brother's is because it *is* the same. The only difference is that your brother or, I assume, one of your parents, had to pay a ridiculous eleven dollars for it, whereas we buy them in bulk for fifty cents each. They break *all the time* because they're cheap and nasty.'

'Not *on the stage*,' said Bianca. 'They never break on the stage.'

'What does it mean?' Sage asked. 'The omen?'

Bianca slowly turned her head to look at her. 'Death,' she said, after a moment's pause. 'It means death. Whenever a magician dies, fellow magicians hold a ritual, where they break his or her wand. It lets their magic escape. Except ... if the wand is broken before the magician dies, in the place where his or her magic is strongest…' She waved a hand to indicate the theatre. 'Then the magician will be cursed, and death will follow soon thereafter.'

Sage shivered, and suddenly wished she was at home. She blinked as she realised that, for the first time, she had pictured home as the crumbling Victorian terrace, instead of her old house near the beach.

'Do you really believe that?' she asked.

Bianca shook her head and tried to smile. 'Not really,' she said, a little tremor still in her voice. 'I'm sure it's bad luck, though.'

Herb rolled his eyes. 'Bianca, the wand-breaking ritual is all very cute and everything, but there is no actual magic in a magic wand. Magicians don't do *real* magic. We do *effects*. Using all sorts of misdirection and sleight of hand. But there is no real magic. Therefore breaking a fake magic wand cannot possibly create bad luck. Because there is *no such thing as real magic*.'

Bianca scowled at Herb. 'Even if you don't believe in the supernatural, you can't deny that many superstitions are rooted in common sense. Like walking under ladders and breaking mirrors – they can both be genuinely dangerous.'

'And just as many are total nonsense,' said Herb. 'Like black cats, or spilt salt, or the number thirteen. And *painted pieces of wood breaking in half*.'

'I still say it's bad luck.'

'Are there lots of theatrical superstitions?' asked Sage. 'I mean, apart from the obvious one.'

Bianca ticked them off her fingers. 'Don't use real money, real Bibles, real jewellery, real flowers or real peacock feathers onstage. Don't wear yellow clothes or new makeup. Don't knit, clap or whistle onstage or backstage. A cat in the theatre is good luck, but not if it runs across the stage. Never rehearse the final line of a performance, or the curtain call.'

'And the other one,' said Sage. 'The famous one.'

Herb's face arranged itself into an expression of crafty innocence. 'What famous one?'

Bianca looked at him suspiciously. 'Don't you dare.'

'Everyone knows it,' said Sage.

Bianca swung round and glared at her. '*Shh.* Don't encourage him.'

'*Encourage* me?' Herb spread his hands wide. 'What would she be *encouraging* me to do?' He sauntered onto the middle of the stage. 'What?' he said, turning back to them. 'Do you think I'm going to stand here and do this?'

He whistled a short tune, and then applauded himself, laughing.

'*Stop it,*' hissed Bianca, glancing around nervously.

'Or I could count the change in my pocket,' he said, pulling out a twenty-dollar note, and holding it between his right thumb and forefinger. 'Damn.' He frowned at the note. 'Looks like I don't have any change.'

He waved his left hand over the note, making it vanish. He showed both his empty hands to Sage and Bianca, and then shook his wrist. A handful of ten- and twenty-cent pieces clattered out from his sleeve, rolling and bouncing on the floor.

'Okay,' Bianca said. 'I get it. You're very clever, and you're enjoying showing off to your pretty new friend. Now cut it out.'

Sage started. Was she the pretty new friend? And what was going on? Why had Bianca's tone suddenly turned so cold?

Herb grinned and held out both hands to Bianca, as if offering a peace treaty. 'Okay, okay,' he said, chuckling. 'Lucky for you I don't have a Bible, peacock feathers, or any candles. And I left my knitting at home. But tell me, does the cat running across the stage thing still work if it's a bunny? Because I could go and wake up Warren ...'

He went to walk offstage, but stopped and grabbed both of Sage's hands, and dragged her into the centre of the stage. 'I'm curious, though,' he said. 'What was the superstition *you* were thinking of?'

Sage opened her mouth to inform him that while she didn't *really* believe in the supernatural, she didn't see the point in taking any chances, but Herb stopped her by laying a finger on her lips. Sage felt her heart start to beat faster.

'Wait,' he said. 'I'll read your mind and tell you.'

He stared into Sage's eyes. His own were brown, flecked with green and fringed with dark lashes, and bright with mirth. A spray of freckles was spattered across the bridge of his short nose, and his cheeks were ruddy and flushed.

'I'm getting the letter *M*,' said Herb. 'And … somewhere very far away. I'm sensing that you don't want me to say something.' He brushed his thumb along her wrist, and she felt suddenly flustered.

'*Herb*,' said Bianca, sounding genuinely upset. '*Please*.'

'I totally understand you don't want me to say anything in front of Bianca,' said Herb, leaning forward and keeping his voice low. Sage could smell his cologne, something spicy and dark, like Christmas pudding. 'But just so you know, I'm very flattered.'

Sage felt her face growing hot, and tried to pull her hands away. Herb hung on for a moment, before letting go and turning back to Bianca. 'You know that the superstition she's thinking of is totally apocryphal, right?' he said. 'The story goes that the Globe burnt down during a production of this particular play, right? Except it didn't. It burnt down during a performance of *Henry VIII*. No superstitions about that one, are there? It's all nonsense.'

Bianca's lips were white and thin. 'Don't say it,' she said. 'Promise me you won't say it. Not in the theatre. If you have to talk about it, call it the Scottish Play.'

'Okay,' said Herb, with a little bow. 'I promise I won't say *Macbeth*.' He paused, then smacked himself on the forehead. 'Oh, I did! I'm so sorry. I didn't mean to say *Macbeth*.'

Bianca's expression turned murderous.

'Cut it out,' Sage told Herb. 'You're upsetting her.'

'Why?' asked Herb. 'Just because I said *Macbeth*? Would you like me to ... what is it? Go outside, spin around three times, spit, curse and knock?'

Bianca turned and stormed out of the theatre, slamming the auditorium door behind her. Herb chuckled.

'That was kind of mean.' This was a side of Herb that Sage hadn't seen before, an arrogant, mocking side. She didn't like it.

'Look,' said Herb. 'I like Bianca. I really do. She's a good assistant, and she's incredibly beautiful. But the superstition thing can get *really* annoying after a while.'

'Still,' said Sage. 'You could at least try to respect her beliefs.'

'Why? She doesn't respect any of mine.' Herb saw the frown on Sage's face, and sighed. 'Fine,' he said. 'I'm sorry. I went too far.'

'It isn't me you should be apologising to,' said Sage.

Herb nodded. 'I'll talk to her in the morning.' He stood and stretched. 'Home time,' he said and started to walk up the aisle towards the foyer.

'Hey,' said Sage, following him. 'How did you know I was thinking of…' She glanced around. 'How did you know what I was thinking?'

Herb paused. 'Lucky guess,' he said over his shoulder.

4. Prediction: it is forecast that a particular thing will happen in the future.

True to his word, Herb apologised to Bianca as they were setting up for the show the following afternoon, producing a beautiful bouquet of silk flowers from an old feather duster. Bianca laughed, and whacked him on the head with them.

'Figure out how to do that with real flowers,' she said. '*Then* I'll be impressed.'

Herb grinned at her. 'I thought I wasn't allowed to have real flowers onstage.'

Bianca rolled her eyes, but Sage could tell her heart wasn't in it. She floated back to her dressing-room to get changed, and Herb asked Sage to help him get the Zigzag Effect equipment out of the storeroom.

'The storeroom?' she asked.

'No,' he said. 'Follow me.'

She followed him up the auditorium aisle to a narrow staircase tucked behind the door to the foyer. It led to a small room with a glass front looking out over the theatre.

'This place was originally built as a cinema,' said Herb when he saw her questioning look. 'Ages ago, when movies were this big new exciting thing. This was the projection booth. It's where we store all the magic stuff we're not using.'

The room was crammed with boxes and trunks that had once been brightly painted, but were now shabby and faded. Cardboard boxes were stacked in one corner, with carefully lettered labels reading *Indian Rope*, *Silk Scarves* and *Fake Daggers*. Sage shuddered at a guillotine collecting dust in a corner, and something that looked like a large and complicated clothes wringer. Next to it loomed a tall, thin box with a scantily clad lady painted on the front, covered in small slots where knives or swords could be inserted.

'Charming,' muttered Sage, taking out her phone and snapping a few photos of the dingy room for her ghost-hunting project.

'You're like an overenthusiastic tourist with that thing,' said Herb.

Sage hesitated, then told him she was trying to get a photo of the theatre ghost. He gave her a flat look. 'Are you serious? You are, aren't you. This is terrible.'

'There has been plenty of documentation of paranormal

activity,' said Sage. 'There are professional ghost hunters.'

Herb stared at her. 'I am a professional *magician*,' he said. 'That doesn't make magic real.'

Sage snapped a few more photos. She knew she wasn't going to convince Herb, and anyway, she still wasn't sure if she believed in the ghost herself. But after a few seconds, Herb couldn't contain himself any longer.

'What documentation?' he burst out.

'Digital recording equipment has captured voices,' said Sage.

'Radio signals, or noise from the recorder itself,' said Herb promptly. 'Next?'

'Electromagnetic field detectors.'

'Can be set off by faulty wiring which is very common in old buildings. Also microwaves and mobile phone signals.'

'Photographs have shown floating orbs of light.'

'*Orbs of light!*' Herb spluttered. 'Come on, do you really think there is any valid scientific explanation as to how a dead human being can transform into a *floating orb of light* that can be captured in a photograph but not by the human eye? You don't think that maybe it's *slightly* more likely to be light reflecting off particles of dust or moisture in the air?'

Sage shrugged. 'There have been some pretty convincing investigations.'

'No, there haven't!' Herb's voice was high and indignant.

'Nobody has ever actually set out to do a scientific, logical, methodical investigation into the existence of ghosts. Every so-called "experiment" is rife with sampling errors and mis-use of equipment. And *feelings*. So many bloody *feelings*. Saying *Ooh, I felt a chill in the air* proves *nothing* other than the fact that you are either a) standing in a draught or b) highly susceptible to the power of suggestion.'

Sage gave up defending herself. 'So where is this Zigzag thing?' she asked, looking around.

Herb ignored her. 'It's like I said before: humans see what they want to see. If you ask the average human to prove a hypothesis, they'll devise tests to achieve positive results.'

Sage couldn't help herself. 'So? Isn't that what you're supposed to do?'

'No!' Herb's outraged shout rattled around the projection booth. 'It's not what scientists do. A scientist tries as hard as they can to *disprove* the hypothesis. It's only by achieving positive *and* negative results that a hypothesis can be proven. But people just love to hear the word "yes", so they only ask questions that they think will yield that answer.'

'But aren't you doing just that?' asked Sage. 'You assume that there are no ghosts. What are you doing to test *that* hypothesis?'

Herb blinked. 'Nothing,' he said. 'You can't disprove a

negative, and it's not up to sceptics to disprove the nonsense spouted by believers. I'm also making no effort to test my hypothesis that the sun is made out of burning marshmallows, or that the universe is ruled by a giant saucy overlord made from spaghetti.'

He savagely yanked a drop cloth from something that looked like a filing cabinet: three boxes stacked on top of each other, with a black-and-white zigzag design painted on it.

'Tell me you're not really going to try and photograph the ghost,' Herb said, his eyes pleading.

Sage shook her head. 'I can't promise that.'

Herb looked disgusted.

'Who you gonna call?' Sage grinned.

'Give me a hand,' said Herb, shaking his head. He pulled at the top of the cabinet, tilting it over so Sage could lift it from the bottom. It was heavier than it looked, and she gritted her teeth as she took its weight. Herb started to back slowly out of the booth and guide it down the little set of steps.

'Do you think Bianca's okay?' asked Sage, steering the conversation away from the supernatural. 'She seemed upset last night, and she still looks a bit weird today.'

Herb grunted under the weight of the cabinet. 'It's hard to tell with Bianca.'

'You've been working with her for two years,' said Sage,

as they hauled the cabinet down the aisle to the stage. 'You must know her pretty well.'

'Bianca isn't the easiest person to get to know,' said Herb. 'When I first started working here, I was only sixteen. Just a geeky magic kid desperate to get involved. I tried to make friends with her. Get to know her properly. But ... sometimes she's just sort of empty, you know?'

'I think she's sad,' said Sage.

'Maybe,' said Herb. 'Here, help me lift it up onto the stage.'

Under the stage lights, the Zigzag cabinet looked faded and cheap. 'Might need a new lick of paint,' said Herb. 'I'll wait and see if Armand really does want to use it.'

They headed back to their poky little office. Sage half-heartedly sorted through the list of phone bookings while watching Herb out of the corner of her eye. He was sketching a complicated-looking device in a notebook. His hair hung in his eyes, and a frown of concentration crinkled his brow. He looked so focused, so intent, that Sage almost didn't want to say anything. He was such a puzzle. One minute he was funny and relaxed and smiling his wide, goofy smile; a moment later he was snarking away at Bianca, saying things he knew would hurt her. And was what Bianca said true? Was his clowning around and showing off all for Sage's benefit?

Did he really like her? That brought up an even more important question: did Sage like him back?

'What are you working on?' she asked.

Herb didn't look up. 'Just something I've been tinkering with for ages.'

'A trick? For the show?'

'An effect,' corrected Herb. 'But not for this show. It's too good for this show. Or at least it will be, if I can make it work.'

He tore the page out of the notebook, screwed it up into a ball, and waved his hand over the ball to make it vanish.

'Is that what you want, then?' asked Sage. 'To have your own show?'

Herb nodded. 'That's the idea,' he said. 'There aren't that many job opportunities for magicians. You're either a designer or a performer, or a fraud.'

Sage decided to try a little experimental flirting. 'What about solving crime?' she asked. 'There seem to be heaps of magicians on TV who solve crime.'

A flicker of his usual grin. 'They're mostly mentalists, not magicians.'

'What's the difference?'

'Magic is... magic. Making things appear and disappear. Mentalism is more about reading people's minds and getting them to do stuff.'

'But you can do that,' said Sage. 'You knew what theatre superstition I was thinking of last night.'

Herb let out a chuckle. 'That's not mentalism,' he said. 'It's the best-known theatre superstition out there. For most people, it's the only one they know. Bianca knew it, she just wasn't saying it because she knew I'd say *Macbeth*.'

Sage winced.

'Oh, now come on,' said Herb. 'Not you too. We're not even on the stage!'

'We're in the theatre,' muttered Sage. 'It still counts.'

Herb pulled the screwed-up paper ball out of Sage's ear, then turned it into a green jelly snake. 'I saved you the last one.'

Sage felt herself blush a little as she took it. This snake was a flirting snake. A delicious, green piece of jelly flirtation.

'What did you mean by "fraud"?' she asked, chewing thoughtfully. 'You said your career paths were designer, performer or fraud.'

Herb shrugged. 'You know,' he said. 'Psychics. Mediums. All those people who prey on the grief of others and pretend to talk to their dead relatives.' His face wrinkled in disgust.

'So you don't believe people can be psychic?' asked Sage.

'Nope, it's all bullshit. You know that, right?' Herb looked at her, suddenly concerned. '*Right?*'

'I don't know,' said Sage, thinking about her ghost photo

project. 'I think that I shouldn't automatically assume something is fake, just because I don't understand it. Not everything is a trick.'

Herb rolled his eyes. 'Just because I don't understand something,' he replied, 'doesn't mean it's automatically *magic*. Don't you think that's kind of narcissistic? To assume that just because we haven't figured out how something works yet, it can't possibly have a rational or scientific explanation?'

'You're so *closed*, Herb.' Bianca was standing in the doorway to the office, wearing a thin cotton dressing-gown over her sequined leotard. Her hair and makeup were done, and she looked like a porcelain doll. 'It's sad, really.'

'Anyway,' said Herb, ignoring her. 'I do understand psychics. I know how it works. There's nothing supernatural about it, it's just cold reading and the Barnum Effect.'

Bianca sighed. 'I supposed you're an expert, then.'

'What's the Barnum Effect?' asked Sage.

Herb looked at her, and cocked his head to one side. 'You really want people to like you,' he said. Sage immediately felt her cheeks grow hot. 'Sometimes you seem extroverted and sociable, but in fact you are quite wary and reserved around people you don't know. You are an independent thinker, and you don't like to feel restricted or limited. You're not achieving your full potential. Even though you're disciplined and seem like you have a lot of self-assurance, in fact you're very insecure on the inside, and often have serious doubts about decisions you've made. You're often self-critical.'

Sage stared at him. She knew what he was trying to do, but his analysis had still been frighteningly accurate. 'So,' she said. 'The Barnum Effect is like horoscopes. You just say general stuff and people assume it applies to them.'

Herb's face split open in a wide smile. 'Exactly!' He turned to Bianca. 'Why can't *you* be that perceptive?'

Bianca sighed.

'There's a classic experiment where psychology students are given a personality test, then presented with a personality profile along the lines of what I just told you. They're asked to give it a score out of five, with five being totally accurate, and zero being not accurate at all. The average score given is 4.3.'

'You're a genius,' said Bianca drily. 'You know all the answers to everything. There are no mysteries left in the universe. Congratulations.'

Herb shrugged. 'Humans want meaning in life. We want to find meaning in everything.' He leaned to yank an extension cord from a powerpoint, and held up the plug. 'Sage,' he said, showing it to her. 'What does this look like to you?'

Sage studied it. The two prongs at the top sloped upwards like questioning eyes, and the bottom prong looked like a nose or mouth. 'It's a face.'

'No,' said Herb. 'It isn't. It's just three bits of metal. But you *see* a face, because you're looking for meaning. People see Jesus's face in the soap scum on their shower screen, or in their breakfast cereal, because they want to. A bunch of people have tried to prove that psychic ability is genuine, using something called the sitter-silent condition, where the subject being read can hear the psychic, but the psychic can't see or hear them, and gets no clues as to how the subject is reacting. The sitters *still* reported that the psychics' predictions were accurate and relevant. But that proves *nothing*. The greatest trick of psychics is that they don't do *anything*. The audience does it all for them. People hear what they want to hear. All a so-called psychic does is to give them back exactly what they want.'

'You don't know what you're talking about,' said Bianca, perching on the desk. 'Have you ever even *seen* a real psychic?'

'There is *no such thing* as a real psychic! Here.' Herb leaned forward and stared intently into Sage's eyes. She swallowed. 'I'm sensing pain,' he said. 'And loss, but you're still trying to hide it behind a façade. I'm getting...April. Something happened in April. The number sixteen. I can see...a dinner table, and a letter in a white envelope. And I'm getting the letter *M*. Michael? Mark? Or is it a *D*? David? Who is this David?'

Sage caught her bottom lip between her teeth. 'My ex-boyfriend's name is Daniel.'

'Daniel, yes! That's it,' said Herb. 'Tell me what happened with Daniel in April.'

Sage thought about it. 'April was when Dad found out he was getting this new job in Melbourne.'

'And did you tell Daniel?'

'I–I thought he'd be more upset. That I was leaving.' Sage remembered the conversation, outside the science block at her old school. Sage had struggled not to cry, expecting a passionate avowal of everlasting love from Daniel, or at least a poignant kiss. But Daniel had just said, 'Wow, that really sucks,' and asked to borrow two dollars for the vending machine. In hindsight, it wasn't surprising at all. Daniel wasn't the passionate-avowal kind of guy, and Sage wasn't the kind of girl guys got passionate about.

Herb nodded sympathetically. 'When did you and Daniel break up?'

'The twentieth of May,' said Sage. 'It was my birthday. He took me out for lunch and told me that there was no point in us being together if I was just going to leave anyway.' She didn't add that Parama had seen Daniel with his tongue down Alice Petricavich's throat at the beach four days later. Alice was definitely the kind of girl that guys got passionate about – all wispy and glimmering, like early-morning sun.

Herb saw her expression and snorted. 'What a douche-bag. That was your sixteenth birthday, right? Did he give you a present?'

'A scarf. Because it gets cold in Melbourne.'

'Was there a card?'

'I think so – yes.'

Herb punched the air and grinned. 'A full strike! I said April – that was when you found out you were leaving. I said sixteen – it was your sixteenth birthday. I said *D* – that's Douchebag Daniel. He took you out for lunch – that was the dinner table I saw, and he gave you a crappy present and a card – which is the white envelope.'

Sage stared at him. 'How did you do that? How did you know about Daniel taking me out for my birthday?'

'I didn't. I just said a bunch of random stuff and you made sense out of it. You did all the work.'

'But everything you said was true,' said Bianca, putting her hands on her hips. 'Maybe you just don't realise that you're channelling stuff from outside of yourself.'

'Don't be ridiculous,' said Herb. 'I got it *all wrong*. I said Michael or David – you turned that into Daniel. I said April, but he actually broke up with you in May. I said sixteen – but I already know you're sixteen because you wrote it down on your employee information form the other day. Then I said a dinner table – but he took you out to lunch. And I said

71

there was a letter in a white envelope, which you decided was a birthday card. Was it even *in* a white envelope?'

Sage thought about it. 'No,' she said slowly. 'There wasn't an envelope at all.'

Herb folded his arms. 'See? You just remembered the things that applied to you, and forgot all the stuff I said that didn't. This is what humans *do*. This is why people buy lottery tickets – because we only remember the extraordinary and the unusual stories of people *winning*, not the millions upon millions of totally uninteresting stories about people who don't.'

Bianca picked up Warren and stroked his ears. 'Fine,' she said. 'But just because you're a crappy fake psychic doesn't mean that the real deal doesn't exist.'

'If it does,' said Herb, 'then there's absolutely no evidence of it. There's a stage magician called James Randi who is offering a million dollars to any psychic who can prove their abilities. He opened the offer in 1968. More than a thousand people have taken the challenge. Nothing so far.'

'So maybe real psychics aren't interested in money.'

'Then how come they're demonstrating their abilities on psychic phone hotlines and daytime TV, instead of using them to actually help people? How come they're not working for the government?'

'How do you know they're not?'

Herb made an exasperated noise. 'It's impossible talking to people like you.'

'Nobody asked you to,' said Bianca.

'You came into *my* office!' said Herb.

'Only to see if Sage can help me with this wispy bit of hair,' said Bianca huffily. She handed Warren to Herb and smiled at Sage.

Sage followed Bianca back to her dressing-room. It was littered with shoes, sequins and discarded feather boas. An ancient couch covered with cushions and blankets took up an entire wall, and above it were various vintage posters for old magic shows.

THE HOUDINI METAMORPHOSIS – *The Greatest Novelty Mystery Act in the World!*

THURSTON THE GREAT MAGICIAN – *The Wonder Show of the Universe*

ALEXANDER – *The Man Who Knows*

T NELSON DOWNS – *Once Seen Never Forgotten*

A little side table held an old sewing machine, and there was a smallish dressing table against the opposite wall, cluttered with little pots, brushes and lipsticks. Above the dressing table hung a mirror, with mostly blown light bulbs surrounding it.

'Thank you,' said Bianca, handing Sage a bobby pin.

Sage pinned the stray wisp of hair back in place, feeling

oddly pleased that Bianca needed her help for something. Bianca shrugged off the cotton dressing-gown, revealing her smooth long limbs and glittering costume.

'Is that a bruise?' asked Sage, frowning at a deep purple mark on Bianca's upper thigh.

Bianca looked down. 'Damn,' she said. 'That was quick.'

'Where did it come from?' The bruise was angry, veined with red streaks. It looked very painful.

Bianca made a face. 'I just ran through the Zigzag Effect with Armand. I haven't done it since I was eighteen, and I was a bit smaller then. The blades are blunt, but they're still very hard when they scrape along your body.'

Sage winced. 'Did you say anything? To Armand?'

'He'd just tell me to lose weight.' Bianca smiled a bright smile that didn't reach her eyes. 'It's fine. I'm a bit out of shape.'

Sage felt furious on Bianca's behalf. 'What a dick,' she said. 'Only a man would say something like that. You don't have to put up with it, you know. Refuse to do it. Go on strike!'

Bianca looked puzzled and strangely touched by Sage's concern. 'It doesn't work that way.'

'Who says?'

'The world. Anyway, it's just a magic trick. It's not important.'

Bianca leaned towards the mirror and touched up her eyeliner with a stubby, worn-down pencil. Frustrated, Sage tried to think of a way to make Bianca understand.

'Are you guys ready?' Herb was standing in the doorway.

'You!' Sage pointed a finger at him. 'Can't you fix the cabinet? Make the blades smaller?'

'Hmm?'

Sage felt her heart sink. Herb was staring at Bianca, not listening to anything she'd said. Of course he was. Bianca was beautiful. Like stupid Alice Petricavich, Bianca was the kind of girl who boys got passionate about. Tall and beautiful, like a delicate long-stemmed flower. Bianca was the kind of girl whose face launched ships. She was the kind of girl people had written poetry and songs about for thousands of years. She was perfect in every way, like a daydream come to life. And it wasn't a sex thing. Even Sage wanted to protect her, make her smile. She was just that kind of girl.

Suddenly everything made sense. Herb and Bianca's constant bickering. The assistant and the magic designer. It was like a romantic comedy. Herb had basically admitted he was in love with Bianca before – when he'd said that she was beautiful and he'd tried to get close to her. And the only role for Sage in this particular rom-com was as the third wheel; the short, dumpy, comic-relief friend with flat brown hair, who would help bring the two lovers together and almost certainly bring the laughs by falling on her bottom several times, in increasingly humiliating circumstances.

'Sage? Are you okay?' Bianca touched her arm.

It was perfect timing, really. Just when it would have been *convenient* for Bianca to play the ice-queen, she turned all nice so Sage couldn't even quietly despise her. But Bianca was lovely. Lovely and sad and in need of protection. Herb was lovely too, and he could help her, be her knight in shining armour. They deserved each other. Sage was sure that the fire of their arguments would very soon mature into a different sort of fire – less antagonistic, but no less heated.

'I'm fine,' she said, plastering on a smile. 'Good luck tonight. Break a leg.'

What did she care, anyway? She hadn't taken the job because of Herb. She didn't need a boyfriend. She just needed enough money to take Yoshi Lear's photography class.

After the show, Sage started to think seriously about asking Armand if she could photograph him. With no sign of Bianca's ghost, Sage wanted something impressive she could show Yoshi Lear, and a shimmering series of magic at work could be just the thing. But how to approach Armand?

Herb was backstage, tinkering with the blades in the Zigzag cabinet, and Sage was sweeping the rose petals off the stage and pondering her best strategy. The door to the foyer banged.

'I can't believe this old theatre is still here,' said a smooth voice from the auditorium. 'I'm surprised nobody's torn it down and put up apartments.'

Sage looked up to see a middle-aged man in a suit standing in the middle aisle.

'I'm sorry, sir,' she said. 'But the theatre's—'

The man walked towards the stage. He waved a nonchalant hand at Sage. 'Don't worry, love,' he said. 'I'm family.' He flashed her a warm, open smile, and Sage couldn't help smiling back.

'Um,' she said. 'I'm not—'

'Jason Jones,' said the man, reaching the stage and holding out his hand for her to shake.

So *this* was Armand's rival magician. Although he wasn't tall or particularly attractive, Jason Jones radiated confidence and charisma. His suit was impeccably tailored, his short black hair perfectly cropped and styled. His teeth were straight and white, and when he smiled, it was like the sun coming out.

'I don't know you,' he said to Sage. 'Are you new?'

Sage nodded and introduced herself, stumbling over the words. Why was she so flustered? It wasn't like she was attracted to Jason – he was much too old for her. But there was something about him … Sage wanted him to like her. She glanced into the wings and saw Herb watching her with amusement.

'And how are you finding the old Lyric?' asked Jason. His gaze locked with hers and filled her with warmth. All his attention was on her, and she basked in his glow.

Out of the corner of her eye, Sage saw Herb roll his eyes and mime being sick.

'It's good,' said Sage. 'Everyone's very nice.'

Jason raised his eyebrows. 'Really?' he said, his mouth curving into a conspiratorial smile. 'Even Armand? I find that hard to believe.'

Sage found herself giggling. What was *wrong* with her? 'He's not so bad,' she heard herself say.

'I'll believe that when I see it,' said Jason. 'Speaking of whom, would you mind telling him I'm here?'

Sage nodded and mumbled something inarticulate before rushing off to Armand's dressing-room.

'Excuse me?' she called through the door. 'There's a gentleman called Jason Jones here. He wants to talk to you.'

There were a few moments of silence, then the door was yanked open. Armand's face was creased with displeasure. Sage took an involuntary step back as he swept past her and stomped down the corridor. She followed, a few paces behind.

Next to Jason, Armand looked like a shabby pastiche – someone from a comedy skit about magicians. Sage hung back in the wings and watched.

'Good to see you, Jason,' said Armand stiffly. 'Have you been well?'

Jason Jones rolled his eyes and shrugged. 'You know how it is,' he said. 'Just so busy putting this new show together. And of course everyone wants a piece of me. I swear, if I get one more phone call from a talk show or journalist, I'll go postal. Sometimes I think I'd like to just pack it all in and become a Tibetan monk or something.'

Sage noticed Herb, still standing in the wings on the opposite side of the stage. His eyes met hers, and he raised his eyebrows slightly as if to say *what a douchebag*. And suddenly, now she wasn't in Jason's spotlight anymore, Sage found herself agreeing with Herb. When he'd been bathing her in his golden light, Sage had felt like he was the most interesting person on the earth. Now, watching Jason with Armand, Sage could see that it was all fakery. A great magician indeed.

'You must be very pleased,' said Armand. 'A show at the Arts Centre.' Armand didn't look pleased at all.

'It's no big deal.' Jason Jones's superior expression implied that it was, in fact, a very big deal.

Armand said nothing.

'Fun show tonight,' said Jason Jones, with an insincere smile. 'I think it's a credit to you that you can always make such old material seem so fresh. I mean, if I had to do exactly the same routine day in, day out, year after year, I'd go crazy.'

'It's not the same routine,' Herb burst out indignantly, stepping out onto the stage. 'What about the floating chair and the rose petals?'

Jason Jones turned his gaze upon Herb with a slight air of confusion, as though he hadn't realised that there were other people in the universe. 'That was yours, was it?' he said. 'I'm impressed. Not bad work for a beginner. I thought it was really ... cute.'

Sage saw Herb's face cloud over. 'I have to ...' He looked around vaguely. ' ... go and do a Thing. Over there.'

He stomped past her, muttering *cute* under his breath. Jason Jones watched him go, and winked at Sage as he noticed her standing behind the curtain. For a moment Sage was sucked back into the vortex of his charm. Then she blinked and it was all make-believe again. Resisting the urge to stick her tongue out at Jason, Sage followed Herb back to the office, bumping into Bianca on the way.

'I wouldn't go out there if I were you,' Sage told her. 'Jason Jones is here. What a creep.'

Bianca craned her head round the wings so she could see onto the stage. 'Jason's here?' she asked. 'Why?'

'He came to the show. He's talking to Armand now, being patronising.' Sage frowned. 'Do you know him?'

'What? No. What makes you think that?'

'You called him Jason. It sounded like you knew him.'

Bianca laughed. 'Oh, I mean, I know him a bit. It's like that in the magic industry. We all know each other. It's not a big field.' She glanced at her watch and frowned. 'I'd better go,' she said. 'I'm meeting friends.'

She turned and started to hurry back to her dressing-room, but stopped halfway down the corridor. 'Oh, Sage?'

'Yes?'

'Thank you,' said Bianca. 'For saying what you did, yesterday. About how things don't always have to be this way. You made me … think about a lot of stuff. I guess sometimes it takes an outsider to remind us how weird this industry is.'

'You're welcome,' said Sage, feeling totally thrilled that she'd gained Bianca's approval.

'It's … it's been a while since anyone said anything like that to me,' said Bianca.

Sage resisted an almost overwhelming urge to give her a hug.

'Girl power, hey?' Bianca giggled. 'Sisters are doing it for themselves!'

Sage nodded, suspecting that Bianca might have totally missed the point. 'Absolutely.'

'See you tomorrow!' Bianca smiled brightly and slipped into her dressing-room.

Sage went into the little office she shared with Herb. He was sitting in his swivelly chair with his feet on the desk, crankily scribbling on a notepad.

'Do you feel special?' he asked, not looking up. 'Now you've been personally condescended to by Lord Jason of Douchebaggington?'

'*So* special,' replied Sage, collecting her bag. 'I shall treasure this day until I die.'

'You fell for it a little bit, though, didn't you?' said Herb.

Sage made a face. 'Totally,' she admitted. 'It was like, for a moment, I was the most interesting person in the universe.'

'He's such a *tool*.' Herb stabbed his notepad savagely. 'He's a master of the backhanded compliment and the humble brag.'

'The what?'

'You know,' Herb struck an aloof pose. 'I ruined my shoes last night, stepping in chewing gum. It was so annoying. I mean, who spits their used gum on a red carpet?' He sighed. 'And this is the *third* awards ceremony I've been to in a week. I mean, I'm totally honoured, but it's getting embarrassing.'

Sage laughed.

'So where's Bianca?' asked Herb. 'Usually she's in here

by now trying to convince me I need my chakras realigned.'

'She had to leave,' said Sage. 'She's meeting up with friends.'

Herb snorted. 'Is that what she said?'

'Why is that so unbelievable?'

'Bianca doesn't have *friends*,' Herb said. 'None of us do. That's why we're here all the time.'

Sage felt taken aback. 'Really? You don't have any friends? Nobody who you hang out with on the weekend?'

'We do three shows every weekend,' said Herb. 'There are some other magic nerds I meet up with once a month to play cards with, but otherwise it's just me and Bianca. And now you.'

Sage frowned. 'That's … kind of sad.'

Herb shrugged. 'That's magic.'

﹀﹀﹀

After Sage heard Jason Jones's ostentatious farewell, she made her way down the corridor and knocked timidly on Armand's dressing-room door, slipping inside when she heard his voice. Armand was sitting at his dressing table, looking over a pile of papers. His expression was sour.

'I was wondering if I could ask a favour,' she said.

Armand raised an eyebrow, but didn't look up. Sage explained about her photography class, and that she wanted to do a series of portraits of him.

'You know,' Sage finished. 'Capture the glamour and mystery of the show.'

Sage saw a flicker of light in Armand's eyes, and he turned away from his table and actually looked at Sage for what felt like the first time ever.

'Tomorrow,' he said. 'You may photograph me tomorrow, before the show.'

Sage grinned. 'Thank you,' she said. 'It won't take long, I promise.'

'It will take as long as it needs to,' said Armand. 'Oh, and don't worry about the accounting query you had the other day. I've taken care of it. It was just a glitch.'

Sage waited for him to explain further, but Armand didn't say anything, just turned back to his pile of papers. Sage walked slowly back to the office, thinking. What kind of glitch would make nine hundred dollars disappear? And why the secrecy? Could Armand be hiding something?

5. Transformation:
something is transformed from one state into another.

Click.

Sage stared through the viewfinder at Armand, astonished. He'd walked onto the stage a bitter and resentful old man, but as soon as Sage had turned on the stage lights and started snapping photos, he'd morphed into something else entirely. Dressed in a long black cloak, Armand prowled about the stage like a jaguar. His movements were powerful and precise. Sage stepped forward for a close-up, and Armand turned to look at the camera. His piercing gaze made her shiver. She'd never felt such a strong *presence* before – she hoped she'd been able to successfully capture the sheer strength of his performance.

'I think I've got enough,' she said after about twenty minutes.

'Very well.' Immediately the powerful magician vanished, and was replaced with Armand's usual sour, unhappy self. 'If you see Bianca, can you please ask her to step into my office for a moment?'

Sage nodded. 'Um,' she said, trying to pluck up a little more courage. 'I wanted to ask you … whether you think the theatre is haunted.'

Armand curled an eyebrow disdainfully. 'Haunted?'

'Bianca says there's a ghost.'

'A ghost?' Armand's face seemed to sag a little. 'There are many ghosts in this theatre,' he said. 'Ghosts of lost careers and long-dead friendships.'

His face took on a stony blankness, and before Sage could say anything else, he slunk off into the wings and disappeared.

〰〰〰

Bianca and Herb had a regular Friday post-show dinner at a nearby Vietnamese restaurant, and they'd invited Sage to join them. She was pleased to be asked, but was also sure that she'd be a third wheel. After all, usually it was just Bianca and Herb. It sounded like a date night to Sage. Maybe they'd just invited her out of politeness. Still, she wasn't going to turn down dinner.

After the show, Sage scrolled through the photos she'd taken of Armand, while she and Herb waited for Bianca to get changed. It was hard to tell on her digital camera's low-quality display, but Sage was almost certain that the photos were going to be amazing. Her favourite was an extreme close-up that captured every stern line on Armand's face. His eyes glowed with energy, and his mouth curved in a hint of a proud sneer. Sage suddenly realised that she'd forgotten to properly thank Armand for taking the time to be photographed.

'I'll be back in a moment,' she told Herb, and headed down the corridor to Armand's dressing-room, only to bump into Bianca coming out.

'Great show tonight,' said Sage.

Bianca looked paler than usual. Her eyes were wide and blank.

'Are you okay?' asked Sage.

Bianca looked at her for a moment, as if she'd forgotten who Sage was. 'I'm fine,' she murmured. 'I'm not sleeping very well, is all.'

Sage remembered the bruises on Bianca's thigh. The shows must be so draining for her. She'd probably been in Armand's dressing-room to ask him if they could cut the Zigzag Effect, and he'd said no. That was why she looked so upset. Sage felt indignant on Bianca's behalf, and resolved not to thank Armand after all. Impulsively, she stepped forward and gave Bianca a hug. She felt the taller girl's shoulders stiffen under her arms. She was so slim, it felt like hugging a bird. Bianca took a deep breath, and pulled away.

'Thank you,' she said. 'You're lovely.'

There was a little catch in her voice, like she was trying not to cry.

'Don't worry about Armand,' said Sage. 'You're amazing.'

Bianca smiled weakly. 'I think I'm just tired. I'm going to go home.'

'Oh.' Had she forgotten about Friday-night Vietnamese?

Sage watched her go, her heart sinking. No Friday-night dinner, then. Looked like another greasy generic-brand peanut-butter sandwich on stale bread when she got home.

'Where's Bianca?' asked Herb, getting up from his desk and stretching as Sage returned to the office. 'Is it dinnertime?'

'Bianca went home,' said Sage. 'I don't think she's feeling very well.'

'Her loss.' Herb picked up his bag and slung it over his shoulder. 'Lucky I've got you. Otherwise I'd be eating on my own, and that's always a classy move on a Friday night.'

'You … you still want to go?' Sage felt a little spark of happiness.

'Of course! I'm not letting Bianca's lameness get in the way of my *cá kho to*. Come on, let's get out of here.'

A strip of light still shone under Armand's door. 'Does he

usually stay so late?' asked Sage as they left the theatre and stepped into the freezing night.

Herb nodded. 'This show is his whole life,' he said. 'When he's not onstage, he's holed up in his dressing-room reliving his glory days.'

'Armand had glory days?' Sage rubbed her hands together to try to warm them up.

'Oh yes,' said Herb. 'He used to be one of Australia's leading magicians. Top billing. He did European tours and everything.'

'What happened?'

Herb shrugged. 'Traditional stage magic fell out of fashion. Now it's all about the flashy Vegas style stuff. You know. Derren Brown, and the ridiculous one who wears eyeliner. That's why Jason Jones is so big right now. It's all that mentalism garbage.'

'What's his show like?' she asked, as they passed boarded-up shopfronts covered in graffiti. 'Jason Jones's, I mean.'

Herb closed his eyes and sighed. 'Really, really good. It's disgusting. As I'm sure you've inferred, I'm not a massive fan of mentalism, but his routine is truly excellent. A perfect blend of misdirection, sleight of hand and brilliant design. It makes me hate him even more.'

The restaurant was wedged between a grotty twenty-four-hour laundromat and a hairdressing salon that looked as if it had closed its doors sometime in the 1970s. Sage thought calling it a *restaurant* was a bit of a stretch – it was just a handful of laminex tables, rickety chairs and no customers. Herb pushed open the door. Sage glanced at her phone. It was just after nine.

'Is it still open?' she asked.

Herb laughed at her. 'It's Friday night,' he said. 'You clearly haven't been in town long.'

A middle-aged man bustled out from the kitchen to show them to a table by the window.

'Hey, Mr Pham,' said Herb.

'Where's Bianca?' replied the man. 'Scared her off, have you?'

Herb shrugged. 'She got a better offer. But I brought a worthy replacement. This is Sage. She's helping out with the show.'

'Very pleased to meet you,' said Mr Pham, shaking Sage's hand. 'Please sit down.'

He plonked a pot of green tea and two little cups on the table, then disappeared into the kitchen. Herb poured the tea and pushed one cup towards Sage.

'Cheers,' he said. 'Welcome to Friday-night dinner.'

They clinked cups. The tea was hot and pleasantly bitter. Sage wrapped a hand around the little cup. 'Is there a menu?' she asked.

'Not for us,' said Herb. 'We get what Mr Pham gives us. You don't have any allergies, do you?'

Sage shook her head.

Mr Pham reappeared with a plate of spring rolls, a giant curl of lettuce, a few sprigs of Vietnamese mint and a little bowl of dipping sauce. Herb tore off a piece of lettuce and wrapped it around a spring roll and mint leaf, and then dipped the whole thing in the sauce. Sage cautiously followed suit.

'So tell me about *you*,' said Herb, between mouthfuls. 'Actually, let *me* tell you about you. It'll be more fun.'

Sage raised her eyebrows. 'Okay,' she said, biting into her own spring roll. The pastry was just the right kind of crispy, and the lettuce around it added an extra layer of cool crunch that was extremely pleasing. The soft, steaming inside was a burst of garlic and ginger and chicken. Sage closed her eyes for a moment and chewed happily.

'Well,' said Herb, after a moment's thought. 'I already know you have a little brother. I'm guessing no other siblings. I know you just moved here, and from your tan and freckles I'd say it was from either Perth or Queensland. I'm going with Queensland – you have a very particular way of shaping your vowels. You moved because one of your parents got a new job here. Statistically speaking, it was almost certainly your dad. Some kind of office job.

Financial sector, maybe?' He glanced at her for confirmation.

'He's a credit analyst,' said Sage, reaching for a second spring roll and trying to hide how impressed she was. 'Keep going.'

Mr Pham came to the table with rice and a hot plate sizzling with chicken. Herb ladled rice into a bowl and grinned at her.

'You told me last week that your birthday is in May, which makes you a Taurus. Because you didn't wholly side with me in that ridiculous psychic argument with Bianca yesterday, I suspect that you read your horoscope and tentatively buy into all that hippy bullshit. Taureans are supposed to be patient, warm-hearted, persistent and placid. You identify with all these traits, even though in fact you are prickly, argumentative, introverted and creative.'

Sage blinked, not sure whether to be surprised or insulted. Mr Pham returned with a noodle dish bursting with prawns. She filled her bowl as Herb watched her carefully.

'You're not a painter,' he said. 'Your fingernails are too clean. Possibly a creative writer. Definitely not acting, dance or any kind of performance – you're not confident enough. Maybe music … but I wouldn't bet on it. No, it's definitely a writer, or …' He narrowed his eyes at her. 'Photography. It's photography, right?'

Sage choked on a prawn.

Herb let out a triumphant laugh and slapped the table. 'I'm awesome.'

'How did you do it?'

He gave her a sly look. 'I knew all along. You were reading a book by Yoshi Lear backstage the other day.'

Sage nearly spat out her prawn. 'That's cheating!'

'It's *all* cheating,' said Herb, chuckling. 'Haven't you been paying attention?'

He was flirting with her. Or, at least, it certainly *felt* like he was flirting with her. Here she was, with a cute guy, alone in a restaurant late on a Friday night. Was this... a date? She covered her awkwardness by filling her bowl again. It couldn't be a date. Herb liked Bianca. Didn't he?

'These prawns are amazing,' she said.

Herb nodded. 'It's all about the lemongrass,' he said. 'Mr Pham is a genius. I seriously go into withdrawal if I don't eat here at least twice a week.'

Maybe that was it. Maybe he just didn't like eating alone.

'Tell me about the new trick Armand put in the show.'

'The Zigzag Effect?' Herb shrugged. 'It's a classic.'

Sage had watched the effect that night. Bianca climbed into the zigzag cabinet, a panel in the top box sliding open to reveal her face. Her left hand poked out of a hole in the middle box, waving a red handkerchief. Her bare left foot emerged from the bottom box, her toes wiggling. With a great deal of drama, Armand inserted two wide, flat blades into the cabinet, at the points where the three boxes met each other. Bianca continued to smile, wave the handkerchief and wiggle her toes. Then Armand pushed at the middle box and slid it over to the left, making it look like Bianca's torso had been severed and pushed to the side. When Sage had seen Bianca's hand still waving the red handkerchief, she'd felt sick. With the middle box to the side, the cabin looked like a sideways *V*, giving the trick its name.

'Did you fix it? So Bianca won't get hurt?'

Herb nodded. 'I did what I could,' he said.

'I suppose you can't tell me how it works? The trick?'

Herb clicked his chopsticks together. 'It's a pretty old effect,' he said. 'The secret is all over the internet if you really want to know.'

'Why don't you save me the bandwidth,' said Sage with what she hoped was her most persuasive smile. 'And just tell me.'

Herb chuckled. 'It's all Bianca,' he said. 'There are black panels at the sides of the cabinet to make it look slimmer than it is. Once she's in, she sort of turns her body to the side. The handle of the blade is as wide as the cabinet, but the actual blade is about twenty centimetres shorter. She has to be careful, but she's skinny. So the blades miss her completely.' He paused here with a frown. 'Most of the time.'

Sage felt a little sick again. She put down her chopsticks. 'Then what?'

'Then she reaches over with her hand as Armand pushes the middle box sideways so it looks like her whole body is moving, but it isn't. That's basically it.'

'It sounds very simple.'

'The good ones always are. But it takes a lot of physical strength from Bianca. She basically has to have the skills of a contortionist. Armand is just there to add some drama.'

'So you think it's a good trick?'

Herb made a face. 'It's *effective*,' he said doubtfully. 'But I'm personally not crazy about it. It requires nothing from the magician at all, and on the whole I'm not big on the cut-up-the-pretty-lady genre of magic effects.'

Sage felt a strange sense of relief. 'Thank goodness it's not just me,' she said. 'Some of those tricks are so *creepy*! I just can't stop thinking about what would happen if those blades really *did* slice her up.'

'It's old-school stuff,' said Herb. 'The best magicians working today have moved on.'

'Do you think Bianca minds?'

'Getting cut up?'

Sage nodded. 'All those creepy tricks. And the fact that she does all the work while Armand gets the credit.'

'Nah,' said Herb airily. 'She knows it's all part of the gig.

95

And you know Bianca: she's pretty cheerful when she's not freaking out about superstitions or her horoscope.'

Sage picked up her chopsticks again, finding her appetite had returned. 'So what about the trick you're working on?' she asked. 'Can you tell me about that?'

Herb refilled their teacups. 'It's an escapology routine,' he said. 'With a historical lesson thrown in for fun.' He saw her dubious look and grinned. 'I really, really love the history of magic. It's fascinating. And it's one of the oldest forms of entertainment we have.'

'If you say so,' said Sage. 'So what's the history of escapology?'

'Mostly Houdini,' said Herb, through a mouthful of broccoli. 'He turned escapology into what it is today. I'm also thinking of adding an homage to the whole locked-room mystery genre.'

'Someone is murdered inside a locked room, there's no sign of the murderer or weapon, and the key is in the lock, on the inside?'

Herb looked impressed.

'I read,' said Sage, helping herself to more rice. 'So how will this trick work?'

'Effect,' Herb corrected her with a slight frown. 'I'm not sure, yet. Escapology routines are usually death-defying – suspended from the Golden Gate Bridge, or trapped inside a block of ice, or sunk to the bottom of the ocean. All of these things are hard to do in a theatre, they work better on TV specials.'

Mr Pham reappeared with a steaming claypot.

'*Cá kho to*,' he said. 'My specialty.'

'I'm so full!' Sage protested. 'I'm sure I couldn't manage another bite.'

'Oh no,' said Herb. 'You have to try this. It's caramelised fish. It's *amazing*. It will literally change your life.'

Mr Pham grinned at him. 'For that, you get a twenty per cent discount.'

'You always give me a twenty per cent discount,' said Herb.

'Well, tonight you earned it. Usually you're just a freeloader.' Mr Pham cleared their empty dishes and went back to the kitchen.

Sage let Herb spoon some of the fish into her bowl. She took a bite.

'Holy crap,' she said, her mouth still full.

'Don't you mean holy *carp*?' Herb chuckled. 'But I know, right? It's like Mr Pham takes the happiest fish in the world, caramelises it in pure undiluted joy, and then smothers it in love-sauce.'

Sage choked out a laugh, and Herb's ears went pink. 'That came out a little dirtier than I'd intended,' he admitted.

Sage helped herself to more. 'So what kind of magic do you want to do?' she asked. 'Be a TV magician, with occasional shows in Vegas?'

'I don't know,' said Herb. 'There's something very special about performing in a theatre that you just don't get on TV.'

Sage nodded. 'So what are you going to escape from? A locked room onstage?'

'I think so. I like the idea that an audience member and I will get locked in the room together, by a second audience member. It'll be a real lock – a padlock or something, on the inside. I'll get tied up first, with chains and more padlocks. Maybe a straitjacket and a hood over my head. The second audience member will lock everything, then slide the key out from under the door. They'll also make sure I'm not cheating.'

'But you will be cheating.'

'Well, yes,' Herb looked slightly put out. 'But not in a *sneaky* way. In a *skilful* and *secret* way. And then at the end I'll not only escape and open the door, I'll also reveal some clever twist, like I swapped clothes with the audience member without them noticing.'

'Can you do that?'

Herb shrugged. 'Well, I've seen it done before. I just have to figure out the logistics. That'll be the tricky bit. Escaping and unlocking the door is easy.'

'I look forward to seeing it.'

He considered her for a moment, and the wide smile crept across his face. 'Do you want to see it now?'

'Now?' Sage looked at her phone. It was just after ten.

'Sure,' said Herb. 'My stuff is in the theatre. It'll only take five minutes to get there, and five minutes for me to show you the effect. You'll be on your bus by ten-thirty.'

His eyes were full of boyish excitement. It wasn't as if Sage's parents would mind if she was half an hour late. She could text them to let them know. It was Friday night. And she didn't want to go home yet.

'Okay,' she said. 'Let's do it.'

Herb practically sprang from his chair. 'Let me pay for dinner,' he said. 'My treat. To welcome you and everything. Mr Pham!'

〰〰〰

'Ladies and gentlemen,' Herb boomed theatrically. 'Over four hundred years ago, Saint Nicholas Owen was tortured to death in the Tower of London. It wasn't his first visit, however. He'd been there before, helping Jesuit priests escape. Today he is known as the Patron Saint of Escapologists.'

They had tiptoed past Armand's dressing-room, where the light was still on, to the storeroom near the end of the hallway, collecting a clinking green bag from their office on the way.

'Sherlock Holmes investigates a murder involving a man, dead of a gunshot wound to the head, in a room locked from the inside. Is it a suicide? The gun in question is still clutched in the victim's right hand. Except according to the layout of items on his desk, the man was left-handed. How did the murderer escape from a locked room? The art of escape is a craft, carefully honed. From the Davenport Brothers in the 1860s to Harry Houdini in the early twentieth century, to the flashy Vegas magic shows of today, highly trained escapologists can still baffle audiences with their death-defying acts.'

A banging sound, like a slamming door, sounded from somewhere else in the theatre. Sage started. Was it the ghost? Then she remembered that Armand had still been in his dressing-room. It was probably him finally going home.

A sly smile crept across Herb's face. It wasn't as wide as his usual smile, but it still lit up his eyes and made Sage smile in response.

'I'll need a volunteer from the audience.'

He looked pointedly at Sage, who, after a pause, raised her hand. 'Excellent! You, young lady. Step into this room with me.'

Sage stepped into the storeroom, and Herb squeezed in after her, flicking on the light. The cupboard smelled of damp mop and disinfectant. Shelves of cleaning supplies ran across one wall, while another held a drape of filthy tarpaulin, hanging from a rack near the ceiling. The narrow back wall held another rack for mops and brooms, and above it there was a tiny grate that let in wisps of fresh air. Herb handed Sage the bag, and Sage nearly dropped it. She hadn't been expecting it to be so heavy. Herb sat on the floor, drawing his legs up against his chest. 'Tie me up.'

Sage snorted. 'I bet you say that to all the girls.'

Herb grinned his ridiculous grin at her, and Sage pulled a length of chain out of the bag, and five padlocks with the keys in them. Following Herb's instructions, she wrapped the chain around his torso, binding his knees and arms tightly to his body. Once finished, she snapped on all five padlocks, and put the green bag over his head.

'Are you ready?' asked Herb.

Sage nodded, then realised that he couldn't see her. 'Yes.'

'Leave the keys outside, and close the door.'

Sage dropped the five padlock keys outside the door, and then pushed it closed. There was a click. The room was suddenly very small. Herb was very close. He smelled like cinnamon. She saw him start to fumble with the chains.

'How are you doing?' he asked, his voice soft and low, slightly muffled by the bag.

'I haven't done this since grade six, playing seven minutes in heaven with Otis Levin.'

Herb chuckled as chains clinked. 'How was it?'

'Not great. Otis burst into tears and told me he was gay.'

'Sounds romantic.'

'It was.' Sage half-wished that Herb wouldn't open the door quite yet. Even if he didn't like her, it was kind of exciting being together in this quiet, cramped space. Anything could happen. She could hear him breathing, sense his warmth on her skin when he accidentally brushed against her.

'Well,' said Herb. 'Here comes the magic.'

He stood up, the chains falling to the ground, and pulled the bag off his head. He grinned triumphantly at Sage.

'Very good,' she said.

He moved toward the door, and Sage heard the doorknob turn. The door didn't open. Herb rattled at it a little, then took a deep breath. Suddenly the storeroom felt very small.

'Herb? I'm ready to get out now,' said Sage.

'Just a minute.'

The minute turned into several minutes. Herb swore.

'Are we ... locked in?' asked Sage.

'No,' said Herb. 'Definitely not.'

He was still for a moment, and then made Sage jump by thumping loudly on the door. 'Hello?' he yelled. 'Bianca? Are you out there? This isn't funny.'

Sage held her breath, listening for movement outside. There was nothing. Herb rattled the handle again.

'Holy carp,' he said.

6. Permeation: a solid object passes through another.

Sage felt panic rise up inside her. She took a few deep breaths, trying to calm her hammering heart. It was fine. They weren't locked in. Herb had said they weren't locked in.

'We're locked in,' said Herb, and banged on the door again. 'Armand?' he shouted. 'Armand, are you still around?'

'Wait,' said Sage. 'Wait. This is stupid. This isn't a Sherlock Holmes story. We have phones. Call Armand and see if he's still here. Or call Bianca.'

Herb relaxed visibly. 'You're right,' he said. 'I'm an idiot. Give me your phone.'

Dread clanged into the pit of Sage's belly like a lump of iron. 'Why can't you use *your* phone?'

'I put it down when we picked up the bag with the chains. It's on my desk.' Herb held out his hand.

Sage swallowed a panicked sob. 'So is mine. I left my

104

bag in the office. I thought we'd only be five minutes.'

She slid down the wall until she was sitting on the floor. Herb banged on the door a few times, then looked wildly around.

'What about the window?' he asked, pointing.

'It's not really a window,' Sage replied. 'More of a grate. Even if we could get it off, there's no way we could fit through there.'

Bianca probably could, she thought ruefully. Skinny, lithe, contortionist Bianca could fit through a plughole if she needed to.

Herb craned his neck to look at the vent. 'Maybe we could take it off, and post a note outside for a passer-by to find.'

Sage nodded. 'Yes!' she said, starting to feel a bit excited and Famous Fivey about the whole thing. 'What's outside the grate? Is it the main road?'

Herb frowned, thinking about it. Then his face fell. 'No, it's the alley. There's nobody out there. Not until tomorrow at the earliest.'

He slid down the wall to sit next to Sage. His shoulder brushed against hers. It was warm and comforting. And he smelled good.

'Well, Sage Kealley,' he said. 'I guess it's lucky we just ate an enormous dinner. We could be in here for a while.'

His breath tickled the side of her face, and Sage felt

something inside her tingle. Suddenly, being locked in a tiny room all night with Herb didn't seem so bad after all.

Except he liked Bianca.

'So, where did Bianca go last night?' asked Sage, trying to keep her voice light. 'When she said she was meeting friends?'

She felt Herb shrug next to her. 'Dunno. Probably hooking up with some guy.'

Sage was surprised. 'Really? How do you feel about that?'

'How do I feel about it?' Herb sounded puzzled. 'I'm not sure. Vaguely nauseated? I hope she uses protection?'

'You're not upset?'

'Why would I be upset?'

Sage attempted a worldly eye-roll. 'Come on,' she said, full of bravado. 'You guys do nothing but bicker. It's clear you're in love with each other.'

Herb was silent for a moment. He looked genuinely baffled. 'Why would us bickering mean that we're in love? I thought the bickering wasn't supposed to show up until at least the fifth year of marriage.'

'Teasing is a sure-fire sign of affection,' said Sage. 'Like when Gilbert Blythe calls Anne of Green Gables "Carrots" and she breaks her slate over his head.'

'Huh,' said Herb. 'Well, there are two possibilities here. One is that I *am* in love with Bianca, but haven't realised it.

The other, and I don't want to pick favourites here, but I suspect this one is more likely, is that I bicker with Bianca because I find her genuinely irritating, and it's difficult working in close quarters with someone who's all *ooh, astrology is a pathway into the soul, crystals, unicorns, Tarot-whatever*.'

Sage felt a strange combination of hope (maybe he wasn't in love with Bianca!) and embarrassment (he clearly thought she was an idiot).

'So tell me about the escapology trick,' she said. 'How do you escape from the chains?'

'Hmm?' said Herb vaguely. 'Oh, the chains. That's the easiest part, really.'

'Oh.' He definitely thought she was an idiot.

'It's to do with the way you sit. You set your knees apart slightly. Even though the chains look tight, when you bring your knees together there's enough slack that you can wriggle out of them. You don't need to undo the locks at all. It never ceases to amaze me how few people figure that out.'

Sage felt her cheeks burn. *She* hadn't been able to figure it out. But she was smart! She knew she was smart. Just maybe not at the same things that Herb was clever at. After all, Herb barely knew how to turn a computer on.

'What if we used the light to signal?' she said suddenly. 'We could flash it on and off. Maybe someone will see.'

Herb sprang to his feet. 'It's worth a shot. Do you know Morse code?'

'I know SOS,' said Sage. 'And SMS, but I'm not sure that's particularly pertinent.'

Herb started to flick the light switch, turning the light on and off in a regular, blinking rhythm. It was like being at a really small, quiet nightclub. Then, with a *plink*, the light went out and didn't come back on again.

'Turn it back on,' said Sage.

'I did.' Herb's voice was bleak. 'I think I blew the globe.'

'Oh.' Sage felt mortification creeping over her once more. It was her fault. Maybe it was Herb's fault that they were locked in the storeroom, but it was definitely Sage's fault that there was no light. At least Herb couldn't see her burning cheeks now. She held out a hand in front of her and wiggled her fingers.

Herb sat down again next to her, but didn't say anything. Sage bit her lip as the minutes passed with excruciating slowness. She considered speaking, making conversation to pass the time, but didn't trust herself not to say anything that would make Herb think she was even more of an idiot than he already clearly did.

Herb shifted awkwardly, like he couldn't bear to stay still in the tiny, cramped room for another moment. His breathing sounded erratic.

'Um,' said Sage. 'Are you okay?'

'I'm fine,' said Herb between gritted teeth.

'Are you claustrophobic?'

'No.' She felt him jiggling his legs up and down.

'Suffer from anxiety of any type? Because you seem like you're freaking out a little bit.'

Maybe he thought she smelled.

'Really,' he said. 'I'm fine.'

'Okay.' Sage looked down at the dim outline of her shoes. She wondered what time it was. Would Zacky be in bed by now? Would her parents be worried? They might not notice she was gone – they'd been going to bed early since they moved to Melbourne, exhausted from unpacking and transition. They'd already been asleep when she'd arrived home from the last few late shows.

Herb let out a sigh that was almost a groan. He sounded like he was in pain. But he clearly didn't want to talk about it, so Sage held her tongue. Again she held up her hand in front of her, and tried to force her eyes to adjust to the gloom. She thought about light, and image, and photography. She thought about the manual film camera that Dad had promised her, and felt a twinge of sadness.

'Fine, I'm not okay,' said Herb suddenly, his voice strangled. 'This is possibly the most embarrassing thing I've ever had to say, and you can't imagine how mortified

I am to have to say it to *you*. But here we are, locked in the storeroom in the middle of the night with no hope of escape, so here I go. I really, really, *really* need to pee.'

As soon as he'd said it, Sage realised that she did too.

'Okay,' she said. 'We'll just have to figure something out. This is a storeroom. There'll be a bucket in here somewhere.' She peered at the dark blocks of the shelves, but couldn't make anything out. She saw the shadowy outline of Herb stand up and heard clinks and scratches as he groped around on the shelves. She followed suit, hoping she wouldn't put her hand on a mousetrap or, worse, one of the escaped white mice. Her fingers closed around the hard, metal rim of something curved.

'Bucket!' she said triumphantly.

Herb was silent for a moment. 'Now what happens?' he said at last.

'Now you ... do whatever you need to do.'

There was another pause. 'I can't,' he said. 'I just can't pee into a bucket with you two feet away from me.'

'I'm not sure you have a choice.'

'It's fine, I'll just hold it. I can hold it. Totally fine.'

Sage nodded, even though he couldn't really see her in the dark. There was another, longer pause, then a sigh.

'Give me the bucket.'

Sage handed it to him.

'I bet this is the most romantic date you've ever been on.'

Sage heard him set the bucket down in a corner of the room, and the unmistakable sound of a zipper being undone. She held her breath. *Date?*

'Okay,' said Herb. 'Operation Most Humiliating Moment of My Life is go. You have to block your ears.'

'What?'

'I can't have you *listening* to me pee into a bucket. I realise that this is going to be a horrific experience for both of us, but there's no need to make it worse. Block your ears.'

'How will I know when you've finished?'

'I'll tap you on the shoulder.'

Sage made a face. 'Without washing your hands?'

Herb sighed. 'Fine, I'll nudge your foot with my foot.'

Sage complied, but even with her ears blocked she could hear the sound of liquid hitting plastic bucket. She tried not to think about how Herb was just a *little bit more naked* than he had been a moment ago. She also tried not to breathe in through her nose.

After what felt like an hour, she finally felt Herb's shoe nudge hers, and she took her fingers out of her ears.

'Do you need to go too?' he asked.

'Yep,' Sage replied. 'But ... it's more complicated for a girl.'

A pause. 'I hadn't considered that. It must make things tricky when you're on a bushwalk or something.'

'You have no idea.'

They stood up and awkwardly exchanged places. Sage felt for the rim of the bucket, screwing up her nose as she did so. There was no way around it. She was about to squat over a bucket of someone else's urine. The fact that it was a cute boy's urine didn't seem to help. What if there was splashback?

'Block your ears,' she told him, and did the best she could.

When it was all over, they found a rubber mat to drape over the top of the bucket, to keep its pungent odour to a minimum. Then they sat side by side as far away from the bucket as they could.

'Well,' said Herb at last.

'Well,' replied Sage.

'I feel like we've certainly got to know each other on a new level.'

'Quite.'

There was another awkward pause.

'At least we didn't have curry for dinner,' offered Herb, and Sage laughed.

'You have a nice laugh,' he said. 'Warm and low. You don't laugh very often, but when you do, I can tell you really mean it.'

Sage felt herself smile. Maybe he didn't think she was an idiot after all. 'Thank you.'

'Thank *you*,' said Herb. 'There's nothing more annoying than a girl who won't accept a compliment. Bianca does it all the time. You tell her that her hair looks nice or something, and she won't accept it. *This? Really? No. I look terrible. You're lying.*'

Sage nodded. 'I hate that too.'

'It's totally a self-fulfilling prophecy, too,' said Herb. 'You tell someone they're attractive, and they say *no, no, I'm hideous*, and lo and behold – suddenly they are hideous.'

Sage chuckled. 'So you think Bianca is hideous?'

There was a pause. 'No,' said Herb thoughtfully. 'Of course she's attractive. But she's so … You know how sometimes you go to an art gallery and see a painting that is totally amazing – you stare at it and stare at it because it is literally the most amazing thing you've ever seen?'

Sage nodded. That was how she'd felt the first time she'd been to a Yoshi Lear exhibition.

'But at the back of your mind, you're kind of thinking *I love this, but I wouldn't want it in my house, because it would overpower everything else.* You wouldn't be able to watch TV, or make pasta, or sit on the couch in your boxer shorts eating ice-cream straight from the tub. Because somehow it would be disrespectful to the painting?'

Sage had a sour taste in her mouth. 'So you don't want to be with Bianca because you don't think you deserve her?'

Herb rubbed a hand through his hair. 'No,' he said. 'That's not it. I'm explaining it all wrong. What I mean is – some things are beautiful, but you don't want to be around them all the time. Because falling in love isn't just about finding something beautiful, it's about being happy and comfortable.'

Falling in love. Sage's arms broke out in goosebumps. 'So what kind of painting *do* you want in your house?'

'One that makes me happy,' he said. 'The kind of painting that, when you look at it, makes you feel warm and content and strong. Like you can do anything, or nothing. A painting that *belongs* with you. That you can't imagine *not* being in your house, because if it wasn't in your house, then your house wouldn't feel like home.'

Sage felt her heart thumping and her cheeks growing red. She wanted to be Herb's painting. She felt him lean in towards her. His hand reached for her face, brushing her hair away from her forehead and cupping her chin. Sage held her breath.

'It's kind of paradoxical,' he said, his voice barely more than a whisper. 'Because it's a feeling that makes you feel safe and happy, but also makes you brave. Makes you do things you didn't think you could do. It's ... exciting. The painting is still beautiful – very beautiful. But it's more of an organic beauty. Like something grew wild and natural, and that's *why* it's beautiful. It's not like the first painting – that painting took years to prepare. Every brushstroke is perfect. But *my* painting isn't perfect. It's *real*, and real is infinitely more beautiful.'

His lips brushed hers. Electricity ran through Sage's body. She was Herb's painting. She was content and strong. She was *warm*, for the first time since leaving Queensland. She felt beautiful. She parted her lips slightly to kiss him back, but it was already over.

'I'm sorry,' said Herb, pulling away. 'I—'

Sage's tingling, electric feeling of *rightness* was replaced with a dull sinking ache. He didn't like her after all. It had all just been a stupid speech. He hadn't been talking about her. She wasn't his painting. 'It's fine,' she said. 'We probably shouldn't – I mean, we work together. It'd be unprofessional.'

'No,' said Herb hastily. 'I didn't mean – I *want* to kiss you. Very much. I've been thinking about pretty much nothing else for the last four hours. It's just…'

Sage's stomach twisted itself into a knot. What was he talking about? Why were boys so confusing?

Herb let out a sigh. 'I just don't want to look back and remember our first kiss, and recall the aroma of urine.'

A relieved laugh bubbling up inside her. 'Of course,' she said, while everything inside her sang *first kiss! First kiss! That meant there'd be more than one!* 'You're totally right.'

At some point, Sage fell asleep. She jerked awake and panicked for a moment in the unfamiliar darkness, then heard
Herb's steady breathing and relaxed. She heard something
else, too. A far-off scraping kind of sound, like someone
was dragging a chair across a concrete floor somewhere in
the building.

Could Armand still be around? Or could it be the theatre
ghost? Herb shifted his position and murmured something
unintelligible, leaning in to Sage. She rested her head on
his shoulder, and fell asleep.

When she opened her eyes again, daylight was coming in through the grate. Sage shifted slightly, and realised
with a start of horror that she had drooled on Herb's shoulder. Moving was a challenge. Everything ached. She sat up
and tried to stretch the crick out of her neck. The smell
from the bucket was worse.

Herb made an indistinct mumbling noise, and opened
his eyes. He looked adorably sleepy and rumpled, his hair
a little squashed, his face all confused and vulnerable. If it
hadn't been for the urine bucket, Sage would have pounced
on him then and there.

'Hey,' he said.

'Hey.' Sage put a hand to her hair, and realised that
although *Herb* looked rumpled and adorable, she probably

looked more like the crazed offspring of a cat-lady and a privet hedge. Also, she wished she'd had an opportunity to brush her teeth. She clamped her mouth shut. 'What time is it?' she asked, tilting her head away from him.

Herb held his wrist up to the light and peered at it. 'Just after six.'

'What time does Bianca usually get here?'

Herb sighed. 'Eleven.'

They played I-Spy until they ran out of things to spy, and then Herb taught Sage how to do a French Drop, disappearing a coin by sneakily changing it to the other hand. Then they talked about what they wanted for breakfast when they got out.

'I'm having the biggest burger of all time,' said Herb. 'Thick and juicy, with onion and mustard and cheese and a whole bucket of fries.'

Sage's stomach growled. 'And coffee,' she said. 'Don't forget the coffee.'

Herb groaned. 'At least a pint of coffee. Two pints.'

'And pancakes. And bacon. And eggs.'

They fell silent again. Sage's mouth watered as she imagined her towering stack of pancakes.

'Why do you like photography?' asked Herb suddenly.

Sage tilted her head to one side and thought about it. 'It's a kind of remembering,' she said. 'It captures moments that you didn't even realise were happening, and then preserves them forever.'

Herb nodded to show that he was listening. Sage wondered how to explain.

'Dad gave me my first camera when I was eleven and we went to the hospital to see Mum and Zacky, just after he was born,' she said. 'I guess Mum and Dad thought that I'd bond with my little brother through taking pictures of him. The first photo I took was of Mum and Zacky. He was breastfeeding for the very first time. I was so excited to meet him, and to see that Mum was okay. Zacky was so beautiful. He had a little tuft of black hair, and the sweetest little face, with big blue eyes that seemed very serious. I fell in love with him right then and there. It wasn't until the photos got developed that I noticed his little hand resting on Mum's chest as he fed, with all his fingers curled into a fist. Except for one.' Sage raised her middle finger to Herb and laughed. 'We were all so entranced with him, none of us noticed he was giving us the finger the whole time.'

Herb's wide smile split into a genuine laugh. The sound of it spread through Sage like sunshine. She grinned back at him, and for a moment, they just stared at each other, grinning like fools. Herb's lips parted as if he were about to speak, then his grin turned rueful and he shook his head slightly.

'Sage Kealley,' he said. 'You really are kind of awesome.'

'You're not too bad either, Herb Jackson,' said Sage, twinkling at him.

Another moment passed. The air was electric.

Herb sighed impatiently. 'Ah screw it,' he muttered, and tugged Sage closer to him, pressing his mouth against hers. Sage forgot about her sore back and growling stomach. She forgot that her parents were probably going to kill her when she got home. She forgot that she hadn't showered or brushed her teeth in twenty-four hours. She even forgot about the bucket of urine in the corner. The rest of the world just melted away, leaving only Sage and Herb and this heart-stoppingly sweet kiss.

When they broke away to breathe, Sage felt like she'd been cut in half. Who needed to breathe anyway?

'Well,' murmured Herb. 'That was …' He shook his head and the goofy smile – goofier than ever before – spread across his face. 'I guess once we get out of here we'd better—'

'Shh!' said Sage suddenly, clamping a hand over Herb's mouth. 'Did you hear something?'

Herb shook his head and leaned in for another kiss. Sage frowned, listening intently. Footsteps. Shoes on floorboards, somewhere in the building. She turned back to Herb, eyes wide. They both leapt to their feet and started banging on the door and yelling. The footsteps stopped, then started again, coming closer, and closer until Sage heard the scraping of a key in a lock, and the door opened to reveal Bianca, in the same floral dress she'd been wearing the night before.

She stared at them for a moment, her eyes wide. 'You scared the crap out of me,' she said, then wrinkled her nose. 'What is that *smell*?'

'Don't ask,' said Herb darkly, pushing past her and gulping down fresh mouthfuls of air.

Bianca looked at Sage's rumpled hair. 'Were you guys in there all night?'

Sage nodded and tilted her head to one side, trying to work out the crick in her neck. 'We got locked in.'

'But why were you in the storeroom in the first place? Surely if you wanted to make out you could just do it in your office.'

Herb glared at her. 'What are you doing here so early, anyway?'

Bianca seemed suddenly flustered. 'Nothing,' she said, looking away. 'I stayed at a friend's house last night, and it seemed easier to come back here and change than to go to my apartment.'

Herb raised his eyebrows. 'One-night stand, eh? You're in the middle of your walk of shame.'

'No need to thank me for rescuing you,' said Bianca coldly.

Herb glowered and stumped off. 'I'm going home.'

Sage felt a little twinge of disappointment. She'd been hoping they would go out for breakfast and drink those pints of coffee, holding hands and perhaps doing some sappy staring-into-each-other's-eyes. On the other hand, she *really* needed a shower. And some deodorant.

'He was trying to show me a trick,' Sage told Bianca. 'An escapology one. But he made a mistake.'

'I did not!' yelled Herb's retreating figure. 'Someone sabotaged the lock.' The door to the auditorium banged shut behind him.

Bianca's expression turned sour. 'It couldn't *possibly* be because he screwed up.'

'There was no one else in the theatre,' said Sage. 'Except maybe Armand. But he wouldn't have done it.'

'Of course not,' said Bianca. 'Men. They can never admit they're wrong.'

Sage giggled. 'Maybe it was the *curse*.'

Bianca raised an eyebrow. 'What curse?'

'You know. The wand-breaking curse. Maybe we made the theatre ghost angry.'

Bianca's eyes grew thoughtful. 'Maybe,' she said softly.

7. Vanish: Something is made to disappear.

Sage only had time for a quick shower and a disappointing breakfast of toast and dirt-flavoured instant coffee before she had to head back to the theatre for the Saturday matinee.

Bianca was sitting on the stage when Sage walked through the door. She looked tired and wan, as though she hadn't got enough sleep. Maybe she really had been coming home from a one-night stand when she'd released them from the storeroom.

'Armand's not here,' she said when she saw Sage. 'Show's off.'

'What's wrong with him? Is he okay?'

Bianca raised a shoulder in a half-hearted sort of way, as if she didn't have enough energy for a full two-shouldered shrug. 'Don't know. He just sent a text.'

She passed over her phone, and Sage noticed an exhausted tremble in her hand. A text message from Armand was on the screen.

NOT COMING IN CANCEL WEEKEND SHOWS

'That's it?' said Sage. 'Should we be worried?' Could this be related to the missing money? Maybe Armand was in trouble.

'Who knows?' said Bianca. 'I should think he'd tell us if there was something really wrong.'

Sage thought for a moment. How did one go about cancelling a show that started in an hour and a half? 'I'd better get on the phone and call everyone who's booked,' she said. 'And make a sign for out the front. Do we offer refunds or anything?'

'Don't ask me,' said Bianca. 'I'm just the beautiful assistant.'

Herb was in their office. 'I heard,' he said, holding up his hand. 'And no, I don't know what's wrong with him. And I don't care. All I know is that our contracts state that we still get paid if the show is cancelled within twenty-four hours of curtain.' He looked pleased.

Sage hovered in the doorway for a moment. Was he going to say anything about their early-morning kiss? Was it going to happen again? Herb shot her a distracted smile, and turned back to the notepad he was scribbling in.

Sage sank into her chair with a sigh, and pulled up the spreadsheet of the weekend's bookings. 'There're fifty names on this list, and we don't have long before they'll start turning up. And then there are the people who have booked into tonight's show. And tomorrow's.' She sighed and turned to Herb. 'Can you help call people?'

Herb gave her a pained look. 'Me? Talk to people? Real live members of the public?'

Sage printed out the list and ruled a red line halfway down it. 'Tell them they can re-book at no expense for any other show. And be *nice*.'

'You owe me,' said Herb, scowling at the list as he picked up the phone.

'You locked me in a storeroom overnight with a bucket full of wee,' Sage informed him. 'I owe you nothing.'

They made their way through the list without too much difficulty.

'So,' said Herb, tearing the spreadsheet into small strips. 'Any plans for tonight?'

'My plans were to work here,' Sage replied. 'Until about an hour ago.'

'Great,' said Herb. 'Come and see Jason Jones's show with me.'

Sage started. 'Like on a date?'

'Sure.'

Sage didn't want to bring up the kiss in the storeroom in case she looked desperate or clingy. She was going to be mature about it – let Herb come to her when he was ready. She'd started to worry that she'd dreamt the whole thing, or that Herb had been out of his mind and the kiss was a one-time-only event.

But a *date*. A date meant something.

'I thought you hated Jason Jones,' she said, trying to sound casual.

'I do,' said Herb. 'But his show is amazing. And he sent Armand a couple of freebies. Armand would rather chew off his own leg than go, so he gave them to me. And I would like to go with you.'

Sage felt a totally involuntary smile spread across her face. 'Great,' she said. 'I'm in.'

The Arts Centre foyer was not like the foyer of the Lyric Theatre. Perfectly maintained red velvet stretched from floor to ceiling. Warm, glittering chandeliers were reflected in the floor-to-ceiling windows that looked out over the equally glittering lights of the city across the river. It was elegant and comfortable, and Sage felt impossibly grown-up. She was on a date, with a nice guy, at a posh theatre. She wished she'd worn a dress, or makeup, or fancy shoes, but she and Herb had come straight from the Lyric, so she was in her usual show uniform of black jeans and a black button-up blouse. At least the blouse had a lace collar, and she was wearing a string of jade beads.

Herb bought her an orange juice and only went a little pale when the uniformed bar attendant told him how much it would cost. The foyer was packed with people dressed up for a night on the town – a very different crowd to the family groups who came to see Armand.

'Is this what you want?' asked Sage, leaning into Herb and feeling daring and desirable. 'This kind of glitz and glamour?'

Herb's expression grew wistful. 'Jason Jones is a lucky bastard.'

The bell rang, and Sage finished her orange juice. 'Are you ready?' she asked Herb, who was watching the people file past the ushers into the theatre.

'Mmm,' he said, not looking at her. Then he snapped to attention. 'What? Yes. Yes, let's go in.'

Sage followed him into the cavernous theatre, where more red velvet covered the walls, floors and seats, and warm lights glinted off polished brass. The stage – also swathed in red velvet – seemed enormous compared to the one at the Lyric. A polite usher showed them to their seats, and Sage sank into the soft embrace of the chair, feeling like a princess. This was definitely the *fanciest* date she'd ever been on.

'Welcome, ladies and gentlemen,' boomed a plump, bearded man in an evening suit. He was lit by a single spotlight. 'Welcome to the Arts Centre. We have an extraordinary night of magic and mentalism for you tonight. Prepare to be amazed and mystified by the incomparable talents of Mister Jason Jones!'

The red velvet curtain rose to reveal Jason Jones standing in the centre of the stage, holding a white envelope. The crowd applauded.

'My friends,' he said, as the MC left the stage. 'I shall require a volunteer.'

Sage settled back into her seat, ready to enjoy the show.

Herb had been right. Jason Jones's show was polished and slick, with just the right touches of humour and pathos. The magic tricks seemed effortless, and Sage had absolutely no idea how any of them were achieved. Jason Jones predicted which word an audience member would choose in a newspaper. He walked through a solid wall and turned the MC into wisps of smoke. Every now and then Sage snuck a look at Herb, who was entirely focused on the show, his face a mix of admiration and envy.

For the show's finale, the MC called for a volunteer from the audience, a man with neat silver hair and spectacles, and had him supervise Jason being blindfolded with a mask, followed by two fifty-cent pieces over his eye sockets, wrapped all around in bandages, with a black bag over his head. He then sat on a chair with his back to the audience. The MC came out into the aisle, holding a microphone.

'Ladies and gentlemen,' he said. 'What do you have in your pockets?'

The audience members near the aisle eagerly dug into their purses and pockets, proffering random objects. The MC accepted one and held up a green plastic cigarette lighter. 'Mr Jones, I want you to try and tell me what this is.'

A camera had been pointed at Jason, and his blindfolded face was projected on an enormous screen. 'It's ... something to do with heat. Matches? No. A cigarette lighter.'

'Please can you tell us the colour?'

'It's green.'

There was a smattering of applause. The MC held up another object – a gold wedding ring. 'Now, I want you to tell me about this one.'

Jason Jones tilted his head to one side. 'It's something precious,' he murmured. 'Something... that belongs to two people at once. It's very valuable, and ... a ring. A gold wedding ring.'

'Anything else?'

'There's an engraving on the inside.'

The MC peered at the ring, and then nodded and showed

it to the people nearby, who also nodded and stared at Jason in rapt attention.

'Now,' said the MC. 'Would you …' He paused dramatically and looked out at the audience. 'I think we should get him to try to guess the inscription, don't you? Would you like to, Jason? Do you think he will do it, ladies and gentlemen?'

Jason held up a hand, as if feeling his way through gauze curtains. 'It starts with … an *A*? No. An *H*. It's a woman's name. It's an old name. Named for a very famous woman. Famous for her beauty.' Jason's head snapped up. 'Helen.'

The owner of the ring stood up and nodded, his face a mask of wonder. The woman sitting next to him clapped her hand over her mouth, her eyes filled with tears.

Sage was impressed. Jason Jones went on to correctly identify a woman's hair-clip that had belonged to her grandmother, an airline boarding pass from the fifteenth of May, and a man's driver's licence including his date of birth and the expiry date. Sage glanced over at Herb, who was wearing a slightly smug smile.

He knows, she thought. *He knows how Jason does it.*

'But Jason's psychic abilities extend far beyond these simple games,' boomed the MC, as the lights grew dim. 'I'd like a volunteer from the audience.'

Hands jumped into the air. 'You, sir!'

A man stood up. He looked completely ordinary, in jeans and a button-down shirt. He made his way to the stage, where the MC positioned him on the opposite side from Jason, who still sat blindfolded in the chair.

'What we've just demonstrated is Jason's psychic ability to look through my eyes,' said the MC. 'And he can form this psychic bond with anyone. Like with you, sir.' He touched the volunteer on the arm. 'But this bond doesn't just reach your eyes. No. He can hear what you hear. Smell what you smell. Touch what you touch. I want you to put your hand in your pocket. Can you feel something? An object of some kind?'

The volunteer nodded.

'Good, good.'

The MC stepped backwards into the shadows, leaving the volunteer standing in one pool of light, and Jason Jones across the stage in another. Jason's head rolled from side to side.

'Your father gave it to you,' he said, his voice slightly muffled by the black bag. 'When you were very young. Eight? Nine? It was your ninth birthday present. He told you it would bring you luck. And it has, right? This object has bought you luck.'

The volunteer was nodding slowly, his face crumpling up like a paper bag. Tears started to roll down his cheeks.

'It's a coin,' said Jason. 'An … an old coin. Like a pound or a penny or … a shilling.'

The volunteer nodded more vigorously, and pulled his hand from his pocket, holding a silver coin. 'It was the first thing he earned,' he said, sniffling. 'When he was a boy. He … he died a few months ago.'

The audience started to applaud as the volunteer left the stage, but the MC held up a hand. 'Just one more, ladies and gentlemen. What if Jason could see into your *mind*? If, instead of guessing a real object, he could reach into your head and pluck an idea from your imagination?'

He selected another volunteer, a woman wearing thick glasses and an ill-fitting floral dress. Her friends giggled as she made her way to the stage. The MC placed a pad of paper and a black marker in Jason Jones's hands, then went to the woman, passing her a small wooden box. He held his hands up in front of her, cupping them slightly.

'I want you to imagine an object here in my hands. It can be anything you like. Now I want you to concentrate on that object. Fill your mind with it. Can you see it?'

The woman nodded. After a pause, Jason Jones started to scribble on his paper.

'Now,' said the MC, 'I want you to transfer that object into the wooden box you're holding, with your mind. Imagine it inside that box. Have you done it?'

The woman nodded again.

The MC made his way back to Jason and removed the bindings over his eyes. Jason stood up and turned around, holding the pad of paper in front of his chest so nobody could see what was on it.

'Please, madam,' said the MC. 'Tell us what your object was.'

She looked uncertainly at him, and he nodded encouragingly. 'It was a unicorn,' she said.

'A *unicorn*!' said the MC, chuckling. 'It must have been a really tiny one to sit here in my hand.'

The woman went red and the audience tittered. The MC turned to Jason, who raised his eyebrows and slowly turned the pad of paper around to reveal the word *UNICORN* in thick, clear letters.

The audience burst into applause. The woman went even redder, and smiled in a flustered way. The MC started to usher her back to her seat.

'Wait,' called Jason Jones. 'You haven't looked in the box.'

The woman glanced up at him, a little shocked, then down at the box in her hands. She opened it and started to laugh, pulling out a small pink plastic unicorn.

'You can keep that,' said Jason. 'A round of applause for our volunteers!'

Sage turned to Herb with a big smile. But Herb was

frowning, slouched down in his seat looking bored and resentful. What had happened? She'd thought he'd been enjoying himself.

'Well?' asked Sage as they stepped out into the street. 'How did he do it? Was there some kind of camera or something in the MC's coat? Or did he wear an earpiece and someone offstage told him what all the objects were?'

Herb laughed. 'It's funny,' he said. 'People used to believe that these effects were achieved using real wizardry. Now everyone assumes it's technological wizardry.'

'It isn't?'

He shook his head. 'The first part was impressively done, but is very straightforward. It's a two-person telepathy code. They assign a number to certain words that the MC can easily insert into his sentences. *I* is one. *Try* is two. *Can* is three. *Will* is four. And so on. Then you can assign those numbers to other things, depending on the context of the question. So I could say '*Can* you tell me which day of the week this bus ticket is for?' And because you know that *can* equals *three*, you know it's Wednesday, the third day of the week.'

'But what about all the other things? Like the wedding ring and the inscription?'

'You create an alphabet code – twenty-six letters for twenty-six numbers. So if you want an S, for example, that's the nineteenth letter of the alphabet, so you need to say *I* and *Now* – one and nine. To make a word, you just build a lot of distinct sentences together. So ... *I now request your attention, ladies and gentlemen. I want you to guess this lady's name. Quickly. If you would.*'

Sage looked at him.

'That was your name,' he explained. '*I* and *Now* is S. *I* again on its own is A. *Quickly* is G, and *Would* is E. *I now request your attention, ladies and gentlemen. I want you to guess this lady's name. Quickly. If you would.* S-A-G-E.'

'Right,' said Sage.

'You can make heaps of these lists,' he said. 'Assign a letter of the alphabet to a common object, so *A* could be *Aspirin*, *B* could be *Bus ticket*, *C* is *Coin*. The MC only chooses objects that are on the list, and there are pre-agreed characteristics that he looks for. So if he chooses a ring, Jason knows that he'll only ever choose a gold wedding ring.'

'Surely it'd take forever to memorise the whole code,' said Sage. 'Wouldn't the hidden camera and microphone be easier?'

'Maybe,' said Herb. 'But not nearly as impressive. That's the whole thing about magic. The effects require far more work and set-up than they're really worth. That's why people believe in them. They don't believe anyone is lame enough to go to all that effort for something so insignificant.'

Sage grinned. 'But you're totally that lame, right?'

'I once spent an entire school holidays perfecting a faro card shuffle.'

'A what?'

Herb grinned, and Sage realised that he'd wanted her to ask. He produced a pack of cards from his pocket, slid them out of the box and gave Sage the box to hold. He then lifted half the cards from the deck with one hand, so he was holding a half-deck in each hand. He then placed one stack above the other, perfectly lined up, and sort of *pressed* them together. The cards flicked against each other and entwined, a bit like a zipper. Herb tapped the deck a few times to make the cards slide down into a single stack once more.

'It's the hardest shuffle,' he said. 'A perfect faro is where you can cut the deck *exactly* halfway, and all the cards are perfectly alternated. It's really useful in magic because if you do a perfect faro eight times in a row, you get your original deck sequence back.'

Sage stared at him. 'You are such a nerd.'

'That's why you like me,' said Herb with a cheeky grin.

'So what about the next bit?' asked Sage. 'The guy with the coin in his pocket. And the unicorn. The MC didn't see those things, so he can't have told Jason.'

Herb's face clouded over. 'No,' he said. 'He didn't. They cheated. The first guy was a plant.'

'He wasn't really an audience member?'

'He was sitting alone,' said Herb. 'Who goes to a magic show on their own? Also I saw him in the foyer before the show, talking to the usher, who clearly knew who he was. And he didn't show anyone a ticket when he entered the theatre.'

Sage felt somehow disappointed. 'And what about the lady?' she said. 'She was with friends. And she looked far too flustered to be a plant.'

'She wasn't a plant,' said Herb, a vaguely disgusted look on his face. 'She was an instant stooge. Like this.' He pulled a black pen out of his pocket, and scribbled something on one of the playing cards, then shuffled them with his usual deft precision.

'You, young lady,' he said. 'The pretty one with the curly hair.' Sage smiled. 'Pick a card, but don't let me see it.'

He fanned the cards out, and Sage selected one. She cupped her hand over it, and examined the card. It was the seven of clubs, but scrawled over it in black biro were the words *JUST SAY YES OR YOU'LL RUIN IT FOR EVERYONE.*

'How did you make me pick that one?' asked Sage.

'Shh,' said Herb. 'We haven't gotten to the actual trick yet. If I were really doing this, that message would be on every single card. Now put it back in the deck.'

Sage did so, and Herb shuffled them again. He then waved a hand over the pack, and it vanished. He felt in his pockets and shook his head, then hovered his hand over Sage's jacket pocket. 'Do you mind?'

Sage shook her head, and Herb produced a card. It was the ace of diamonds.

'Is this your card?' he asked.

'Yes,' said Sage. 'Oh, I see. So he had *UNICORN* written on his hand, and he showed it to her when he asked her to imagine something. But what if she hadn't gone along with it? What if she'd said something else?'

'They never do,' said Herb. 'You have to be careful about who you choose. Women are more likely to play along than men. You pick timid, friendly-looking people – people who wouldn't dream of outing you because it'd be rude and spoil the show. You never, ever pick a drunk person.'

'And you think Jason Jones did that tonight? Picked an instant stooge?'

Herb nodded, his face still clouded with disgust. 'There are a million ways to do that effect without using a stooge! It just requires a little bit more effort and skill. He's getting lazy.'

'Why do you hate it so much? The stooge thing?'

Herb looked at her like it was totally obvious. 'It's cheating.'

Sage laughed. 'It's *all* cheating,' she said. 'You're not actually *doing magic*.'

'Yes, but to create an effect properly should take skill and practice. Just telling someone what to say is reprehensible. How do you think that poor woman is going to feel? She's leaving the show with this ugly little secret that ruined the whole show for her, and she knows if she tells anyone it'll ruin it for them as well. She'll probably never go to another magic show again. The illusion has been destroyed. Magic has been spoiled for her, forever. It's disgusting.'

He stopped walking, and Sage realised they were at the entrance to the train station.

'Sorry,' said Herb, shaking his head. 'I get a bit carried away sometimes. Will you be all right getting home?'

'I do it every night after the show,' Sage reminded him, hoping he might get carried away with something else. Like kissing.

He nodded, looking slightly distracted. Then he shifted his weight a little. 'My train is coming in a moment.'

Sage wondered where Herb lived. Did he live with his parents? Or alone? Or in a share house? What was his bedroom like? Messy, she imagined. But *interesting* mess.

Herb reached out and gently tucked a loose lock of Sage's hair behind her ear. She held her breath. He smiled, a gentle, soft smile that was quite different to his usual goofy grin.

'I had fun tonight,' he said, his voice low.

'Me too.'

They gazed at each other for a moment that for Sage seemed to last for hours. Then a barely noticeable crinkle of puzzled frown creased Herb's forehead, and he took a step back.

'Well,' he said. 'I guess I'll see you on Wednesday.'

He touched his cap like an old-fashioned gentleman. Then he turned and walked away.

Sage stood and watched him go, a sinking feeling in her stomach. He hadn't kissed her.

Had he changed his mind? Maybe every time he got close to her he was reminded of the smell of stale urine. Maybe the kiss hadn't been as amazing for him as it had been for her.

Or maybe he just didn't like her after all.

Sage was determined not to be one of those girls who dithered about whether or not a boy would call, so she stuck her phone in her underwear drawer and swore she wouldn't look at it until she next saw Herb. She wasn't going to stew or mope. She was going to *do* things. She sprang out of bed on Sunday morning and helped Mum make breakfast. She put on a load of washing. She had a shower and shaved her legs. She used some of Mum's face mask gunk and left it on until it cracked. She unpacked two boxes of books in the living room. She pored over her latest batch of theatre photos, looking for any signs of ghostly activity. She tidied her room and sent an email to her friends back home, telling them all about her new job and about Herb.

Then she looked at the clock. It was three minutes past ten. She thought about the phone in her underwear drawer. No. She wouldn't look at it. She was stronger than that.

Maybe she'd just *glance* at it. What if someone else had called? One of her friends? Or Bianca? What if they needed her to do something at the theatre? It was her job, after all. She had a responsibility to look at her phone. Just once. Then it could go back in the underwear drawer.

She crossed the room and yanked the drawer open. The phone was nestled in there, among her Bonds hipster briefs. She picked it up.

No missed calls. No text messages. Nothing.

She dropped it back in the drawer and shoved it closed again with somewhat more force than was necessary.

Herb hadn't kissed her again. She wasn't his painting after all. He didn't think she was wildly, organically beautiful. She had been kidding herself all along. She was just dumpy, mousy-haired Sage Kealley. Little Miss Unremarkable. Probably the only reason why Herb had even noticed her was because they were locked in a cupboard and there was nobody else to talk to.

She sighed and went downstairs.

Mum was sitting at the dining table, leafing aimlessly through a catalogue of wallpapers and interior furnishings. A pile of printouts from an employment website lay discarded on the floor.

'Is Dad at work again?' Sage asked.

Mum nodded. 'Do you think we should go for a clean, modern look in here?' she asked, nodding at her catalogue. 'Or try to recreate the original period style of the house?'

Sage privately thought that it didn't much matter, given that they had no money for wallpaper or couches or fancy doorknobs. They didn't even have enough money to get the sagging roof or the leaky taps fixed.

'I don't know,' she said. 'I like the old-fashioned stuff, but it might look a bit ... you know. Like a museum.'

Mum nodded and sighed. 'Are you going to the theatre today?' she asked, closing the catalogue.

Sage made a noncommittal noise. 'It's cancelled.'

Mum looked as though she was about to say something, but the front door banged open and Zacky came roaring in with Roman in tow. Roman was a little smaller than Zacky, with a halo of blond curls that made him look like a cherub. The pointy wooden wand gripped tightly in his fist indicated that he shared Zacky's obsession with magic.

'Mum,' said Zacky breathlessly. 'I don't want to alarm you, but there's a *possibility* that we might be being chased by a basilisk. Hi, Sage.'

Sage waved.

'I see.' Mum nodded. 'But I shouldn't be alarmed because ...?'

'Because we're going to defeat it!' piped Roman. 'With magic,' he added helpfully.

'Great,' said Mum. 'Then we won't worry.'

'Good,' said Zacky. 'We're going to do this spell that might be a bit noisy. There might be a big bang and a flash of light.'

'Okay,' said Mum.

'And ...' Zacky glanced at Roman. 'And one of the ingredients we need for the spell is chocolate biscuits.'

Mum laughed. 'You can have two each. They're in the pantry.'

Zacky and Roman tore out of the room, heading for the kitchen.

'You used to be like that, you know,' said Mum with a smile. 'Always making things up. The first time we went on a plane, you were absolutely glued to the window, because you were convinced that there were fairies living in the clouds.'

'I remember,' said Sage. 'I was so desperate to meet a

fairy. I used to leave out little dishes of fairy bread and check them each morning at dawn. For a while I was convinced the fairies were coming, because the dish would be empty each morning. Then one day I caught a possum eating it.'

Mum chuckled.

'It was a really fat possum,' said Sage. 'I guess it had eaten a lot of fairy bread.'

'When did you stop believing in them?' asked Mum. 'Fairies, I mean.'

Sage thought about her plan to get a photo of the theatre ghost. 'I'm not sure I ever did,' she murmured.

'Sage!' said Zacky, bursting through the living-room door again. 'Can you help me and Roman make wizard robes?'

'Sure,' said Sage, secretly relieved to finally have something to keep her busy. 'Do you want just capes? How about some pointy hats?'

After two empty cereal boxes had been decorated with silver foil stars, and Mum and Dad's extra-large bath towels had been fashioned into capes, Sage taught the boys how to do a French Drop, making a coin vanish by pretending to pass it from one hand to the other.

'So it's all just tricking?' said Roman, looking a bit disappointed. 'The coin never really vanishes?'

'Never,' said Zacky, with an infinitely superior toss of his head. 'It's all just pretend.'

'But it takes a lot of practice,' said Sage. 'A stage magician has to be *very* clever to trick an audience.'

'Not as clever as a *real* magician, though.'

'I guess not.'

Sage thought about Herb. She closed her eyes, and saw his face – his wide mouth and smile, his soft brown eyes. She mentally scolded herself. She was *not* one of those girls. She didn't care if he called or not. She thought about the phone in her underwear drawer.

'Come on,' she said to the boys. 'We'll make cupcakes, and you can decorate them like golden snitches.'

She played with the boys until Roman had to go to his grandmother's house for lunch, then she and Zacky watched *Harry Potter and the Chamber of Secrets* for the fifty millionth time, while Zacky slowly drifted into a cupcake-induced sugar coma. Sage pulled the coin she'd been using to teach the boys the French Drop from her pocket and toyed with it.

Herb had shown her a few different coin tricks and techniques, besides the French Drop. In this latest one, Sage placed the coin on her palm, and curled her fingers around it into a fist. Then she turned her fist over and started to rub it with her free hand, pinching and pulling at the skin.

On the TV, Harry, Ron and Hermione had taken polyjuice potion and were transforming into Slytherin students.

Sage pinched and pulled until she revealed the coin on top of her still-closed fist, as if she had pulled it through the flesh of her hand.

'Do that again.' Zacky was awake and watching her, open-mouthed.

Sage remembered something Herb had said, and shook her head. 'Nope,' she said. 'Once is enough.'

Maybe that was why Herb hadn't kissed her again. Maybe he knew how impressed she was by the first kiss, and didn't want to give away his secrets. Maybe he'd just been trying to show off his skills.

'Show. Me.' Zacky's face darkened, and Sage could sense a tantrum approaching like a heavy thundercloud.

'Maybe later,' she said. 'After dinner when Dad's home.'

The thundercloud wavered. 'Promise?'

Sage nodded. 'I promise.'

∿∿∿

Zacky held Sage to her word. As soon as Dad's key turned in the front lock, he dragged Sage into the living room, where Mum was curled on the couch with her laptop.

'Do it,' he said with an imperious wave of his hand. 'You promised.'

Dad slipped off his coat and exchanged a look with Mum, who shrugged and looked at Sage.

'It's just a coin trick,' said Sage. 'It's pretty crappy.'

'Do. It.' Zacky's teeth clenched.

Dad perched on the arm of the sofa. 'Go on, then,' he said with a smile.

Sage did the trick again, making a fist around the coin and pinching and pulling the back of her hand until the coin magically passed through her skin.

'It's still in your fist,' said Dad. 'There're two coins.'

Sage opened her clenched fist. There was no second coin.

Zacky punched the air. 'That is *so cool*,' he said. 'Will you teach me how?'

Sage looked over at Mum and Dad. They were both grinning at her, their eyes alight. 'That was great,' said Mum. 'Did you learn that at the theatre?'

'It's a trick coin, right?' asked Dad. 'I bet you won't let me look at it.'

Sage felt a surge of triumph. She'd tricked them. They were completely fooled. She handed the coin to Dad, who examined it suspiciously.

'It's just an ordinary dollar coin,' she said.

Dad squinted at her. 'Then the second coin is up your sleeve.'

Sage removed her cardigan and shook it to prove there were no coins hidden inside, and passed that to Dad as well. Dad looked up at her, baffled.

'So how did you do it?' he asked.

Never, ever reveal your secrets, said Herb inside her head. Sage smiled enigmatically at them. 'I think I hear my phone ringing,' she said innocently. 'I'd better go check.'

She swept from the room, feeling like the greatest magician who had ever lived. The feeling lasted until she got to her room and peered into her underwear drawer.

He hadn't called.

8. Exposure: a magician's secrets are revealed.

Sage struggled to fall asleep that night. The scene outside the station after Saturday night's show kept playing over and over in her mind.

Why hadn't Herb kissed her? Why hadn't he called? Why did she *care*?

Sage was disgusted with herself. She told herself she was overcompensating because she was in a big new city and Herb was the first friend she'd made here. She told herself that she was really worried about Armand, and that the whole Herb thing was to distract her from Bianca's unsettling stories of curses and ghostly magicians.

But the fact was, she *liked* Herb.

And it had seemed as if he liked her back.

Maybe she needed something. Warm milk. People in books always drank warm milk when they couldn't sleep.

Sage climbed out of bed and slipped from her room, making her way down the stairs.

She stopped halfway down when she heard voices.

Light spilled from the half-closed living-room door. Mum and Dad were still up, talking in low voices. She sank down on the stairs and leaned her head against the peeling wallpaper. She didn't really want to talk to them, but it was comforting to hear the murmur of their voices.

'I just don't know,' Mum was saying. 'We've been together from the beginning. Do we really have to split up?'

Sage felt her blood turn to ice. She leaned forward, trying to make out the words.

'... Just doesn't work,' said Dad. '... go back ...'

Go back? Did Dad want Mum to go back to Queensland? Were her parents splitting up? Sage remembered the conversation she'd overheard. What if they hadn't been talking about one of Dad's clients? She heard Mum sigh.

'It'd be easier if we could stay together,' Dad said. 'It's much more economical.'

Economical? Sage felt sick. He wanted them to stay together because it was *economical*? What about *family* and *togetherness*? What about *love*?

'Then it's settled,' he said. 'Sage will stay with you. I'll call tomorrow.'

Call *who*?

'And Zacky?'

'We'll cross that bridge when we come to it.'

Sage heard movement, and she scampered back up the stairs and dived under her doona and extra blanket, still shivering with cold. Mum wanted to take her back to Queensland. Back home, where it was warm all year round, and Sage's friends would be waiting.

But what about Zacky? What had Mum meant when she said *we'll cross that bridge when we come to it*? Surely if Mum and Sage were moving home, Zacky would come too.

But not Dad. Dad would stay here, in this big cold house, all alone.

Did Mum and Dad not love each other anymore?

And what about her job? What about the magic show? The Yoshi Lear photography course started on Tuesday – would she have to miss that?

And what about Herb?

Sage felt like she was in the cabinet for the Zigzag Effect, her head in one place and her heart being pushed in a different direction. She was freezing. She slipped out of bed and found some thick woollen socks and a cardigan. Then she climbed under the doona again and waited for sleep to come.

Next morning, Sage arrived in the kitchen feeling sick with fear.

What would her parents say? Would they tell her and Zacky together, or separately? Would it be a temporary separation, or were they getting divorced?

Dad had already left for work, and Mum was reading the paper, hands wrapped around a mug of tea.

'Morning, darling,' said Mum. 'Did you sleep well?'

Sage stared at her. She looked *fine*. Not upset. Not like her marriage was falling apart. What was *wrong* with people?

'Fine,' she replied, and grabbed an apple from the fruit bowl.

'Any plans for today?' asked Mum, taking a sip of her tea.

Sage made a noncommittal noise. Clearly Mum had moved on already. Like Herb had.

Well, fine, Sage thought. *I can move on too.*

She wasn't going to think about her parents, or going back to Queensland, or the theatre, or stupid Herb anymore. She wasn't going to be all twisted in zigzags. She was moving on.

Tomorrow was her very first Yoshi Lear masterclass, and she had lots of preparation to do. What was the point in stressing about everything when she had a Yoshi Lear masterclass to look forward to?

〰〰〰

There were about nine other people in the seminar room, and Sage was the only one under forty. She picked a seat

151

in the middle – she didn't want to seem too eager, or too apathetic. She wanted Yoshi Lear to know that even though she was young, she was just as determined, dedicated and talented as everyone else.

Yoshi Lear was a slight, quiet man with thinning dark hair and trendy black-rimmed glasses. He had a way of smiling where his eyebrows curled upwards, so they seemed like some kind of obscure musical notation. He insisted immediately that everyone call him Yoshi, and told them to ask questions at any time. Sage decided that she liked him.

She had thought that the masterclass would be highly technical. She'd spent all day reading up on apertures and shutter speeds and white balancing. But instead, Yoshi Lear clicked on a projector, and an image leapt to life on the interactive whiteboard.

Sage didn't recognise it. It was in black-and-white, and feathered around the edges. She made out the corners and contrasts of roofs and buildings.

'This is the oldest known photograph,' said Yoshi. 'It was taken by Joseph Nicéphore Niépce in 1826. It was the view from a window. In a letter to a friend, Niépce described his discovery as "downright magical".' Yoshi's eyebrow-curling smile surveyed them. He clicked the remote in his hand, and the photo vanished, replaced by six white words on a black background.

A PICTURE TELLS A THOUSAND WORDS

Yoshi then took them through some famous photographs – images of wars, famine and tragedy. The bizarre photos of Philippe Halsman and the beautiful soft images by Man Ray. Sage had seen all the photos before. Usually, she would relish the opportunity to drink them in again, in the company of the great Yoshi Lear.

But she couldn't help herself.

Her mind kept wandering to her parents, Zacky, the theatre, Armand, Herb.

What if Bianca was right? What if there really was a ghost in the theatre? What if they had made it angry, and it had somehow spirited Armand away?

Yoshi Lear clicked to a slide presenting a line of white words against black.

THE CAMERA DOESN'T LIE

Of course there was no ghost. There was no such thing. Nobody had ever captured a photo of a ghost, had they? Surely if ghosts were real, there would be some hard evidence.

'Photos have made people believe in magic.'

Sage snapped to attention.

'There are photos of the Loch Ness monster,' Yoshi was saying. 'And of Bigfoot. There was a craze in the early twentieth century for Kirlian photography, which could allegedly capture the aura of a living creature. Were any of these things genuine?' He smiled a slow, knowing smile. 'Let me tell you a story about some little girls who took photos of the fairies that lived in the bottom of their garden.'

Sage had a sudden flashback to being small, putting out a saucer of bread and milk for the fairies that she just *knew* lived somewhere in her garden.

'Two English girls, Elsie and Frances, borrowed Elsie's dad's camera in 1917, and took three photos.'

Yoshi Lear clicked through to his next slide. It was a black-and-white photo of a girl, her chin in her hands and a crown of flowers perched on top of her loose dark ringlets. She gazed sleepily at the camera, while in front of her four tiny, elegant ladies danced barefoot on a mossy log. Three of the creatures had patterned wings, like butterflies, and the fourth played a pipe or flute. Sage smiled dreamily. They were *exactly* how she'd imagined fairies would look when she was little – wild, beautiful and exquisite.

'Elsie and Frances's parents were unimpressed – they assumed the girls were just mucking around. But word got out about the fairy pictures, and reached the eager ears of Arthur Conan Doyle, best known as the author of the Sherlock Holmes mysteries. Conan Doyle was a spiritualist, and desperately wanted to believe in the supernatural. He believed he'd finally found evidence in these photos. He sent them to Kodak, Ilford and a photography expert named

Howard Snelling to be verified. All reported back with the same information. There was no photographic trickery going on here. The negatives had not been tampered with. Conan Doyle pounced on this response with glee. The photos were genuine! Fairies were real. But he overlooked something. Snelling, in his response, said "these are straightforward photographs of whatever was in front of the camera at the time".' Yoshi paused for a moment, considering the photos.

They were mesmerising. The languid eyes and soft faces of the little girls added to the dusky romance of the photos. Compared to the slightly fuzzy lines of the girls, the fairies seemed sharp and solid, as if they were somehow more real, or existed in a world that was somehow more in focus, more bright and defined. Sage imagined that in order to really see a fairy, you had to slide your vision sideways a little, until the lines around the everyday things became indistinct and allowed you to see all the other things. The things that were there all along, unnoticed. Such as fairies.

'Years later, the girls admitted that the photos were faked,' said Yoshi. 'Elsie had copied pictures from a book of fairies, and cut them out. They supported the cutouts with hat pins, and then dumped the evidence in the creek when they were done taking photos.'

Sage felt oddly disappointed, just like when she'd discovered the possum eating her fairy bread. Of course the fairies weren't real. She had never really believed that they were. But still … fake cardboard cutouts was such a mundane explanation. How on earth had everyone been taken in by it? How had Arthur Conan Doyle fallen for it?

'Except there was one last mystery. Frances insisted that the last photo they took was genuine.'

He clicked through to a new slide. It was a close-up photo of grass and wildflowers, with a blown-out white sky behind and above. In among the flowers were three translucent figures with delicate wings, and silkily draped robes. Sage found herself holding her breath. The photo was beautiful – artless and poorly framed, but capturing an impossibly magical moment.

'These fairies differ from the others, because of their transparency. The others are, to a cynical modern eye, clearly cardboard cutouts. But these ones are barely visible, blending so completely into the grass and flowers that, if you unfocus your eyes, they vanish entirely.'

Sage squinted, blurring her vision. It was true, the fairies really did disappear into the tangled grasses.

'Frances claimed she took this photograph, and that the fairies in it were genuine,' said Yoshi. 'Even after she confessed to faking the others, she stood firm on this one. The funny thing? Elsie also claimed to have taken this photo.' He paused again. 'Photography is not the truth. Pictures lie. But everyone believes them. Even poor Frances Griffiths believed in them. She knew she never saw any real fairies. She helped make those cardboard cutouts, and pin them to trees and grasses. But because a photo exists that she couldn't explain, she assumed that it must be the genuine article. She took a photo of some flowers, with no fairies. But the developed photo shows fairies. Therefore fairies must exist.' Yoshi shook his head.

'Was she lying?' asked one of the other students.

'She wasn't lying,' said Yoshi. 'But they also weren't really fairies. I'll leave it to you to puzzle it out.'

Sage wondered how someone like Arthur Conan Doyle could believe in fairies, when Sherlock Holmes was so analytical and logical. She thought about Bianca, and her certainty that the Lyric Theatre was haunted. Herb would have said that people like that were illogical, and unable to look at things objectively. Sage wondered if they were just good at believing in stuff.

'The fairy hoax would have been much easier to pull off if the girls had had access to Photoshop,' said Yoshi, and a murmur of laughter rippled through the classroom. 'But photographic manipulation has been going on for as long as photos have existed. Early last century, it was common practice to assemble a family portrait out of several photos, if the family members were unable to be in the same place at the same time. Historical figures like Mussolini, Mao Zedong and Adolf Hitler all had images doctored to remove certain undesired individuals or elements. One of the most famous portraits of Abraham Lincoln is faked, where Lincoln's face is pasted on top of the body of another politician named John C. Calhoun.'

Sage's mind wandered again. She remembered getting a family portrait taken with Mum and Dad and Zacky, a few Christmases ago. It had been in one of those cheesy shopping-centre studios, and it had taken forever. The photographer had a pink bunny to wave to make three-year-old Zacky look at the camera. The bunny had been old and threadbare, and it had terrified Zacky. He'd burst into tears, and in every photo he had his eyes screwed up, and his mouth a long, wailing *O*. Sage had hated the whole experience, and Mum had sworn they'd never do it again. *A waste of money*, she said. But now Sage felt a pang of longing for that tacky photography studio with its soft-focus glamour shots and oversaturated photos of babies in flower pots. What if that was the last family photo they'd ever take together?

'Today it's almost impossible to see an undoctored photo in the media. Bulges are slimmed, teeth are whitened. People are added and removed. In the original British version of the famous photo of the Beatles crossing Abbey Road, Paul is holding a cigarette. On the American album cover, he isn't.

Photography is a kind of magic, and nowadays nothing is beyond the scope of our manipulations.

'There is, however, a kind of innocent charm to these pre-Photoshop photos.' Yoshi looked up at the fuzzy, semi-transparent fairies again. 'So that's your first assignment. I want an undoctored photo that tells a lie. You may interpret that how you will – I'm very happy for you to think outside the box. But you can only take a photo of what's in front of the camera. There is to be no doctoring of the negative, or any digital manipulation.'

He clicked to a new slide. It was one of his most famous photos, a photo of a fifties-style family. The husband sat at the kitchen table, reading a newspaper and smoking a pipe. A pretty wife in an apron stirred something on the stove. Through the window, you could see two children playing with a dog. Everyone had huge smiles on their faces, revealing white teeth. But their eyes were dead, giving the impression that they were all only pretending to be happy, and that inside they were all screaming.

A photo that told a lie.

Sage knew this photo was also a lie because the handsome, square-jawed man in the photo was actually Yoshi's husband.

Sage thought of a photo she'd taken just after they'd arrived in Melbourne, of Mum and Dad unpacking boxes

159

in the kitchen. They'd been horsing around laughing. Dad put a copper pot on his head and bent down on one knee before Mum, with a wooden spoon in his mouth. Mum was laughing so hard, tears were running down her cheeks.

Had that photo been a lie?

Sage arrived at the theatre on Wednesday an hour before the evening show to find Herb and Bianca sitting on the stage. Bianca wasn't in her costume, and the stage wasn't set for the show.

'Armand sent another text,' Bianca told her. 'Apparently there's been some kind of family emergency, and he's had to leave town for a few days.'

Sage frowned. 'Are we sure he's okay?'

'Who cares?' said Herb. 'I just want to know when he'll be back. We'll have to cancel *again*.'

Bianca yawned, and Sage noticed how tired she looked. Maybe the one-night stand hadn't just been one night after all. 'Well,' she said, standing up. 'I'm going to tidy up my dressing-room. Then I'm going home.'

She disappeared into the wings.

'Have you tried calling him?' Sage asked Herb, hoisting herself up onto the stage to sit next to him.

Herb nodded and scowled. 'He's not picking up.'

'And you don't think that's kind of weird?'

'What can I say? Armand's a weird guy.'

'Has he done this before? Disappeared with no warning?'

Herb shook his head. 'Not that I know of.'

They sat in silence for a moment, Sage enjoying the feeling of his warm arm next to hers, and wondering if he was planning on putting that arm around her.

'About the other night—' Herb started to say, before he was interrupted by the sound of Bianca screaming.

They jumped to their feet and sprinted down the corridor to Bianca's dressing-room to find Bianca standing in front of the mirror, her hands clasped over her mouth and her eyes wide with horror.

Sage felt a chill around her heart as she looked at the mirror. On it, in blood-red letters, was written a single word.

RETRIBUTION

'Is – is it blood?' asked Sage.

Herb walked up to the mirror and touched a finger to the glass. 'Lipstick,' he said, sniffing his finger. 'Is this some kind of joke?'

Bianca stared at him. 'Why would I write that?' She turned to Sage. 'I think you were right,' she whispered. 'About the curse.'

Sage blinked. 'What? No. I was just joking.'

Bianca swallowed. 'I did some research on the theatre ghost,' she said. 'It's the spirit of a magician who used to perform in a variety show here, in the 1920s. His name was Renaldo the Remarkable.'

Herb sighed. 'Let me guess,' he said. 'Remarkable Ron died onstage, performing an effect.'

'How did you know?' Bianca turned wide eyes on him.

'Using my incredible powers of clairvoyance,' said Herb wearily.

Bianca's eyes narrowed slightly, and she tossed her head. 'You're right, it was an escapology routine. He died right here on the stage, in front of everyone. Heart attack.'

'Really?' said Sage. The scrawled red letters on the mirror seemed to shift and take on meaning. Everything felt different, as if the spilled life force of a human being still inhabited the creaking walls of the theatre.

Bianca nodded. 'The story goes that he still haunts the theatre. People have said they've seen him sitting in the audience. And strange things have been known to happen here. Maybe we … we made him angry. When we broke the wand and Herb showed such disrespect for the theatre spirits.'

'So what, the ghost of some dead magician wrote on your mirror in lipstick?' Herb's voice dripped with sarcasm. 'Why? Retribution for what?'

'The curse,' said Bianca. 'We angered the spirit by breaking a magic wand onstage. The spirit of Renaldo the Remarkable.'

Sage shivered. The theatre seemed to take on a kind of musty consciousness. She felt like the walls were watching her, and listening to every word she spoke.

'Do you think that this is related to Armand's disappearance?' she asked.

Herb groaned. 'Not you too,' he said. 'Tell me you don't buy her bullshit.'

Bianca ignored him. 'N-no,' she said slowly. 'No, I don't think it's related.'

'Why your room?' asked Sage suddenly. 'Why not our office? I'm the one who broke the wand, and Herb was the one who was such a dick about it.'

'Hey!' said Herb.

'Sorry,' said Sage. 'But you *were* kind of a dick about it.'

He pouted. 'Maybe. But you didn't have to come out and *say* it like that.'

Sage thought somewhat resentfully that she should be able to say what she liked, especially since Herb had taken her out on a date, practically ignored her the whole time and then hadn't called for *three days*.

'I don't know why it's in my dressing-room,' said Bianca. 'Maybe Renaldo's spirit knows that I'm the only one who'll listen to him.'

Sage nodded. 'I wonder if there's anything on Armand's mirror.'

Bianca looked uncomfortable. 'He *hates* it when people go into his dressing-room,' she said. 'He's very private.'

Herb started towards the door. 'Let's do it,' he said. 'I've actually never been in there.'

Bianca pulled a tissue from a box and started to clean her mirror. 'You can go ahead,' she said. 'I'm staying here.'

Herb shrugged. 'Suit yourself.'

Sage hesitated for a moment, then followed Herb out into the corridor. Someone had to keep an eye on him.

9. Switch: one item is covertly exchanged for another.

Armand's dressing-room was much bigger than Bianca's, with a little ensuite bathroom off to one side. It was sparsely decorated, unlike the feminine clutter of Bianca's room. A few books on magic rested on a small shelf. A trunk that Sage assumed contained various kinds of magic equipment was tucked up against the dressing table. Armand's suit hung on a wire hanger, the coat-tails just brushing the floor.

Warren was asleep on the dressing table. Herb shook his head. 'I have no idea how he gets into closed rooms.'

'So what are we looking for?' Sage whispered.

'Why are you whispering?' asked Herb in a normal voice. 'Afraid the ghost might hear you?' He laughed.

'I don't know,' said Sage, no longer whispering but unable to raise her voice to its normal speaking volume. 'I just feel like we're breaking in – like we're somewhere forbidden.'

'You've been spending too much time with Bianca.' Herb emptied the wastepaper basket onto the floor. 'To answer your question, we are looking for clues.'

'Clues?'

Herb pulled open the drawer of the dressing table and rifled through its contents. 'I don't really know Armand,' he admitted. 'I don't know anything about him. I don't know where he lives. I don't know whether he has a wife, or a girlfriend, or a boyfriend. I don't even know his real name.'

Sage blinked. Of course Armand wasn't his real name. He was about as French as Warren was. 'You're worried about him, aren't you?'

Herb ran a hand through his hair and nodded. 'Yeah. At first the idea of an Armandless theatre seemed pretty appealing. But it's not like him to just vanish like this. He's usually the one who makes other things vanish.'

Sage looked at Armand's desk. The pile of papers he'd been studying was gone. Sage wondered again about the missing money, and told Herb.

'How much was missing?'

'Not much, about nine hundred dollars. But that was just what I found. There could be more. He seemed *weird* when I asked him about it. Really weird. Maybe he's in debt, or made a bad investment or something. Maybe that's why he's had to go away, to try and sort something out.'

Herb nodded. 'Maybe,' he said. 'Who could tell with Armand? He does a great job of being mysterious. A great magician is like glass – your gaze just slides over him, like he isn't really there. You never consider looking any deeper.' He pulled out a handful of objects. 'On the other hand, I am very clever.' He dropped the objects on the table and spread them out. 'Bianca!' he yelled. 'Come in here!'

Bianca appeared at the door. 'You rang, Your Majesty?'

'I thought you might be interested in watching my display of psychic ability or, as I like to call it, cold reading.'

Bianca rolled her eyes. 'Get on with it then,' she said. 'I still don't think we should be in here.'

'Armand is a smoker,' said Herb, holding up a crumpled but almost full packet of cigarettes. 'But he's trying to quit. I found these in the bin.' Herb held up a Medicare card. 'His real name is Louis Smyth, and he's fifty-three years old. He doesn't return library books.' He waved a printed-out email with the subject heading *OVERDUE BOOKS*, then picked up a small electric razor. 'And he trims his nose-hair. Or ear-hair. Or both.'

'I don't really see how this is helpful,' said Bianca with a sigh. 'It's just nosy.'

'It's *interesting*. And interesting is always helpful.' Herb slid a folded piece of yellowed newspaper from underneath

Warren, and smoothed it out. 'Well, well,' he said softly. 'Will you look at that.'

He passed it over to Sage. It was a clipping, an article from fifteen years previously.

THE GREAT ARMAND: THE NATION'S MOST BELOVED MAGICIAN

The article was about how Armand had just returned from a successful world tour, and was selling out major venues throughout the country. There was also going to be a TV special, during which he'd promised to make the prime minister's suit change colour.

'Look,' said Herb, pointing at the photo accompanying the article.

'Armand looks so young,' said Sage. The man staring out at her was barely recognisable. The confident sweep of his arm, the arrogantly cocked head. Armand looked strong and powerful – not like the slightly shabby, cranky man that she knew.

'Look harder,' said Herb.

Sage frowned, staring at the photo. Armand was posed onstage, a glittery assistant beside him on one side, and a black-clad stagehand hanging towards the back. Sage squinted.

'Is that ...?'

'It's Jason Jones,' said Herb. 'Huh. Jason Jones used to

work for Armand. No wonder Armand hates him so much. Also, how *old* is Jason? Is he taking some sort of unicorn-blood youth tonic?'

'So?' Bianca took the article. 'It's a small industry. Everyone has worked with everyone else. I'm not in the least surprised.'

'But Armand was really famous,' said Sage. 'What happened?'

'Things change,' said Herb. 'Magic isn't cool anymore, unless it's fancy mentalism, or that big showy stuff, like Criss Angel making all of Las Vegas disappear or whatever. I guess Armand couldn't keep up with the changing times.'

'That's sad,' said Sage.

'That's life,' replied Herb.

Bianca said nothing, just stared at the photo, her expression even more distant and sad than usual. *She misses him*, thought Sage. *Even though he's horrible to her. It's still her job. Without him she's nothing.* She made a face. It was an awful thought.

'I don't know about you two,' announced Herb. 'But I'm starving. I'm so hungry I could eat Warren.'

Warren's ears twitched at the sound of his name, but he went on sleeping.

'Anyone up for burgers?' asked Herb.

Bianca shot him a cold look. 'So that's it, is it? A ghost writes a creepy message on my mirror, and you want to get a burger?'

Herb looked confused. 'I have to eat,' he said. 'I can't survive on the smell of a cucumber like you can. I get low blood sugar.'

Bianca stalked back to her dressing-room. Herb turned to Sage with a lopsided grin. 'Just you and me then, I guess. Come on, we can do the cancellation phone calls later.'

Sage felt a confused twisting inside. The last time she and Herb had gone out for a meal, there had been kissing. Admittedly there had also been urinating in a bucket, but Sage was choosing to focus on the kissing.

'I love this bit of the city,' said Herb, as they walked the five blocks to the CBD.

'Are you kidding?' said Sage. 'It's like a ghost town that's been taken over by fast food chains and crappy laundromats.'

'That's why it's so awesome,' said Herb. 'At first glance, it's all cheap and nasty. But then you look up …'

He pointed at a shop selling cheap mobile phone cases. It had a handwritten sign in the window and barely any shop fittings. Sage tilted her head and gasped.

Although the ground floor just looked like an ordinary shopfront, the first and second storeys of the terrace building were beautiful. Pale blue paint flaked away from grey stone, and from the intricate plaster roses that wound around the window frames. A crumbling gargoyle clung to the drainpipe at the very top of the building, leering over the edge of the roof and laughing at commuters below.

'Just about every building in this area is like that,' said Herb.

Sage kept her head tilted up as they walked. She saw a KFC that sprouted shingled turrets, and an accountant's office with an elaborate wrought-iron balcony. Everywhere she looked there were art-deco friezes and Grecian pillars.

'I had no idea,' she murmured.

'You have to look up in this city.' Herb steered her around a fire hydrant. 'All the best things are above street level.'

They squeezed into a tiny, nondescript café and perched on stools by the window, watching commuters scurry by, hunched over against the icy wind.

'Does it ever get warm?' Sage asked, thinking longingly of her old home.

'Oh yes,' said Herb. 'Horridly so. Baking heat, and of course nobody has an air conditioner.'

Sage sighed. 'I miss the heat.'

'You won't when it comes around. I bet you a million dollars that by January you'll be longing for winter.'

Sage felt a smile tug at her mouth. Would Herb still be around in January?

'What happens when the show finishes?' she asked.

'It doesn't,' said Herb, slurping at his lemonade. 'We have a few months off during term time, then open up again for the September school holidays. Then another break, then back on from November to February. But it works pretty well – most of the shows are in the evenings, so there's plenty of time to hang out at the beach during the day.'

'I don't believe that this city has a beach,' Sage said. 'It's just not possible.'

Herb grinned. 'You will *love* the beach,' he said. 'There're buskers and street performers and lots of interesting food trucks. You'll see.'

Sage nibbled on a chip, trying not to look too pleased. Herb clearly thought that she'd still be around for summer. Then her stomach plummeted. Maybe she wouldn't be. Maybe she'd be back in Queensland with Mum. Sage put down the chip and changed the topic of conversation.

'Don't you believe Bianca?' asked Sage. 'About the magician who died in the theatre?'

'Not particularly.'

'You think she's lying?'

Herb frowned. 'Have you seen any evidence of this

Ron the Rambunctious? Any newspaper clippings? Tried a Google search?'

Sage hesitated. 'But why would Bianca lie?' she said at last.

'To *win*,' he said. 'To scare the pants off you to get you onside with this ridiculous spiritualism-believing nonsense.'

'No.' Sage shook her head. 'She wouldn't.'

Herb hesitated for a moment, then sighed. 'You're right. She wouldn't. She's far too bloody *moral*.'

'So what, then?' asked Sage. 'If she's not lying, isn't there a possibility that it's true?'

'There's a possibility that lots of things are true,' said Herb. 'There's a possibility that the universe was created by a giant flying spaghetti monster. But it's pretty unlikely.'

'Don't you ever just get a *feeling*?' asked Sage. 'In a building or something? Don't you think that places can be affected by the things that have happened there?'

'Only because of the emotions and memories that people bring to a space. If everyone thinks that a building is haunted, then they'll feel clammy fingers touching them, and hear whispers in their ears. Draughts will become ghosts passing through them. Water damage becomes the Virgin Mary's face. It's called pareidolia – when a random stimulus is perceived as being significant.'

Sage watched a couple walk past, huddled together against the cold. The girl had her hand in the pocket of her boyfriend's coat, and they were laughing. She scowled at them. They made it look so easy.

'Does it happen often?' she asked, trying to get her mind off Herb's ridiculous mixed signals. 'Magicians dying, I mean. Are there lots of magic tricks that are really dangerous?'

Herb thought about it. 'Well, there're plenty of spectacle magicians who do things like being buried alive or escapism underwater. One guy had himself entirely encased in ice. But they're all under extremely controlled conditions. Often the tricks that *look* the most dangerous are actually entirely safe. Like sawing a lady in half.'

'So what's the most dangerous magic trick?'

'The bullet catch.'

Sage knew this one. 'The magician gets shot, and catches the bullet in his teeth?'

Herb nodded.

'But surely that's all faked.'

'Most of the time. There are plenty of illusory effects that go with it – people use wax bullets, or blanks. There's one guy who used to do it for real, wearing a steel mouthguard.'

'And it worked?'

'Yep, although I'd hate to be his dentist. Plenty of

people have died trying to do even the trick version.'

Sage blinked. 'Really? Died?'

'Yep. The first recorded performance of the bullet catch was in the 1600s, by a magician called Coullew.'

'And it failed? The bullet killed him?'

Herb let out a short bark of laughter. 'No. He pulled the trick off perfectly. But an angry spectator thought he must be some kind of demon, and beat him to death with his own gun.'

'That's terrible.'

Herb nodded. 'It's a bit of a cursed trick. In the nineteenth century a magician called Torrini de Grisy accidentally shot his own son. Another guy around that time shot his wife – a real bullet was accidentally loaded into the gun. A few times, a member of the audience has sabotaged it – putting shrapnel in the gun, or just standing up and shooting the magician from the audience.'

Sage shook her head. 'Why do they do it? If it's so dangerous?'

'It's a challenge. Probably the most famous bullet-catch disaster is Chung Ling Soo. He was this mystical Chinese magician early last century. Always worked with an interpreter. Nobody ever heard him speak. He did the bullet catch one night, and it went wrong. The audience saw sprays of blood coming from his chest, but they thought it was all part of the act, and applauded wildly. Then his crew ran onstage to help him, and the cheering turned to screaming. But then something strange happened. Soo spoke. He said, in perfect English, *My feet are cold*. He died a few minutes later, and when an ambulance came to cart him away, they realised Soo's greatest trick of all.'

'He could speak English?'

Herb grinned. 'He was an American. He wasn't Asian at all. It was just makeup and trickery.'

'Wow.'

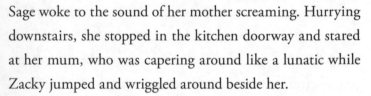

Sage woke to the sound of her mother screaming. Hurrying downstairs, she stopped in the kitchen doorway and stared at her mum, who was capering around like a lunatic while Zacky jumped and wriggled around beside her.

'Mum?'

Sage was thrown against the wall as her mother barrelled into her with a fierce, lung-squeezing hug. 'Oh, Sage!'

'Did we win the lottery?'

'Better. I got a job. A *really* good one at a design firm. I start on Monday!'

Sage felt a rush of emotions and questions whirl around her. 'A job?' she said. 'Here?'

'It's in the city.' Mum did a little dance.

'Does this mean we're not moving back home?'

Mum frowned. 'What? We were never moving back. Your father's job—'

'But I heard you,' said Sage, and glanced at Zacky. She lowered her voice. 'I heard you and Dad the other night. Talking about … splitting up.'

Mum stared blankly at her. 'You mean … splitting up our family contract?'

Sage felt panic rise up inside her. 'What does that *mean*?' she almost wailed.

Mum started to laugh. 'For our phones,' she said. 'You, your father and I are on a family mobile phone plan. But your dad can't get a decent signal at his new office. So we're splitting up the family plan so he can go to a different provider.'

Sage felt as if she was about to burst into tears. Her parents weren't splitting up. That was a good thing. But she wasn't moving home. She wasn't sure how she felt about that. She was in the stupid Zigzag cabinet again, being pulled in different directions.

'You should be more explicit when you have these conversations,' she growled, feeling embarrassed and confused and exhausted from having spent all week worrying about it.

'You shouldn't eavesdrop on private conversations,' said Mum, still chuckling. 'But seriously, darling, your father and I are definitely not splitting up. I know this move has been hard, but now I've got this job, things are going to get *much* easier. We'll have more money again, and we can fix up this old house. I know it's weird adjusting to a new place, but I promise that within six months, you'll *love* it here. Okay?'

Six months seemed like an awfully long time. 'Okay,' said Sage without much conviction.

'Now be excited about my job.'

'Hurrah,' said Sage. 'Congratulations.'

'What about me?' Zacky tugged on Mum's sleeve. 'What will I do when you're at work?'

Mum ruffled Zacky's hair. 'Well, Sage can look after you on Mondays and Tuesdays because she's not at the theatre. And I'll be home on Fridays. I've asked Kate next door if you can go and play with Roman on Wednesdays and Thursdays until school starts.'

Zacky's eyes went wide. 'All day with Roman?'

Mum nodded. 'If that's okay with you.'

Zacky's face split open in a toothy grin. 'We're training to be wizards,' he told Sage importantly. 'We're going to learn how to limitate.'

Sage laughed. 'Don't you mean *levitate*?'

'No-o,' scoffed Zacky, giving her a superior look. 'Obviously you don't know about magic, even though you work for a magician.'

Herb summoned Sage to the theatre that afternoon. A spark of hope in Sage's heart suggested that maybe it was so he could get her alone, but that spark was quickly doused when she walked into the auditorium to find Bianca there as well. Of course he didn't want to get her alone. All the kissing and flirting had meant nothing to him.

Bianca looked wan and limp, as if she was a flower that someone kept forgetting to water. *She's just putting on a brave face*, thought Sage. *She's more worried about Armand than she's letting on.*

'I'm taking over,' Herb announced.

Bianca's mouth fell open. '*What?*'

'The show. We can't just keep cancelling it. I know Armand's whole routine. We'll spend tonight going over it, and reopen tomorrow night.'

Bianca looked doubtful. 'I–I don't know,' she said.

Sage felt her face pulling into a scowl. 'Why can't Bianca take over?' she asked. 'Surely she knows Armand's routine even better than you.'

'Sure,' said Herb, barely looking at her. 'But she can't do Armand's routine.'

Sage looked indignantly at Bianca, who shrugged.

'You think she can't do it because she's a *girl?*' said Sage, as a dangerous feeling started to swell inside her.

'Precisely,' said Herb, still looking totally unconcerned. 'She can't fit an orange in her pocket, and she certainly can't hide Warren anywhere on her person. Not in that spangly little number.'

'What if she wore a suit?'

Herb shook his head. 'When an audience sees a beautiful girl in a loose-fitting suit, they immediately get suspicious. It just doesn't work. And anyway, if Bianca were the magician, who would be the fabulous beautiful assistant?'

Sage's mouth fell open.

'Sage, just leave it,' said Bianca softly. 'He's not totally wrong.'

'He's a *misogynist*!'

'I'm a realist,' said Herb. 'Look, I'm not denying that the assistant is a vital part of a magic routine. The assistant has to be much, much more skilled than people think she does. She ends up carrying many effects all on her own – effects like Zigzag and Impaled rely solely on the skills of the assistant. And Bianca is an extremely good assistant.'

'But?'

'But she's not a magician. She hasn't trained as a magician. I'm sure she could if she wanted to – she's very talented.' He turned to Bianca. 'But I don't think you do want to. You're more interested in women's magic.'

'*Women's magic*?' spluttered Sage.

'Just ignore him,' said Bianca. 'You'll only encourage him.'

'*Women's magic?*'

Herb shrugged. 'You know, all that Tarot, crystal-ball bullshit.'

Sage wanted to break something over his head. 'So you're saying women can't be traditional magicians?'

'I'm not saying that at all. There are plenty of great female magicians.'

'Name one,' said Sage.

'Dorothy Dietrich,' Herb responded immediately. 'One of the greatest magicians alive or dead, as well as being a notable historian, collector and debunker of spiritualism.'

Sage glanced at Bianca, who nodded. 'Everyone knows Dorothy Dietrich,' she said. 'She's one of the best.'

'Fine,' said Sage. 'Name me another.'

'Princess Tenko. Melinda Saxe. Dell O'Dell. Madame Hermann. Eusapia Palladino. Talma. Iona.'

Sage had no idea if he were making the names up, but his smug look of satisfaction filled her with rage.

'But apparently you don't think Bianca . . .' Sage trailed off as she realised she didn't actually know Bianca's surname.

'Bareldo,' supplied Bianca helpfully.

'You don't think Bianca Bareldo can be on that list.'

Herb threw his hands up in the air. 'Sure,' he said.

'Bianca Bareldo can be the greatest magician of all time. Hell, so can Sage Kealley. Is that what you want? You want to run the show? Go right ahead. Good luck designing all the effects.'

Sage stared at him, for a long, cold moment.

'Um,' said Bianca awkwardly. 'I'll be in my dressing-room. Try not to kill each other.'

She slipped away. Herb sighed. Sage stared at him, shaking her head slowly from side to side.

'What?' Herb glared at her.

'*Women's magic?*'

'Okay, that was a dumb thing to say. But it's still true,' said Herb. 'The vast majority of those TV psychics and palm readers are women. Fact.'

'What about John Edward? Or Uri Geller?'

'There are always exceptions. There are some amazing female magicians too – specifically the ones I just mentioned. But there aren't many of them. I'm not saying it's right. I'm not saying the industry isn't sexist. But that's just the way things are.'

Sage made a face. 'I bet that's what a whole bunch of guys said when women wanted to vote.'

Herb made an exasperated noise. 'I'm not trying to *prevent* anyone from becoming a magician! I just think that in terms of who takes over while Armand is away ... I designed half the effects, I know how they run – it makes sense. I can do Armand's job. I'm sure Bianca can as well, but the fact is I can't do *her* job. I can't fit in half those boxes, and I'm not sure I can pull off the sparkly leotard look.'

'Why didn't you say any of that before?'

'I was *trying* to,' he ground out. 'Except you kept interrupting to call me a misogynist.'

Sage shook her head. 'I'm going to see Bianca.'

Herb waved a hand. 'Give her my best regards,' he said. 'Why don't you have a seance or something while you're in there?'

Sage ignored him.

∿∿∿

Bianca was sitting at her dressing table. She'd cleaned the writing off the mirror, but there were still reddish smudges where she hadn't quite managed to get rid of all the lipstick.

'Sorry about that,' said Sage, taking a tentative step into the room. 'I got a bit carried away.'

Bianca turned to face her. 'Don't apologise,' she said. 'We're all a bit on edge.' She stared at her reflection through the red smudges. 'I'm not crazy. There's something going on here. Something *weird*.'

Sage nodded slowly. 'I think you might be right,' she said. 'I can't think of any other explanation for what's going on. I wish there was something *concrete*.'

'What do you mean?'

'I keep thinking about what Herb would say. He'd demand evidence. All we have are hunches and weird feelings.'

'What about the noises you heard? And Armand's disappearance? And the message on my mirror? And you and Herb getting locked in the storeroom? How much evidence do you want?'

Sage frowned. 'I don't know,' she said. 'I just wish there was something more tangible.'

She wanted a photo. She didn't want to admit it, but she wanted a photo of the ghost. And she didn't want it for any high-and-mighty mystery-solving reason, she wanted it to impress Yoshi Lear. And also to prove Herb wrong. If he were here, he'd say there was always another explanation, and just because people couldn't figure out what it was, it didn't automatically make it supernatural. He'd put on his smug face and talk about how primitive people didn't understand what made it rain, so they assumed that a spirit or a god did it when they performed a certain ritual and a sacrifice. And Sage would admit that everything he said made sense.

But if she had a *photo*. Then everything would change.

Bianca sighed loudly, jerking Sage from her reverie.

'Are you okay?' she asked.

Bianca smiled a wan smile. 'Sure,' she said halfheartedly.

Sage immediately felt guilty. Here she was, wanting a photo to show off, and poor Bianca was suffering. It was *her* mirror, after all. And Armand's disappearance was worrying her.

She stood up and gave Bianca a swift hug. 'Everything will be fine. You'll see.'

Bianca swallowed and nodded, but her expression faltered. Sage felt uneasiness creep into the pit of her belly. Something was very, very wrong at the Lyric Theatre.

10. Steal: to secretly obtain a required object.

The uneasiness got worse. Bianca came out of her dressing-room, and they all sat down to discuss their next move. Sage's toes grew stiff with cold, and the back of her neck prickled. She kept feeling like there was someone behind her, but every time she turned around, the theatre was empty.

'So how's this going to work?' asked Bianca. 'Who's going to do the sound and lights if you're on the stage?'

'Sage.'

Sage blinked. 'Really?'

'It's not that hard,' he said, obviously trying to sound reassuring. 'I can teach you.'

Sage's lips stretched in a smile. She knew she should be flattered to be entrusted with such an important job. Herb thought she was capable. That was a good thing. But something just didn't *feel* right. Herb seemed too eager to take over from Armand. It was as if he'd already planned out his steps beforehand, of how he'd take over the show and slot her and Bianca into their assigned roles.

He hadn't even *asked* her if she wanted to do the lights.

Bianca frowned. 'Can anyone else smell ... flowers?'

'No,' said Herb. 'You're probably just having a stroke. Can we run through Zigzag? I've never done it before. I know there's not actually much for me to do, but I'd like to get the timing right.'

Sage closed her eyes and saw Armand slide the wide metal blade into the Zigzag trunk. She shuddered. 'I thought you said that Zigzag was overkill,' she heard herself say. 'That it's too similar to the sword cabinet at the end.'

She opened her eyes and looked at Bianca, who was staring at her with a strange expression on her face.

'Did I say that?' said Herb, chewing on his bottom lip. 'Well, I'm usually right.'

'So pick another trick,' said Sage. 'One that doesn't involve cutting Bianca into bits.'

Herb glanced at Bianca. 'Any thoughts?'

Bianca tipped her head onto one side. The corners of her mouth twitched in a smile. 'How about Assistant's Revenge?'

Herb snorted. 'You'd love that.'

'No, seriously,' said Bianca. 'It's a good trick. Everyone likes seeing the magician vanish.'

Herb narrowed his eyes, considering it. 'We'll have to go over it a few times tonight,' he said. 'I know the routine, but I've never done it onstage before.'

'I can help you.' Bianca looked pleased. 'I think it'll be ... *seriously*, can't you smell that?'

'Smell what?'

Bianca looked around. 'The *flowers*,' she said.

And then suddenly Sage *could* smell it. The scent was overpowering, like being drowned in flowers. It choked her nose and throat, and for a moment she thought she might be sick.

'Did you spill something?' Herb asked Bianca. 'A bottle of perfume?'

Bianca shook her head. 'No, I've been smelling it on and off all day. Ever since I arrived at the theatre.' Her eyes grew wide.

'Don't say it,' said Herb. 'I'm sure it's coming from outside. Someone's giving away free perfume samples or something, and the smell is coming in through the air-conditioning vents.'

Bianca opened her mouth to protest, but Herb silenced her with a glare. 'Now,' he said. 'Assistant's Revenge. Do we have enough chains?'

Sage felt as though a rubber band was stretching inside her, getting tighter and tighter as she listened to Herb and Bianca bicker over the set-up of the trick. The smell was making her head ache. She knew she wasn't beautiful like Bianca. She knew she didn't have that glimmering *something* that made people flock to girls like Bianca adoringly. She knew she wasn't the kind of girl that boys wrote poetry about. But that didn't mean she was entirely devoid of worth or feelings. Herb had kissed her, and she hadn't imagined it. He'd kissed her and it had *meant* something. People didn't just kiss other people like that because they were bored – she knew this for a fact, because her ex-boyfriend Daniel had often kissed her because he was bored, and it hadn't been anything like the kiss with Herb.

It was as if the smell had soaked right through her. It streamed in through her nostrils, her eye sockets, every hair follicle and skin pore.

She needed some air.

'I'm going to the office,' she murmured, standing up.

Herb and Bianca didn't even acknowledge her existence. Why would they? She wasn't important.

Sage wandered back to the office. The scent clung to her in clouds, but at least she could breathe again. Warren was sitting on her desk, chewing on a stack of invoices. She sighed and offered him a carrot from the bucket on the floor. Warren dropped the invoices and shuffled over to her, making a contented grunting noise. She stroked his rabbity soft ears, but he shrugged her aside, turning his back on her so he could focus all his attention on the carrot.

The rubber band stretched tighter. Even Warren took her for granted.

'Sage!' Herb strode into the room looking distracted. 'You can sew, right? There's some fabric in the storeroom that I need you to turn into a curtain.'

Sage scowled at him. 'What, no magic word?'

Herb looked confused. 'I don't really *do* magic words,' he said. 'Not part of my routine. But did you know that *Abracadabra* is derived from an Aramaic word meaning *I have created*? It was used to ward off illnesses by Roman emperors and Gnostic priests, and people painted it on their doors during the Great Plague in London. Nobody's really sure where *Hocus pocus* comes from. Some say it's the corruption of a Latin phrase taken from a religious Mass. Others reckon it's a reference to Ochus Bochus, a sorcerer from Norse folklore. But more likely it's just a meaningless phrase that sounds cool.'

Sage said nothing. The rubber band inside her stretched so tightly that it started to hum gently.

'Anyway,' said Herb. 'We need the curtain sooner rather than later.'

Sage felt the rubber band snap, the two ends flying apart with a *twang*. 'Do it yourself,' she said coldly, and pushed past him, stomping down the corridor, through the auditorium and out into the foyer. She charged outside and stood on the footpath, taking deep breaths and trying not to cry. It had been raining, and the gutters ran brown with little rivers of dirty water.

She wrapped her arms around herself and shivered. Why did it have to be so damn *cold* in this city? She wanted to be warm again. She wanted to hang out on the beach with her friends. She wanted to go back to her world where magic and theatres and vengeful spirits were just stuff she saw on TV, and Herb was something she sprinkled over a salad for extra flavour.

Maybe she could just go home. She didn't really *need* this job, after all. She almost had enough money saved to finish Yoshi Lear's photography course, and now that Mum had a new job, surely she could pay for the rest. And she didn't need a new camera. Then she wouldn't have to see Herb's face again. She could just imagine his confused, hangdog expression when she walked back in. As if her outburst had been entirely unexpected and irrational. As if she was just being a typical hysterical girl with a stupid crush.

But they needed her. Especially with Armand gone. Sage needed to operate the lights as well as run the office and sell the tickets. They couldn't do it without her. She didn't want to be the one who ruined the show.

The stage door in the alley beside the theatre banged shut, and Sage turned, her traitorous heart thrilling with the thought that it might be Herb. But it was Bianca, hurrying down the steps in a thick red duffel coat, a notebook tucked under her arm. Had Herb sent her out to placate Sage? Coward. She started to raise her hand to wave, but Bianca didn't see her. Good. Sage didn't really feel like talking anyway. Bianca ran across the road, dodging puddles, and opened the door of a black car parked near the corner, getting into the front passenger seat. For the brief moment before Bianca pulled the door shut behind her, Sage could see into the car. The man behind the wheel looked ... familiar. Dark hair. Suit. Sage frowned.

It couldn't be.

Why would Bianca get into a car with Jason Jones?

Sage thought of all the possibilities. Could Bianca be having an affair with Jason Jones? The very idea made Sage shudder. Surely Bianca knew she could do better than Jason Jones? Surely she didn't fall for his phoney charm? Sage remembered being bathed in Jason's glow, and how important and valued she'd felt in those few moments. Bianca was lonely and sad. Maybe she *would* fall for it? Maybe after being ignored by Armand for so many years, was she hungry for some attention, even if it was all fake? Or ... maybe Bianca was meeting Jason Jones to audition. With Armand out of action, it made sense she'd be looking for other options. And Jason Jones was a big-time magician who toured the world. Maybe his next show required an assistant. And maybe Bianca wanted to be that assistant.

That had to be it. The black car pulled away with a wet rumble, and Sage felt a tingling sensation. She shivered, the tips of her fingers growing numb. The hair on her arms stood up, and she felt washed with cold, alert with adrenaline. Something was wrong. She thought of ghosts and vengeful spirits. She was in danger. She could *feel* it.

She heard steps behind her, and felt a hand on her arm. She spun round, her heart pounding, and suddenly she was pressed up against Herb, and he was kissing her. The cold feeling of danger dissolved, and was replaced by a soft, spreading warmth. It was just Herb. Everything was fine. Everything was *better* than fine. She'd been jumping at shadows, and now Herb was here, and he was kissing her. His hands cupped her face and wound into her hair, and he smelled like cinnamon and jelly snakes and he was warm and strong and she totally forgot she was angry with him. Her hands crept around his waist and she sighed softly as she relaxed into the kiss.

He'd been right. It was *much* better without the smell of urine.

'You meant *please*,' he said. 'The magic-word thing. Sorry. I get in my own head sometimes. I totally took you for granted, and I sincerely apologise. I was wrong.'

Sage's lips were buzzing. She wanted more. 'It's okay,' she said. 'There's a lot going on. We're all wound a little tight.'

He nodded. 'I was still a dick, though. And I was wrong before that, as well. About the female magician thing. The only reason there aren't more female magicians is because dicks like me keep saying there can't be.' He shook his head. 'I'll apologise to Bianca, too. She's incredibly talented, and I know that Armand often treats her like crap. I imagine lots of people treat her like crap, because she's blonde and beautiful and people automatically think she's dumb.'

Sage remembered first meeting Bianca, and how she had totally assumed that Bianca was a typical dumb blonde.

'I mean, don't get me wrong,' Herb was saying. 'Bianca is absolutely pants-on-the-wall insane. All that spiritual curse mumbo jumbo sets my teeth on edge. But that doesn't mean she's not talented. She could have an awesome solo magic show if she wanted. So I apologise unreservedly to her, and also to you. Do you forgive me?'

Sage tried not to smile.

'Come on,' said Herb. 'Name your price. I'll do anything, just forgive me.'

'Anything?'

'Anything. Make it as humiliating as you like. Want me to do the whole show with my fly undone?'

Sage thought about knives slicing into bare skin. 'Drop the sword cabinet from the show.'

Herb looked taken aback. 'Why?'

'I hate it. It's creepy.'

'But we've already dropped Zigzag…'

Sage gave him a cold look. Herb sighed.

'If I drop it, you'll forgive me?'

Sage nodded.

'Then consider it done. We'll move Assistant's Revenge to the finale. So I'm forgiven?'

Herb's eyebrows wrinkled pleadingly, making him look like an oversized, hopeful puppy. Sage laughed, and the eyebrows shot all the way up.

'Is that a yes?' asked Herb, leaning forward. 'Does that mean I can kiss you again?'

Still laughing, Sage nodded, and Herb moved in, tilting her chin up with his hand and lowering his face to hers. Sage felt a warm, tingling happiness spread all the way down to her toes. She liked this boy. She liked him a *lot*.

'Come on, then,' he said at last, offering her his arm. 'I'll walk you to your bus.'

'But don't we have to go through the show?' Sage asked. 'The lights…'

'We'll do it tomorrow,' he said. 'You deserve a night off.'

'What about the curtain?'

'I'll do it myself. I'm pretty handy with a sewing machine.'

'Such a well-rounded gentleman,' said Sage, grinning at him.

He grinned back. 'I'll even walk on your left side,' he said. 'In case a carriage wheel should splash mud on us. However, I draw the line at putting my coat over a puddle. I really like this coat, and I don't have a spare.'

They ambled down the street. Sage thrilled at the warmth of him, up against her side. They passed an old man pushing a walking frame, who smiled indulgently at them. Sage swelled with pride. Herb was walking down the street with *her*. He'd chosen *her*.

Finally.

'Why didn't you kiss me the other night? After the Jason Jones show?' she asked him.

Herb looked surprised, swinging his head around to look at her. 'Why didn't *you* kiss *me*?'

Sage spluttered.

'Oh, I see,' said Herb, taking on a knowing, lofty air. 'So what you're saying is that women should have all the same opportunities as men, and should be totally equal in every-thing, and shouldn't have to be the spangly-clad assistants to magicians. *Except* for when it comes to kissing. Kissing isn't equal at all, because the boy has to make the first move. Am I right?'

Sage glared at him. 'Seriously?' she said. 'After that whole lovely heartfelt apology, you still want to win this fight?'

He shrugged. 'I think I just did.'

'You are infuriating.'

The goofy grin widened. 'But you like me.'

Sage wasn't sure whether she wanted to hit him or kiss him again. She settled for the latter, pulling on his arm to make him stop and reaching up on tiptoe to wrap her arms around his shoulders. A car honked at them, and she felt Herb's lips stretch in a smile under hers.

She wasn't even cold anymore.

The bus pulled up just as they turned the corner. It started to rain again, fat drops that slid down the back of Sage's jacket and plastered her hair to her forehead. She leaned in for a quick kiss, and then dashed to meet the bus, skipping over puddles and feeling light as a feather. She felt like Gene Kelly, springing and whirling through the rain.

She climbed on board the bus, and the bus driver gave her an amused smile. She grinned back as she swiped her card, and sank damply into a spare seat. Herb still stood on the corner, getting steadily wetter. She waved, and he waved back. The bus pulled away from the corner with a groan, and Herb finally turned and started to walk back to the theatre. Sage let out a little squeal, and pressed her fingers to her still-buzzing lips. It wasn't until she was halfway home that she remembered seeing Bianca with Jason Jones. She'd forgotten to tell Herb about it. Maybe that was for the best. Tensions between Herb and Bianca were running high, and knowing that Bianca might be planning to defect to Jason Jones certainly wouldn't make things any better.

Her mother was waiting for her when she got home. She was wearing a neat grey business suit with stylish black heels. Her hair was swept back. Sage stared at her. She hadn't seen her mother in anything other than jeans and a baggy knitted jumper for weeks.

'I thought you didn't start until Monday?'

'I don't. Today was just a preliminary meeting.' Mum's smile was so wide, Sage was afraid her teeth might fall out. 'It's *great*,' she said. 'I have my own office with this gorgeous view out over all those higgledy-piggledy rooftops. Everyone is absolutely lovely, and the work is so *interesting*. First up I'm going to be working on a design project for a bicycle company.'

'That's excellent.' Sage opened the fridge and squealed a little. It was full of food. And not cheap-brand basics. There was hummus and olives and the expensive organic ham that Sage loved and at least four kinds of cheese. Sage pulled it all out, grabbed the fresh loaf of sourdough bread that lay on the kitchen counter and made herself a sandwich.

'There's just this one thing,' said Mum. 'Kate next door is totally happy to look after Zacky during the days you're at work. But there's one night next week when Roman has a piano lesson, and I have to take a late client meeting. I won't be back until nine.'

Sage took a blissful bite of her sandwich. 'Mhmm.'

'Do you think you could take Zacky to the theatre with you?' asked Mum. 'Just on Wednesday night?'

Sage chewed and raised her eyebrows. She swallowed. 'I don't know,' she said. 'It's pretty hectic backstage during the show. I wouldn't be able to keep an eye on him all the time.'

'Couldn't he sit in the audience?'

Sage thought about it. 'I suppose so,' she said doubtfully.

Mum smiled understandingly. 'I know it's a bit of a pain, but I really appreciate the help. And I want to make it worth your while.' She reached under her chair and drew out a white plastic bag.

'What is it?' Sage took the bag and opened it, and almost dropped her sandwich.

It was a camera. A proper film camera. It was *her* camera, the one she'd spent hours staring at online. The one that Yoshi Lear used. She reverently removed it from the box and gripped it in her hands. It was real. It was *hers*. She looked up at her mother, who smiled.

'I know it's been hard,' said Mum. 'The move, and everything. But now I have this job, we're going to be fine. A plumber is coming on the weekend to have a look at the pipes and fix the heating, and I've made an appointment with a builder to come and patch up the damp spots in the ceiling. Then maybe during the next school holidays you can help me pick out some new paint and carpet, and help with the design for a new kitchen.'

Sage nodded dumbly, and looked back down at her camera. Her fingers itched. She suddenly thought of the theatre. What an incredible series of photos she could take! Backstage at a magic show – it was a photographer's dream. She knew exactly the kind of lenses and filters she'd use to bring the slightly grungy, worn old theatre to life.

'So next Wednesday?' Mum asked. 'You don't mind taking Zacky along with you?'

'Of course not,' said Sage, her mind elsewhere. 'It'll be fun.'

11. Force: a subject is offered an apparently free choice, but the magician is in control of what will be chosen.

Sage sought Bianca out in her dressing-room the next afternoon. 'I've been thinking about Armand,' she said. 'Have you got any more text messages?'

Bianca leaned towards her mirror and applied eyeliner with expert sweeps of the pencil. Sage watched jealously. She was utterly confounded by makeup, and couldn't manage anything more complicated than lip gloss and mascara.

'There was one yesterday,' said Bianca. 'That he'd be back soon.'

'Did he give a date?'

'Nothing specific.'

'I think he's hiding something,' said Sage. 'Do you remember when I told him that I'd discovered some missing money?'

Bianca shook her head.

'It was the first time I ever met him,' said Sage. 'You were there. I told him that I'd noticed some accounting errors. He acted really weird about it, and told me not to investigate any further. Then the next day he told me he'd sorted it all out.'

'So? If he sorted it all out, then what is there to worry about?'

'I think he was lying. I think he knew exactly what had happened to that money. And I think maybe now he might be in trouble.'

Bianca pulled a baby wipe from a container and dabbed at an unwanted smudge. 'Surely if he was in trouble, he would have mentioned it in one of his texts.'

'What if he's in *big* trouble? What if he owes someone a bunch of money? What if he has a gambling addiction? Or a drug addiction?'

'The only thing Armand is addicted to is attention,' said Bianca. 'I really wouldn't worry about him if I were you. We have bigger things to deal with.'

Sage watched as Bianca painted several layers of glittery eyeshadow in different shades of green.

'Where did you learn to do that?' she asked.

Bianca shrugged. 'Oh, you know. My mother. Magazines. Hours of practice.'

Sage bit her lip and plucked up her courage. 'Um,' she said. 'Did I see you with Jason Jones yesterday?'

Bianca's hand froze, brush poised above her eyelid. 'What?'

'I thought I saw you get into a car with Jason Jones.'

Bianca's lips pressed together. 'Wasn't me,' she said, and her hand unfroze and continued applying eyeshadow.

'Oh,' said Sage. 'I could have sworn it was.'

'Nope.' Icy stillness settled over Bianca's features.

Sage watched her for a few more minutes. She was sure about what she'd seen. But why would Bianca lie?

~~~

'So this fader goes up to about forty per cent,' said Herb, pointing to the little lighting desk. 'And then up to full once I bring Warren out for the second time.'

Sage looked up from the sheet of cues that Herb had made for her and an entirely involuntary smile spread across her face. Herb twinkled at her and Sage's insides went all melty, like chocolate syrup.

'Do you think this would be an appropriate time for me to make some kind of sleazy comment involving your ability to turn on a light?' asked Herb.

Sage snorted. 'Try it,' she warned. 'See what happens.'

Herb reached out and entwined his pinkie finger with hers.

Sage cleared her throat. 'So what's the next cue?'

'Hmm?' Herb started to tug gently on her little finger.

Sage nodded towards the lighting desk. 'I think we were up to Warren's second appearance. Is that where I bring up the blue wash?'

'Warren,' said Herb, his voice low and warm. 'Blue wash.'

He tugged harder, pulling her towards him. His lips brushed hers, and his other hand snaked around her waist.

'Is this really appropriate for the workplace?' Sage murmured against his lips.

'Do you want to file a complaint?'

Sage shook her head and leaned into the kiss.

There was a sudden crash and a short, sharp cry from the stage. Herb sprang to his feet and sprinted out the door. Sage followed.

Bianca was sprawled in the centre of the stage, surrounded by broken glass and a lump of black metal.

'What happened?' asked Herb, crunching through the glass to her.

Bianca raised herself into a sitting position. 'One of the lights,' she said, wincing with pain. 'It fell from...' She looked up to the lighting grid, and then cried out sharply and bent over.

'Where does it hurt?'

'My ankle.' Bianca's eyes filled with tears.

'There's an icepack in the freezer,' said Sage. 'I'll go and get it.'

'Are you sure it's not broken?' asked Herb as Sage left the stage.

'It's happened before,' she heard Bianca say through gritted teeth. 'Just a sprain.'

Sage pulled the icepack out of the freezer, the cold seeping up through her hands into her heart. Weren't the lights supposed to be secure? Had someone rigged it to fall? Someone or . . . something?

She shivered. Could Bianca be right about the curse? Was there a vengeful theatre spirit trying to sabotage the show? And what if Bianca was wrong? What if it was connected to Armand's disappearance?

She hurried back to the stage and handed Bianca the icepack.

'We have to get you to a doctor,' said Herb. 'I'll call us a cab.'

'No,' said Bianca. 'I'll be fine. My ankle used to go out all the time when I was a teenager. I'll just take a painkiller and go lie down in my dressing-room for a bit. You need to prepare for the show.'

The show. Sage saw Herb's face fall. They couldn't do the show without Bianca.

'You can totally do it,' said Bianca. 'Just do the solo effects

– the carrot swap with Warren, some close-up card stuff, cups-and-balls. You know a bit of mentalism, even though you always whinge about it. There are heaps of magicians who work solo.'

Herb nodded slowly. 'We'll have to drop the finale though,' he said. 'I can't do Assistant's Revenge on my own. Unless...'

Two pairs of eyes turned to Sage.

'What?' she said, looking back at them. '*What*?'

～～

'So basically I strap you in here,' said Herb, pulling back the curtain to reveal what looked like a medieval torture device. A wooden frame supported a human-sized leather harness, plus several lengths of heavy chains, fastened with proper padlocks.

'In there?' Sage looked dubiously at the contraption. 'That doesn't look like much fun.'

Bianca snorted. She had taken a painkiller, and was lounging in one of the front-row seats, her ankle propped up on a box and a cushion. It had taken nearly an hour of cajoling and flirting from Herb to get Sage to agree to participate in the trick, and she still wasn't sure about it. On the other hand, without her the trick wouldn't happen at all, and Sage didn't want to be held responsible for ruining the show.

'It's fine,' said Herb. 'It's all fake. Here, I'll show you.'

He led her into the harness, and buckled it all up around her, fastening the locks. The straps were tight around Sage's wrists and waist, and she felt a sudden rising panic.

'I don't like this,' she said. 'Let me out.'

He grinned at her. 'Let yourself out. Just step backwards.'

He showed her how to move sideways half a step, which released a hook, allowing the whole harness section to swing open like a door. Sage stepped out, and Herb explained that the wrist and ankle straps were buckled and padlocked on the front, but were actually velcro around the back. Sage released herself, feeling bizarrely relieved.

'So here's what happens,' said Herb. 'I buckle you in, and you look all cranky that you're being tied up.'

He ushered Sage back into the device and buckled it all up.

'Then I pull this curtain around.' A floaty red curtain billowed around the wooden frame, like a shower curtain. 'And as I do so, you escape out the back and grab the other end of the curtain. I strap myself into the device...' They awkwardly exchanged places, the red fabric making it difficult to see. '...And you take my place and pull the curtain open, revealing that we have magically exchanged places.'

Sage walked around the device, pulling the curtain open. Herb was strapped into the device, leather straps buckled around his wrists and ankles, chains wrapped around his torso.

'Is that it?' said Sage.

Bianca snorted again. 'It takes a lot of practice to get the timing right,' she said. 'It has to be one smooth movement, no pause around the back while you swap places.'

Sage looked at the contraption. 'Don't people guess how it's done?' she asked. 'It seems so simple.'

Herb and Bianca exchanged a glance and laughed. 'They *never* figure it out,' said Herb. 'Ever. Precisely because it's so simple.'

'Okay,' said Bianca. 'Time to make the *real* magic happen.' She limped up the stairs and down the corridor to her dressing-room, calling out for Sage to follow her.

Bianca inched her way down onto her chair, keeping her ankle straight, and bent over to open a large steam trunk in a corner of the room. 'I'm sure I'll have something your size in here,' she said, pulling out bits and pieces of costume.

Sage watched as Bianca produced a jewelled crown, a velvet cape, a furry tail, a pair of lederhosen and a pair of moose antlers. 'Ah!' she said at last, holding up something blood-red and sparkly. 'Try this on. I think I've got some shoes in here too.' She disappeared back into the trunk.

It was a spangly, glittery number – a little more conservative than Bianca's, but not by much. It had a tasseled fringe skirt and a close-fit, sequined bodice. Bianca politely averted her eyes while Sage squeezed into it. It wasn't easy. Sage looked at herself in the mirror. Bits of her bulged from underneath the tight elastic.

'No way,' she said. 'I look ridiculous.'

'You look gorgeous. You just need a little makeup, and a bucketload of confidence.'

'Nope,' said Sage. 'Not gonna happen.'

Bianca smiled sympathetically. 'Let me tell you a secret,' she said. 'The secret to being beautiful. You can make *any-thing* look good, as long as you wear it with a little sass. Hold your head up, throw your shoulders back and *own it*.'

'That's easy to say when you look like a supermodel,' muttered Sage.

Bianca shook her head. 'It's all in the attitude. I'm telling you. Here.' She handed Sage a pair of red high heels.

'I can't wear these,' said Sage. 'I *never* wear heels. I'll fall over. There'll be *two* sprained ankles.'

Bianca rolled her eyes. 'You'll be *fine*,' she said. 'They're dancer's shoes, anyway. Very comfortable.'

Sage doubted that very much.

'Now sit.' Bianca pulled over a second chair and grabbed a little bottle of foundation.

Sage sat. 'I can't believe I'm doing this.'

'You'll be fine,' said Bianca.

'This was never a position I imagined finding myself in,' said Sage. 'I remember once when I was little, my grandma told me I was pretty, and that if I grew taller I could become a model. I told her that models were brainless coathangers with eating disorders and cocaine addictions, and that, as a feminist, I wanted to be valued for my mind, not my body.'

'How old were you?'

'Eight.'

Bianca chuckled.

'And yet here I am, having my face painted, wearing ridiculous shoes and a skimpy, sparkly outfit. A professional bimbo.'

Bianca's smile faltered a little, and she looked away.

'Oh, Bianca! I'm sorry,' said Sage. 'I didn't mean it like that. Of course you're not a bimbo. You're amazing and clever and I know that being an assistant is *so much more* complicated than just smiling and looking beautiful. I'm just scared because I know I can't do any of the complicated stuff that you do, *and* I'm not beautiful or glamorous enough.'

'Don't be silly,' said Bianca. 'You're definitely beautiful enough.' She swung Sage's chair around so she could look at her reflection.

'I look stupid,' said Sage, staring at the red-lipped, smoky-eyed girl in the mirror. 'Like a hooker.'

'You do *not*,' said Bianca. 'I know it looks a bit over the top up close like this, but trust me, under the theatre lights you'll look like a million dollars.'

'Wow,' said Herb when he saw her, but it didn't sound like a good *wow*.

He was dressed in his own costume – a dark suit with a white shirt and skinny black tie. It made him look older, and Sage felt like a little kid playing dress-ups next to him.

'You're supposed to say she looks beautiful,' said Bianca with a stern look.

Herb raised his eyebrows. 'She looked beautiful before. Now she looks ridiculous.'

Sage felt her cheeks go hot with mortification. Bianca hissed something angry to Herb as she headed back to her dressing-room. He gave Sage a cheerful smile.

'You look great,' he said. 'Really. You look like a magician's assistant. Remember the thing I said about the painting? You look like a very expensive masterpiece.'

'I feel like a Jackson Pollock,' she told him.

'No, no, no,' said Herb. 'Something classy and elegant. Like Georges Seurat's *Sunday Afternoon*.'

Sage gave him a flat look. 'Okay from a distance, but all blotchy close up?'

Herb coughed to hide a laugh and moved in closer to

her, pressing his forehead against hers. 'You look pretty awesome close-up,' he said, his voice low. 'I just like you better when you're wild and natural.'

Sage forgot the spangly leotard for a moment and felt herself start to glow gently. She leaned into him.

'Thanks for doing this,' murmured Herb, brushing his lips against her forehead. 'I really appreciate it.'

Sage's anxiety about the routine, her stupid outfit and ridiculous makeup drained away, and was replaced by a kind of singing joy.

'Let me take you out for dinner tonight,' said Herb. 'To Mr Pham's. My treat. As a thank you. And a celebration of my debut as a performing magician, and yours as a magician's assistant.'

'Well, it is Friday night,' said Sage. 'I'd hate to disappoint Mr Pham.' She turned her head to kiss him, a slow, melting kiss that made her entire body hum.

'Just promise me you'll wash off all this gunk before we go,' said Herb, pulling away. 'You're covering me in glitter.'

〰〰

Sage knew they were in trouble from the beginning, when Warren escaped from the special hidden pocket in Herb's jacket and lazily made his way offstage, to uproarious laughter from the audience.

Things went downhill from there.

Herb fumbled a coin vanish, the coin falling and bouncing on the wooden boards of the stage with a ringing clatter. The wrong top hat had been set on the stage, so instead of pulling out a bunch of flowers, Herb pulled out an empty plastic bag. His patter became more and more frantic as he tried to compensate for the failing tricks, and his hair stuck to his forehead as he sweated and puffed. Sage missed nearly every single lighting and sound cue, and Bianca kept forgetting to open and close the curtains.

As Assistant's Revenge drew closer, Sage felt a heavy, twisting sickness growing in her stomach. Her teeth started to chatter. Onstage, Herb accidentally swore out loud as he failed to guess which card a little boy had selected from a deck. The boy's eyes opened wide, and there was a murmur of disapproval from the adults in the audience, along with much giggling from the children. Bianca nudged Sage, who slowly rose to her feet and shrugged off the cotton dressing-gown that had been covering the sparkly costume. She felt almost numb with cold.

'You'll be fabulous,' whispered Bianca, as she slid into Sage's seat in front of the lighting console.

Sage stood in the wings next to the Assistant's Revenge set piece, which was all ready to be wheeled into place. Herb finally guessed the correct card and closed his eyes with relief as he sent the boy back to his seat. His eyes flicked over to Sage, and his mouth twitched in the tiniest of smiles. It was time.

Sage placed her hands on the metal railing of Assistant's Revenge and pushed. It rocked as the casters bumped over the uneven stage. Sage hesitated. Was she seriously about to do this?

'Go on,' hissed Bianca, gesturing to the stage. Sage took a deep breath and stepped through the wings. The bright lights made it almost impossible to see anything, and she stumbled forwards, teetering in the ridiculous shoes. She dimly heard Herb say something about a beautiful assistant, and she wheeled Assistant's Revenge into place and clicked the brakes on the casters with one glittery toe.

As Herb guided her into the restraints, Sage looked out into the black void that she knew contained approximately seventy-five paying audience members. She swallowed. They were all watching her. Looking at her. This wasn't how it was supposed to be. She was a photographer. She was supposed to be the observer, not the observed. As her eyes adjusted, she saw dim outlines of people sitting in rows. Sage felt a jolt of recognition as her eyes slid over the front row, partly illuminated by the light spilling from the stage. Jason Jones was there. Jason Jones was there, watching them. Witness to their humiliating attempt at a magic show. He held a thin, flat box wrapped in gold wrapping paper on his lap, and had a lazy, sardonic smile on his face. Sage glanced at Herb, who nodded with a grim look on his face.

'I know,' he said under his breath. 'I noticed him straight away. But let's face it, it's not like the show can get any worse.' He squeezed her arm reassuringly as he buckled the last strap.

Sage wanted to disagree with him, but it was too late. Herb walked a measured circle around her, drawing the curtain closed. As he disappeared from the audience's sight, Sage stepped out of her bonds and Herb slipped in, their bodies briefly pressing together as they squeezed past each other. Herb was radiating heat, his brow moist with sweat, and Sage wanted to curl into his warmth and stay behind the curtain forever. But she stepped out and took his place, as he buckled the chains around his ankles and wrists with the velcro straps. Sage grasped the curtain and completed the circle, pulling the curtain open again and revealing Herb restrained within, his face twisted into a comic approximation of indignant rage. He scowled at her, and she walked around one final time. When the curtain parted again, the device was empty. Sage acted shocked, putting her hand over her mouth and shrugging. She peered behind the curtain. She lifted the black silk hat on Herb's card table to reveal Warren sleeping underneath. The audience laughed.

Then Bianca raised the house lights to reveal Herb

standing at the very back of the theatre, wearing a completely different suit. The audience burst into wild applause.

Herb made his way back onto the stage, and offered Sage his hand. Sage took it and they stepped forward together. Herb pulled her hand up into the air, and then down again in a bow. The audience cheered and whistled.

Sage felt a kind of fizzing bubbling in her chest. It had worked! The trick had worked! They'd fooled everyone! A smile spread over her face and, glancing over at Herb, she saw the goofy smile firmly plastered on his. He winked at her, and the fizzing feeling took on a rosy warmth.

The curtains swung closed, and Herb grabbed her in a bone-crushing hug. 'Well done!' he said. 'You were awesome. A natural.'

Sage breathed in the smell of him – cinnamon and theatre-dust. She could get used to this. The applause died down, and Sage heard the sounds of the audience getting to their feet and shuffling out of the theatre. Herb gave her a final squeeze, and released her.

Bianca limped out onto the stage. 'Well,' she said. 'That certainly was … a show to remember.'

Herb closed his eyes for a moment. 'Don't even start,' he said. 'It was a disaster. With the exception of Assistant's Revenge, not a single effect went right.'

'It wasn't that bad,' said Sage, trying to look reassuring.

'And it was partly my fault. I kept missing the lighting cues.'

'It was definitely that bad,' Herb replied. 'And none of it was your fault. Well, almost none of it.'

'I think we all sucked,' said Bianca. 'Sorry about the curtains.'

'Don't be,' said Herb. 'I sucked the most. I'll have to apologise to Armand when he gets back. The whole live-on-stage magician thing is harder than it looks.'

Bianca made a noncommittal noise and limped off towards her dressing-room.

Herb took a deep breath. 'Go change,' he said. 'I want to see the real you. Then to Mr Pham's. I'm going to need a lot of *pho* to drown my sorrows.'

Sage was suddenly starving. She'd left her clothes in a bag under her desk. She ducked into the office and bent down to pull it out. It was so much further to bend because of the red high heels. She slid into her chair for a moment to pull them off, and noticed a white envelope sitting on her desk, addressed by hand to *The Lovely Assistant*.

She opened it, and pulled out a sheet of very thin, white paper. The writing on it looked as though it had been typed on an old typewriter – the letters were uneven and smudged. Sage felt her theatre high drain out of her as she read.

'Oh my god,' she said to herself, and then sprinted

barefoot out to the theatre, where Herb was resetting the props for the next show.

'I hope Mr Pham has a well-stocked kitchen,' he said, without looking up from the black table. 'Because we are going to require an *epic* dinner tonight. The most awesome dinner of all time. Possibly followed by ice-cream. Do you like ice-cream? Of course you do, everyone likes—'

He turned, and instantly crossed the stage to Sage's side. 'What's wrong? You look like you've seen a ...' He shook his head. 'You look upset.'

Sage held the letter out. Her hand trembled.

'What is it?' Herb took the letter – and recoiled in disgust.

```
Painted Jezebel.
I want to tie you up and saw you in half.
Make you vanish.
```

12. Simulation: to give the impression that something has happened when it has not.

'Jesus.' Herb handed Sage a steaming cup of tea. 'Are you sure you're okay?'

She nodded. 'I'm fine,' she said. 'Just a bit shocked.'

'It wasn't meant for you.' Bianca was standing in the doorway to their office, leaning on the frame to keep the weight off her ankle. She held a sheaf of papers in her hand. 'It was for me. It's not the first time.'

She handed the papers to Herb, who leafed through them. They were letters, all with the same wonky typewriter text on the same thin paper.

'People suck,' Bianca said, her face twisting. 'You'd think I'd get used to it.'

'How long has this been going on?' asked Herb.

Bianca shrugged. 'This guy? A few months. But there

have been others over the years. Lots of cheesy pickup lines and come-ons. If I step on Armand's head during the glass-walking routine, I get foot fetishists. There was one guy who wanted to know if he could get a replica of my costume in his size. I don't mind those ones as much as the people who write in about the bondage stuff – when I get tied up or sawn in half. They…' She shook her head. 'I told you we were cursed.'

'This isn't a curse,' said Herb, raising his voice and hitting the pile of papers with the back of his hand. 'It's a *threat*. Why didn't you say anything before?'

'It's nothing new,' said Bianca. 'Nothing unusual. Just part of the job, I guess.'

Sage shivered. Some job.

'We have to call the police,' said Herb.

Bianca let out a hollow laugh. 'Do you think I haven't tried that already? I used to take every single creepy letter down to the police station. They would listen sympatheti-cally, and then tell me there was nothing they could do.'

Sage stared at the letters, trying to understand why someone would do such a thing. 'We have to figure out who's sending them,' she said. 'There has to be a clue or at least something we can take to the police as evidence. Do you still have the envelopes? Maybe someone could analyse the handwriting.'

Bianca sighed. 'Feel free,' she said. 'I've never had any luck.' She turned and hobbled slowly back to her dressing-room.

Herb watched her go, his forehead creased in a frown. 'I'm sorry,' he said to Sage. 'This was supposed to be a fun, happy night, celebrating the utter failure of my performance debut. Do you still want to go to dinner? Or if you like I can take you home.'

Sage managed a weak smile. 'Dinner, please,' she said. The cheerful brightness of Mr Pham's would lift her spirits. 'I'm starving.'

Herb gave her a squeeze. 'Excellent,' he said. 'How about I head over there now while you wash your face and get changed? I'll make sure there are mountains of spring rolls awaiting your triumphant entrance.'

'Sounds great.'

Fifteen minutes later, Sage walked into the Vietnamese restaurant, breathing in the smell of fried garlic and mush-rooms with relief. She looked around for Herb . . . but he wasn't there. There was a couple sharing a steaming bowl of *pho* in the corner, and a man in a suit reading a newspaper and sipping hot tea. But no Herb.

'Miss Sage!' Mr Pham came bustling out of the kitchen. 'Are you alone? Where is Mister Herb?'

'I was hoping you could tell me,' said Sage.

Mr Pham looked confused. 'He hasn't been in since last Friday, with you. Is everything okay?'

Sage smiled. 'Sure,' she said. 'Just a misunderstanding.'

She left the restaurant and headed back to the theatre. Maybe she had misheard Herb. Maybe he'd got held up with something. Sage hunched over against the cold, which soaked right through her, making her fingers and ears ache. Each breath she drew in filled her lungs with what felt like tiny ice crystals, scratching and scraping against her throat. She breathed out great billowing white clouds.

What if something had happened to Herb?

She cupped her hands over her face and breathed out slowly, hoping the warmth of her breath would thaw her frozen nose. It didn't work.

He'd be fine. It was just a misunderstanding. He'd be back at the theatre.

He wasn't.

As Sage slipped into the auditorium, Bianca was making her way gingerly up the aisle, with her red duffel coat and bag, a thick scarf wrapped around her neck.

'What are you still doing here?' asked Bianca. 'I thought you went home ages ago.'

'I was supposed to meet Herb at Mr Pham's,' Sage told her. 'But he wasn't there. Is he still here?'

Bianca shook her head. 'Herb went home about twenty minutes ago,' she said. 'He said you guys weren't going to dinner anymore because he was too angry about the letters.'

Sage stared at her. 'He went home?'

'Didn't he tell you?'

'No.' Sage's mood plummeted. Herb had cancelled their dinner, and forgotten to tell her. He had stood her up. Her cheeks grew hot and tears pricked her eyes. She gritted her teeth together. She wasn't going to cry over a boy in front of Bianca.

'What a tool,' said Bianca. 'I mean, I know we're all on edge because of everything that's been going on, but there's just no excuse to act like a jerk.'

'I guess he was upset,' said Sage.

'Don't make excuses for him!' Bianca jabbed a finger at Sage. 'He is a weasel and a toad.'

Sage swallowed. Herb *was* a weasel and a toad. There was a ghost haunting the theatre, *and* a crazed stalker sending creepy fan mail, and he'd let her walk the streets at night on her own. *And* stood her up. What kind of a boyfriend did that?

She sighed. One who wasn't a boyfriend. Herb was sweet and funny and an excellent kisser, but maybe he just wasn't boyfriend material. He was so focused on his magic career, Sage wasn't convinced there was room in his life for anything else.

'You're right,' she said, her voice sounding surer than she felt. 'Herb *is* useless. I mean, all he does is show off and get all sarcastic whenever anyone mentions something he doesn't understand.'

Bianca nodded. 'That's my girl. Now, what are we going to do tonight?'

Sage looked at her.

'I'm not letting you go home all broken-hearted and dejected,' said Bianca. 'We have to *do* something.'

'What?'

Bianca cocked her head to one side. 'Let's stay here. Overnight. Maybe we'll see the ghost.'

Sage felt uneasy. 'Stay here? All night?'

'I sleep here all the time. It'll be fun. Like a sleepover.'

Sage opened her mouth to protest that staking out a haunted theatre overnight wasn't exactly her idea of fun, but Bianca was already limping past her to the door, her face alight.

'I'm going to Mr Pham's to grab some provisions,' she said. 'You wait here.'

Sage stared at her. 'Now?' she asked. 'Tonight? What about your ankle?'

'My ankle's fine. I've got blankets and pillows in my dressing-room. Why not tonight?'

Sage could think of about a million reasons, but she

chose the one she thought would work best. 'What about the curse?'

Bianca tossed her head. 'You and Herb stayed here overnight,' she said. 'In the storeroom. And nothing bad happened to you. Except for being locked up in a storeroom with Herb. I suppose that's pretty bad.'

Sage thought about the bucket of urine, and of Herb's soft, slow kisses. 'It depends on your perspective,' she said, and her heart broke all over again when she remembered how he'd stood her up.

'Gross,' said Bianca with a laugh. 'Now come on. Will you do it? Stay here with me tonight?'

'I'm just not sure—'

'You don't have to.' Bianca stood up again. 'I'd like you to. But you don't have to. I can do it on my own.'

Sage imagined the theatre, all dark and closed down. It was the perfect time to hunt for ghosts. She could set up a time-lapse exposure on the stage, and see if she could capture a glimpse of some long-dead theatrical spirit.

'Okay,' she said with a firm nod. 'I'll text my parents and tell them I'm staying at your house.'

'Great! I'll be ten minutes.'

She hobbled through the auditorium door. Sage heard a scuffling noise from the stage and started. Warren's pink nose emerged from behind the red curtain, twitching and sniffing. He loped out and sat centre stage. Sage dug in her bag for her old film camera, and snapped a photo.

'Well,' she said. 'It's just you and me, Warren.'

The rabbit looked away, uninterested.

The theatre seemed ... different at night. The cheap paint and lumpy chairs seemed less shabby and more romantically dilapidated. Draughts brushed through the auditorium, like the theatre was sighing to itself.

Sage set her digital camera up on a tripod in the auditorium, hidden among the chairs, pointing at the stage. She adjusted the exposure to two seconds, taking the low light into account, and set the timer to open the shutter every two minutes. That should be enough to catch any ghostly presence. Then she pulled out her new film camera and snapped a few atmospheric photos.

Click.

A wide shot of the empty auditorium.

Click.

Peering into the wings at the side of the stage.

Click.

Herb's props arranged neatly on the black velvet-topped card table.

Click.

A broom resting against the brick wall behind the stage.

Click.

Warren loped into view, dragging a red silk scarf behind him.

Click.

Sage followed him down the hall, snapping photos all the way.

Click.

Sage felt her heart leap into her throat as she heard the auditorium door bang open.

'Sage?' Bianca's voice drifted down the corridor.

Sage took a deep breath. 'I'm here.' She was going to have to calm down, if she didn't want to experience a heart attack.

'Mr Pham loaded me up,' Bianca called. 'I've got noodles and spring rolls and that really amazing caramelised fish thing he makes.'

Sage's stomach growled its approval, and she turned and made her way back up the corridor, Warren softly padding along beside her. Bianca had already transformed her dressing-room into something resembling a nine-year-old's sleepover. A blanket covered the couch in the corner, and more blankets and pillows were spread out on the carpeted floor. Bianca was sitting on a cushion, her bad leg stretched out at an angle that Sage wouldn't even dream of attempting, removing lids from plastic takeaway containers.

'Help yourself,' she said. 'This is going to be fun!'

Sage sat down and spooned noodles into one of the

bowls Bianca had brought. The smell of Vietnamese food
· sent her insides spinning, reminding her of her first dinner
with Herb, where he had been funny and interesting, as well
as the crushing moment of humiliation when she'd realised
he'd stood her up. She took a savage bite of a spring roll. She
wasn't going to let Herb ruin Mr Pham's culinary genius.
She just needed to take her mind off him.

'So how did you find out about the guy who died here?'
she asked Bianca.

'Renaldo the Remarkable?' said Bianca, her chopsticks
hovering delicately over her bowl. 'I know some people in
the industry – I kind of grew up around the theatre. I asked
if anything strange had ever happened before in this theatre,
and this guy I know – Bill – told me about Renaldo. Then
I went to the library and looked it up on the microfilm and
found a few newspaper clippings.'

Sage fed Warren a morsel of lettuce. 'How did he die?'

Bianca closed her eyes. 'It was horrible,' she said. 'They
were doing this trick where he was locked inside a wooden
chest, and a blacksmith's anvil was placed on top – so he
wouldn't be able to escape. Then he was supposed to escape,
and appear somewhere else. But the wooden chest became
weakened during rehearsal, and it broke under the weight of
the anvil – crushing Renaldo to death in front of everyone.'

'That's awful,' said Sage.

Bianca nodded. 'There have been plenty of sightings of him since then. Apparently he's sometimes seen sitting in the front row, the fifth seat along from the aisle. People have reported the feeling of cold fingers on the backs of their necks, and hearing strange sounds and smelling weird things. Some people think his wife is here too.'

'His wife?'

'And assistant. It's really the most tragic part of the whole story. They fell in love while touring the world together. When he died, all the other magicians wanted to hire her, but she said she'd never work again. Can you imagine, watching your husband die in front of hundreds of people?'

Sage closed her eyes for a moment, and heard the clamour of applause fading into screams. She rubbed her hands together – her fingers were freezing.

'She disappeared after Renaldo died,' said Bianca. 'Most people thought she just moved to another city, away from the public eye. But some people say she came back to this theatre and locked herself in the basement, and killed herself.'

Sage shivered.

'I'm going to pop these in the bin,' said Bianca suddenly, stacking up the empty plastic food containers. 'I'll be right back.'

The cold spread through Sage, rising from the tips of her fingers through her hands, her wrists, her arms, and creeping slowly down her chest into her heart. Her toes went numb and she wiggled them, hoping that friction might generate warmth. It didn't.

What if Bianca didn't come back? Sage had seen enough horror movies to know how things worked. Whoever said *I'll be right back* was almost certainly doomed to die. On the other hand, it was the beautiful blonde girl who always foiled the killer and survived. The dumpy sidekick was just one more corpse.

Sage heard footsteps sound in the corridor, and held her breath. She picked up Warren and held him close, feeling his soft fur against her cheek. She could hear his little heart beating. He struggled halfheartedly.

'Don't be silly, Warren,' she whispered. 'It's just Bianca coming back. Nothing to be frightened of.'

It was Bianca, holding two steaming mugs.

'See?' murmured Sage to Warren, putting him back on the floor.

'Here,' said Bianca, handing her a mug. 'Coffee. It'll help us stay awake.'

Sage didn't think she'd have any trouble staying awake. Who could fall asleep when they were in a creepy, empty theatre, in the middle of the night, with either a vengeful ghost or a murderous stalker possibly appearing at any moment? She wrapped her hands around the mug and felt life tingle back into her fingers. She took a sip of coffee – it burned her mouth but spread delicious warmth throughout her. She took another sip and started to feel human again.

'Oh, and there's chocolate.' Bianca handed Sage a fancy box.

Sage took a chocolate and frowned at the box. She glanced at the wastepaper basket under Bianca's dressing table, and saw torn gold wrapping paper. She remembered Jason Jones sitting in the front row, holding a thin, flat box.

'These are great,' she said. 'Where did you get them from?'

Bianca shrugged. 'An admirer,' she said. 'Occasionally you get something nice among all the creepy fan mail.'

Sage chewed on her chocolate thoughtfully. She was sure now that there was something going on between Bianca and Jason Jones. She didn't care what Bianca said, she had definitely seen her get into Jason's car. And these chocolates were from him. But was his interest in her romantic or professional? Sage took another chocolate. They *were* excellent.

'You said you grew up in the theatre,' she said through a mouthful of praline. 'Were your parents performers?'

Bianca nodded. 'My whole family,' she said. 'My grandfather owned a theatre in the country.'

'So how did you get to be a magician's assistant?'

'My dad was a magician,' said Bianca. 'And my mum was

his assistant. I grew up around magic shows. I trained as a gymnast for a while, but this stupid ankle meant I could never compete seriously.'

'That must have been fun,' said Sage. 'Growing up backstage at a magic show.'

Bianca blew on her coffee to cool it down. 'Not really,' she said. 'Mum and Dad were always busy rehearsing. Dad was a real perfectionist. Every trick had to be exactly right. I remember one time he got Mum to escape from being tied up with rope so many times that her hands started to bleed.'

'Wow,' said Sage. 'That's certainly some dedication to your craft. Are they still working?'

Bianca said nothing for a moment, then sighed. 'When I was fifteen, Mum retired and Dad got a new assistant, Estelle. He ran away with her after three months. I haven't seen him since. I think they're working on a cruise ship somewhere.'

'I'm sorry,' said Sage.

Bianca shrugged. 'Mum got very sad, and I just wanted to get out of the house. We knew a lot of magic people – when I heard that Armand was looking for a new assistant, I applied. I started working for him when I was sixteen.'

'How does your mum feel?' asked Sage. 'About you being in the magic business.'

'I don't know,' said Bianca. 'I don't really see her anymore.'

'Is it common?' asked Sage. 'Do many magicians marry their assistants?'

Bianca smiled a little sadly. 'Many?' she said. 'Try *all*. Every single last one of them. Even if they're already married to someone else. It's one of the reasons why I like working with Armand.'

Sage giggled. 'You've never been tempted?'

'*Please.*' Bianca made a face. 'Not in a million years. I'm pretty sure he's gay, anyway. I saw him once with some guy.'

'Huh,' said Sage. 'I never would have guessed.'

'It's why I've never left Armand,' said Bianca. 'I've had plenty of offers from other magicians, believe me. But when my dad left my mum, I made myself a promise. I was never going to be that stupid.'

Bianca looked down at Warren, her face suddenly miserable. Sage thought about the box of chocolates and decided to be bold. 'What about Jason Jones?'

'What about him?' Bianca tried and failed to look casual.

Sage gave her a flat look. 'I did see you with him the other day,' she said. 'And these chocolates are from him, right?'

Bianca closed her eyes for a moment and bit her lip. 'It's nothing,' she said quietly. 'Just a fling. Nothing serious.'

'How long have you been seeing him?'

'Not long. A few months. He came and saw the show and

asked me out for a drink afterwards. It's hard to say no to Jason, he's so charismatic. And one thing led to another…' She blushed.

'Isn't he about a million years older than you?' asked Sage.

Bianca shrugged. 'I like to think of him as *experienced*. He is *amazing*, you know. In the bedroom.'

Sage felt suddenly aware that even though Bianca was only six years older than her, they were a *really important* six years. 'Cool,' she said, and then felt like the biggest dork in the world.

'Sorry,' said Bianca. 'I often forget that you and Herb are younger than me. You seem so mature.' She frowned. 'You do, that is. Not so much Herb.'

So Bianca had fallen for Jason's phoney charm. Suddenly the chocolates didn't taste so good. Sage pushed the box away.

'You're disappointed, aren't you?' There was a little tremble in Bianca's voice. 'I'm sorry. I know Jason can be unbearable, but he's nice to me and makes me feel special. Please don't hate me. You're the only real friend I have.'

Sage felt a wave of sympathy. 'Of course I don't hate you. But I think you can do better.'

Bianca smiled a sad smile. 'Maybe,' she said. 'It's hard. This industry. People tend to judge you based on how you look, not who you are.'

'And does Jason judge you based on who you are?'

'Probably not. But he does a good job of faking it.'

'Would you work with him?'

Bianca shook her head firmly. 'Absolutely not. I made myself that promise. But you won't tell anyone? I know how much Herb and Armand hate him. Armand would probably fire me on the spot.'

'Of course I won't tell.'

Bianca stroked Warren's fur for a minute, and Sage caught a glimpse of how lonely Bianca was. Could it be true that Sage was her only real friend? Then Bianca rolled her eyes and laughed.

'This is all very maudlin!' she said. 'Let's talk about something fun. Like you and Herb.'

Sage made a face. 'I hate all boys.'

Bianca made a sympathetic noise. 'You really liked him, didn't you?'

'It doesn't matter,' muttered Sage. 'He's an idiot. I'm moving on.'

'Did things...go very far? Between you guys?' Bianca put her hands over Warren's ears and whispered. 'Tell me everything.'

Sage felt her insides twist. She didn't really want to talk about it. 'Um,' she said. 'I'm not sure there's much to tell. We kissed—'

Bianca let out a squeak, and Warren looked up sleepily. 'When?'

Sage told her about the kiss in the storeroom, and again on the street the other day.

'But I guess it didn't mean anything after all,' she said glumly. 'It turns out that my Year Eight PE teacher was right: all boys are the same, and they do all just want one thing.'

'Oh, honey.' Bianca reached over and gave her arm a squeeze. 'I'm sorry. I should have warned you about Herb.'

Sage swallowed a mouthful of coffee and suddenly felt sick. 'Has he done this before?'

Bianca looked away. 'He doesn't exactly have the best romantic track record.'

'What do you mean?'

'I don't really think I should say. I—I know that Herb is annoying, but he's my friend too.' Bianca looked uncomfortable. 'I just don't want to cross a line.'

Sage felt a strange, sickly heaviness inside, like her blood had turned to lurching treacle.

'Do you think you'll stay?' asked Bianca.

'Stay where?'

'Here. With us. I mean, I'd hate to lose you. But I'd understand. It must be very hard to be around someone you … have feelings for.'

Sage frowned. She hadn't yet considered leaving. Maybe it would be for the best. But how would she pay for her photography classes?

'I want to stay,' she said slowly. 'I like working here. And … and I don't want to give Herb the satisfaction, you know? If I feel awkward around him, then he's going to feel awkward around me too. He deserves that.'

Bianca stiffened. 'Did you hear that?'

Sage closed her eyes and listened. She *could* hear something. A knocking sound. It sounded like it was coming from beneath them.

'You said there was a basement. Where Renaldo's wife died.'

'There was,' said Bianca. 'But the stairway was blocked up years ago.'

'Maybe it's just an old pipe or something,' said Sage.

'Maybe …' Bianca levelled a meaningful *or a ghost* look at Sage, who shivered.

The knocking noise sounded again. Bianca said something, but Sage couldn't quite get her ears to work. She felt foggy, somehow, as if she was underwater and every movement was an effort. Bianca was looking at her as if she'd just asked a question.

'Hmm?' said Sage. Her head felt fuzzy. She was so *tired* all of a sudden. The coffee hadn't done anything.

'I'm just going to put my head down for a moment,' she said. Or at least she tried to say it. She wasn't sure if it came out right or not. She looked over at Bianca, but she was already asleep, her golden hair spilling out over her pillow.

'So much for the coffee,' Sage murmured, before sinking into sleep.

⋀⋀

Someone was shaking her awake. Sage struggled to open her eyes, the clawing hands of sleep trying to pull her back down. Someone came blearily into focus. Was it Bianca? She looked different. Paler. Her hair was long and dark, instead of its usual blonde. She wore a long, loose white dress, like an old-fashioned nightie. Her lips moved, but Sage couldn't hear anything.

Foggily, she wondered if this was the theatre's ghost. Maybe it had taken on Bianca's appearance so as not to frighten her. She slowly got to her feet. The room spun around a little. Sage's head felt as though it were full of cotton wool, and for a moment she started to sink down again. Maybe she should just go back to sleep.

Images floated around her. She was on the stage at the Lyric Theatre. Then she was among the empty seats in the auditorium. Faint shapes loomed in the corners of her eyes. Dimly, she made out the sharp black-and-white lines of the Zigzag cabinet. Then she felt herself sinking back into darkness.

The ghost grabbed her hand, with icy cold fingers, and pulled her up into a sitting position. Sage looked around as the world undulated gently around her.

She was in a small, cramped room bathed in strange red light. There was another door on the opposite side of the room, and a dirty sink. And sitting in the very centre of the room, there was a desk. Sage struggled to her feet, the floor twisting and buckling underneath her. She took a few tottering steps forward. It looked like Herb's desk. It had Herb's notebook, Herb's plaster Houdini bust, Herb's stack of magic magazines, Herb's chair. The bucket he had used to drop dollar coins sat on the floor. A half-chewed carrot belonging to Warren was on the seat of the swivel chair. It was definitely Herb's desk. Except... there was a typewriter on it that hadn't been there before. Sage leaned forward to read what was typed on the white sheet that fed through the typewriter.

PU UOY EIT OT TNAW I

Sage frowned. It looked like one of the letters from the stalker. She looked at the other sheets of paper on the desk. They were all covered in what looked like gibberish. Sage's tongue felt as if it were made of carpet. She pressed the heels of her hands into her eyes, trying to shake off the fuzziness. She looked at the papers again. It was backwards. All the writing on Herb's desk was backwards. She gazed at the sheet of paper in the typewriter again, squinting.

I WANT TO TIE YOU UP

Sage tasted something metallic. There was a flyer for the magic show to the left of the typewriter. Sage felt her heart start to hammer. Someone had cut out the eyes from The Great Armand's picture. The flyer had been impaled on a mail spike – the sharp silver spike erupted through Armand's forehead.

13. Misdirection: to lead attention away from a secret move.

Sage looked up to where the ghost was … or had been. She was gone. In her place on the floor was a sprig of green leaves with small white flowers.

Suddenly Sage understood.

She was dreaming.

The secret room, the desk of backwards writing, the typewriter. The ghost.

She was dreaming. Sage felt her knees go weak with relief. All she had to do was wake up. She sank down onto the floor, pressing her cheek against the cold concrete, and closed her eyes. When she woke up, everything would be normal again.

'Sage?' It was Bianca, back to being blonde, wearing her floaty hippy dress. Definitely not a ghost.

Sage sat up, putting a hand to her aching head. Her mouth felt dry and tasted disgusting. She wondered if this was what hangovers felt like, and pre-emptively swore never to find out. She looked around and saw she was in Bianca's dressing-room.

It *had* all been a dream.

'Are you okay?'

'No,' said Sage, her voice croaking. 'I feel awful.'

Bianca put a cool hand on Sage's forehead. 'You're pretty warm,' she said. 'Maybe you're coming down with something. You were out cold all night. You should go home and get some rest. Herb and I can handle the matinee.'

Sage shook her head. 'No, I'm fine, I just have this headache. And ...' She glanced at Bianca. 'I had the weirdest dream.'

'Really?' said Bianca. 'Weird how?'

Sage told her about the Bianca-ghost, and Herb's desk, and the creepy note. Bianca's face grew pale, almost as pale as the ghost's had been.

'It was Renaldo,' she said in a choked whisper.

Sage shook her head. 'It was a woman,' she said. 'She looked like *you*, but with darker hair.'

'Maybe it was a warning,' said Bianca. 'A vision. Maybe they want us to leave the theatre.'

Sage shook her head. 'No, it was definitely just a bad dream. The ghost turned into a sprig of flowers at the end.'

Bianca's head snapped up. 'What kind of flowers?'

'Um,' said Sage, trying to remember. 'White ones.'

Bianca's eyes grew wide. 'Jasmine?'

'Yes.' Sage frowned. 'How did you know that?'

'Remember last Wednesday when we all could smell jasmine?'

Sage nodded. 'Was that what it was? Okay.'

Bianca leaned forward, her expression intense. '*Renaldo's wife was named Jasmine.*'

Sage looked around Bianca's dressing-room. Could she smell the jasmine now, faintly? Or was her mind playing tricks on her?

'Holy crap,' said Bianca. 'It was Jasmine. It was Renaldo's wife. She probably appeared looking like me because she was his assistant, and she knew that you'd link her to me. Maybe she's trying to get revenge for her husband's death! Did she say anything? Mention the curse?'

Sage thought of the mail spike through Armand's head. 'Not exactly,' she said. 'But it was … sinister. And there was a note – like the ones you've been getting. It said *I want to tie you up.*'

Bianca made a face. 'Ugh,' she said. 'That sounds like our guy. Maybe it's the ghost that's been sending those letters all along, though. Maybe it's Jasmine.'

'Why would a dead magician's assistant be sending

creepy notes to another magician's assistant?'

'I don't know. Maybe because she's jealous that I'm still performing.'

Sage opened her mouth to tell Bianca about the time-lapse camera she'd set up, and to suggest that it might reveal some sort of clue. But she suddenly remembered Herb explaining how humans wanted to find meaning in everything. *Pareidolia*, he'd called it. Seeing random things and interpreting them as significant. What if that was what her brain had been doing, in her sleep? What if her unconscious brain had put together all of the random clues and occurrences, and came to a logical conclusion?

And what if that conclusion was correct?

'Bianca, what if it wasn't a ghost or a dream? What if it was my *mind*? What if my unconscious mind has figured out something terrible? Something about…' Sage couldn't say it out loud.

Bianca stared at her. 'About Herb.'

Sage flinched. 'How did you know that's what I was trying to say?'

'It's obvious,' said Bianca. 'You had a portentous vision featuring Herb's desk with all the creepy letters on it.'

'That's crazy, right?' asked Sage, hoping with everything she had that Bianca would agree.

'Is it crazy to suggest that Herb is sending creepy notes

and trying to sabotage his own show? Yes. But…' Bianca hesitated. 'Is it crazy to suggest that your subconscious is feeling wounded by Herb, and wants you to stay away from him? Maybe not.'

'It was stupid,' said Sage quickly. 'I shouldn't have said anything.'

'I think it was definitely the ghost, though,' said Bianca. 'It *has* to be Jasmine. That explains everything – my mirror, you guys getting locked in the storeroom, the fallen light, your dream. It's the only explanation.'

Sage nodded, but she wasn't at all sure. Hopefully her time-lapse photos would hold the answers she was looking for.

She arrived home just after nine to find her mother applying lip gloss in the hallway mirror.

'Oh good, you're home,' said Mum. 'Did you have a fun sleepover?'

Sage thought about the ghost dream, and the mail spike. 'Yeah,' she said. 'It was great.'

'Good. Now, I really need to pop out for a few hours and do some shopping. Roman's got a cold, so can you watch Zacky until I get back? I'll be back by lunchtime, and I can drive you to the theatre for your matinee. Is that okay?'

Sage thought longingly of combing through all the

time-lapse photos on her digital camera, but she nodded, and Mum pecked her on the cheek. 'Oops,' she said and swiped at Sage. 'Lipstick.'

'Thanks, Mum.'

Zacky came tearing down the stairs as Mum rushed out the door. 'Sage!' he bellowed. 'We are going to have the *best* adventure! We're going to discover buried treasure and fight some baddies and make potions!'

'Great!' said Sage, as her whole body suggested vehemently that crawling into bed and sleeping for twelve hours might be a preferable activity. 'But I need to have a shower first.'

Zacky nodded. 'Okay. Can I watch TV while you do that?'

Sage set him up with a *Horrible Histories* DVD in the living room, then went upstairs. She plugged her digital camera into her computer and set it to import all the time-lapse exposures she'd taken. Then she headed to the bathroom and peeled off her clothes, stepping under the hot stream of water with a weary sigh as the ancient pipes groaned and clanked.

She couldn't get the image of Armand's flyer on the mail spike out of her head. Did she even *believe* in ghosts? It had been a *very* weird dream, but people had weird dreams all the time, right? But if it wasn't a ghost... Sage remembered the hot, rushing feeling she got when Herb had kissed her. She *liked* Herb. She didn't want him to be a crazed kidnapping loon.

On the other hand, even if he wasn't responsible for Armand's disappearance, he'd still stood her up and lied to her. Sage felt a lump of misery rise in her throat, and she turned up the hot water defiantly. She wouldn't cry over him. He wasn't worth it. The pipes screeched their protest and the water sputtered, then without warning turned icy cold.

Sage yelped and leapt away. She turned the cold tap off entirely, but it made no difference. The hot water wasn't coming back, and Sage had a head covered in shampoo.

Wrapped in a towel, she headed back to her bedroom, pink and trembling with cold. Cold showers were supposed to be healthy, right? Something about pores or circulation? She certainly hoped they were good for you, because otherwise they had no redeeming features whatsoever.

Pulling on a clean pair of jeans and a black T-shirt, Sage glanced at the images popping up on her computer screen from the camera.

She dropped the ball of socks she was holding, and stared at the screen. Then she hurried over and hit buttons until she was looking at one photo, blown up so it filled her entire monitor.

Every photo from the time-lapse was exactly the same.

The stage, dim and silent. Except for this one photo. In the centre of the stage, there was a glowing figure, crouching low, with two white arms reaching up and outwards, like someone was begging for something. Sage peered at it. The figure was blurred and indistinct, but it was there, pale and ethereal. It looked … like a crouching woman.

She'd taken a photo of the theatre ghost.

〰〰

Zacky was sprawled on the couch, his eyes glued to *Horrible Histories*, but he leapt up when Sage entered the room.

'Adventure time!' he said. 'I want to play in the garden.'

They went outside into the grey, dreary morning. Sage watched Zacky zoom around the tiny patch of mossy brick paving on his broomstick, shouting out spells and waving his wand at invisible monsters. The icy terror she'd felt when she'd seen the photo thawed under the onslaught of Zacky's cheerful enthusiasm, and she started to wonder if maybe she'd been mistaken. It could have been anything, really. A bit of fluff on the lens. Some kind of reflection off dust motes. Or maybe the digital file was somehow corrupted.

They sat on the back step and drank glasses of milk, looking out over the tangled vines and bent shrubs of the backyard.

'How far back does it go?' asked Zacky, squinting.

'Not far,' said Sage. 'It's not a very big block.'

'It looks like the forest that surrounded Sleeping Beauty's castle,' Zacky observed. 'You'd need a brave knight with a sword to hack through it.' His face brightened. 'I could use one of Mum's big kitchen knives.'

'No knives,' said Sage. 'Definitely no knives.'

Zacky scowled. 'Stupid garden.'

Sage stared at the grey and green tangle of ivy. She couldn't believe anything else would ever grow there, because it never seemed to get light. Everything was dark and damp and grey. Their old garden in Queensland had featured a swimming pool and a mango tree, and it had been at least three times bigger than this one. Sage remembered the lush green ferns and tropical flowers, and the warm, honey-soft sunlight. She remembered playing Loch Ness Monster with Zacky in the pool, and building a fairy bower out of bright purple trails of bougainvillaea.

'Do you want to hear a story?' she asked. 'About some little girls in England who found some fairies in their garden?'

She told Zacky about the Cottingley fairies and Arthur Conan Doyle, leaving out the bit where the girls confessed to faking the whole thing.

'D'you think there might be fairies in *this* garden?' breathed Zacky, his eyes wide.

Sage shrugged. 'You never know.' She imagined the kind

of fairies that might want to live in their backyard. They'd be all brown and twisted, like the roots of trees. She wasn't sure if they'd be *nice* fairies. Certainly not the dainty, beautiful creatures that Elsie and Frances had photographed.

'Grab your camera!' shouted Zacky. 'Let's see if we can find one!'

Sage went inside and unplugged her camera from her computer. The ghostly photo was still up on her monitor, and she shuddered at the sight of it, feeling suddenly cold again.

She should tell Bianca.

Except Bianca would instantly believe in it. She needed a more neutral opinion. The opinion of a photography expert, perhaps. Sage hit Print, and slid the resulting page into her photography portfolio.

'I found something!' she heard Zacky shout.

She hurried outside again. Zacky had crawled through the tangled ropes of ivy, and was near the back fence. She followed him, bending low to duck under branches. Ivy trails wrapped themselves around her ankles, and with a shudder Sage remembered that the forest around Sleeping Beauty's castle was filled with the bones of all the knights who didn't make it.

'It's a trapdoor!' said Zacky, pointing at the ground.

Underneath dried old leaves, twisted ivy roots and a good deal of dirt, Sage could make out a few slats of wood.

She crouched down further, and rapped on one. It gave a hollow sound.

'Do you know,' she said to Zacky. 'I think you're right. It's some kind of door.'

She pushed away the leaves and dirt. The trapdoor was about two feet square, and looked very old.

'Do you think it leads to a *secret tunnel*?' Zacky hopped up and down with excitement, causing dry brown leaves to rain around them. 'Or *treasure*?'

'I don't know,' said Sage, tugging at the door. It came free with a shower of dirt and wriggling things. The wood was so old that Sage was afraid it would fall apart in her hands. Zacky's excitement was infectious. What if it *was* a tunnel? Or an old bomb-shelter, or a secret cache full of fascinating historical secrets?

They peered into the hole. It wasn't a tunnel. It was just a small, square space carved into the dense clay earth. It looked as if it had once held a box.

'It's empty,' said Zacky, his voice suddenly small and sad.

He was right. The space was completely empty. Sage snapped a few half-hearted photos, but the light was so grey and dull that she doubted they'd amount to much. Zacky kicked the wooden door resentfully.

'No buried treasure,' he said.

'Maybe there was once,' suggested Sage. 'But they were

251

afraid someone would find it, so they moved it somewhere even more secret.'

Zacky's face cleared. 'D'you think there might be another tunnel somewhere else?' he asked hopefully. 'Or a secret passage? Or a hidden room?'

Without waiting for Sage to reply, he sprinted back into the house. Sage stood up, brushing dirt from her knees, and swung the wooden gate back over the hole. She followed the muddy footprints through the house, and found Zacky in the living room, tapping on the walls with his eyes closed, listening intently.

'Any luck?' asked Sage.

'Not yet,' said Zacky, and got down on his hands and knees, tapping on the musty floorboards. 'D'you think there's a cellar?'

'I don't think this kind of house has a cellar.'

'How about a basement?' asked Zacky. 'Or is that the same thing?'

Sage frowned, remembering something Bianca had said last night. She'd been talking about Jasmine, Renaldo's wife.

Most people thought she just moved to another city, away from the public eye. But some people say she came back to this theatre and locked herself in the basement, and killed herself.

Sage thought of those white, ghostly arms, reaching up. Pleading.

'Sage?' Zacky stood up and poked her in the ribs. 'What's the difference between a cellar and a basement?'

'I think a basement is bigger,' said Sage slowly. She looked down at Zacky and smiled brightly. 'And this kind of house definitely doesn't have a basement. Sorry, kiddo.'

Zacky groaned loudly. 'Fine,' he said. 'Can we at least go up the secret stairs to the attic? There might be a treasure map or something up there.'

'Sure,' said Sage. 'It's definitely worth a look.'

Zacky tore up the stairs and Sage followed slowly, turning something over and over in her mind.

Did the theatre really have a basement? And if so, how did you get down there?

~~~

'You're here.' Bianca looked surprised when Sage stuck her head around Bianca's dressing-room door.

'Of course I'm here,' said Sage. 'Why wouldn't I be?'

Bianca shrugged. 'You know,' she said. 'The dream you had. Herb. I thought you might not come back.'

'Don't be silly.' Sage thought about the ghost photo in her folder. Why would she leave now, when things were starting to get interesting? 'I'm hardly going to quit my job just because some stupid guy stood me up for dinner.'

'Good for you.' Bianca flashed Sage a dazzling smile.

Their second show without Armand was much better,

but it still felt a little flat without Bianca's sparkling glamour. Herb was visibly nervous, but he got through each trick with only a few stumbles. Sage felt completely twisted in knots every time she looked at him. She tried to avoid him backstage, and didn't meet his eyes when they took their curtain call together after Assistant's Revenge.

After the matinee, he burst into their office, his eyes shining. 'I think I'm ready!'

'Oh?' said Sage, hoping she'd sink into the ground and disappear.

'My new effect.' He bounced up and down on the balls of his feet, unable to contain his excitement. 'My masterpiece. I'm going to debut it tonight.'

'Great,' said Sage, trying to look busy. She wanted to ask him why he'd stood her up, but didn't want him to know how upset it had made her. Plus there was her dream. The spike through Armand's head. What if there was more to Herb than met the eye?

'I've made some changes since our ... er, rehearsal in the storeroom. I think it's perfect. I can't wait for you to see it.'

Sage nodded and smiled what she hoped was a distantly polite smile. Herb's own enthusiastic grin faltered.

'Are you okay?' he asked.

'Sure,' said Sage. 'I'm fine. Just a bit of a headache.'

'Well, then,' he said. 'Let's drop Assistant's Revenge.

I'll do my masterpiece as a finale. I'm calling it Houdini's Return. It's mostly a solo thing, but there're a couple of lighting cues I'd like to go over with you, if you feel up to it.'

'Sure.' Sage remembered with a wave of misery what had happened the last time they went over lighting cues. 'Just let me grab my notebook.'

〰〰

The Saturday-night show was a triumph. Every little thing that had gone wrong the previous day was now perfect, as if Herb was a well-oiled machine who had been performing the routine for years. Throughout the show Sage could feel his energy, fizzing off him in waves. He was practically *vibrating* with excitement and anticipation, and it was hard not to get caught up in his enthusiasm. Even Warren was infected, waggling his ears comically when Herb produced him from the top hat. Sage found herself grinning at him from the wings when he produced the ace of spades from an audience member's wallet, and for a moment she forgot about everything else. For a moment he was just Herb, doing what he loved.

But then the vision of the spike through Armand's head snapped into Sage's mind, followed by the white blur in the ghost photo, and her world zigzagged back to strange and complicated.

When the finale drew close, Sage helped reset the stage with a velvet curtain (repurposed from Assistant's Revenge) with a comfy, old-fashioned armchair in front of it. Next to the armchair there was a small side table with two brass candlesticks holding long white candles. Sage also rolled a heavy wooden wine barrel onto the stage, and set it up on the other side of the chair, in front of the curtain, with a third candlestick on top.

Then she returned to her position in the wings, and dimmed the lights.

Herb walked onto the stage, holding an empty wine glass. Removing the candlestick, he lifted the lid from the barrel and dipped the glass into it, filling it halfway with red wine.

'For the past hundred years,' he said, 'a battle has been fought. A battle between the magicians and the spiritualists.'

He leaned over and set the wine glass on the side table, then produced a hammer and nails and proceeded to hammer the lid of the wine barrel back into place. Then he lit the candle by waving a hand over it, and placed it back on top of the barrel.

'Two of its greatest warriors are names I'm sure you'll all know: Harry Houdini, the world's greatest escapologist, and Arthur Conan Doyle, creator of Sherlock Holmes, the world's most logical literary detective. Houdini was a renowned sceptic, and devoted much of his life to debunking spiritualists at seances. Conan Doyle literally believed there were fairies at the bottom of the garden.'

Herb lit the two candles on the side table, and Sage faded out the stage lights completely.

'At first, Conan Doyle and Houdini were firm friends. But Houdini was scathing of seances and mediums, and did everything he could to expose spiritualism as fraudulent. Conan Doyle, on the other hand, was convinced that Houdini himself was psychic, but just didn't know it. Houdini laughed this off. *Applesauce*, he said. *Hogwash.*'

Herb sat down in the armchair, took a sip of his wine, and nodded to Sage, who hurried out from the wings carrying several links of padlocked chains.

'Houdini was best known for his escapology routines,' Herb went on, as Sage looped the chains around his arms, legs and waist, fastening padlock after padlock. 'He escaped from water-filled milk cans and beer-filled barrels. He was buried alive and submerged in a lead coffin at the bottom of a swimming pool. He was suspended from a crane in a straitjacket, and could escape in two minutes and thirty-seven seconds. Once he even escaped from the belly of a beached whale. But could he escape death? Could anyone?'

Sage snapped the last padlock into place and returned to her position in the wings, leaving Herb chained tight to the chair. He leaned over with difficulty, and blew out the candles.

The stage was plunged into darkness. Herb's voice floated out, quiet and calm.

'Houdini proposed an experiment with his wife, Bess. He told her a secret keyword – *Rosabelle believe* – and told her that if it were possible for a spirit to return to the world of the living once dead, he would return and deliver that keyword. It was to be his ultimate proof against the claims of the spiritualist. After Houdini's death, Bess lit a candle next to a photo of him.'

One of the candles on the side table sputtered into life. Sage could see members of the audience leaning forward, peering at the armchair and murmuring.

'She kept that candle burning for ten years, and every year on the anniversary of his death, she held a seance. Houdini never made an appearance. After the tenth seance, Bess blew the candle out. *Ten years is enough to wait for any man*, she said. So it appears that Houdini was very good at getting *out* of things – barrels, coffins, safes – life itself. But he wasn't so good at *getting back in*. And I've been thinking – what if you wanted to get back in? What if there was someone else in that locked cabinet or whale belly? Someone you wouldn't mind being trapped with?'

Sage's cheeks grow hot. She felt wretched.

'When Houdini escaped from underwater,' Herb's voice continued, 'he invited his audience members to hold their breath along with him, and see how long they could last.'

Sage couldn't help herself. She held her breath as she counted to twenty, as Herb had asked her to do. Then she slid a fader up, bringing a soft glow of light to the stage.

Herb was gone. The chains were still wrapped around the armchair, their padlocks unopened. There was another long pause. Sage's ears started to pound, and she saw spots in front of her eyes. She let our her breath with a *whoosh*, and gulped in air. She glanced at Bianca, who was standing on the other side of the stage, concealed from the audience by the wings. Bianca twitched her head from side to side. *Wait*, her expression said.

Sage felt fear rise up in her throat. Where was Herb? Why hadn't he appeared yet? Why hadn't she asked him more about the trick, so she'd know whether this was part of it?

The audience started to murmur. Had something gone wrong?

The wine barrel rocked very slightly, and Sage bit back a yelp. Herb was in the barrel.

14. Ditch: to secretly dispose of an unneeded item.

Sage signalled to Bianca again. A frown had creased Bianca's brow. She shrugged slightly at Sage. What to do? Did Herb have a contingency plan?

Seconds passed. The barrel rocked again.

Sage felt like her heart was in her throat. She felt dizzy and sick as adrenaline coursed through her. This was wrong. Something had gone wrong.

The barrel didn't move again.

Bianca stumbled onto the stage, pushing the barrel over, and knocking the lid free. Herb spilled out with a rush of water, coughing and gasping for air.

Sage ran out to him, crouching down. 'Are you okay?' she asked. 'Herb?'

His face was pale, his eyes wide, heaving great breaths. Sage grabbed him under the arms and hauled him upright, digging her shoulder under his arm so she could support his weight.

'Thank you for coming, ladies and gentlemen,' announced Bianca with a beaming smile as Sage half-led, half-dragged Herb backstage.

Bianca closed the curtain and flicked on the houselights, to confused murmurings from the audience. There was no applause.

'Who did this?' hissed Herb, his face purple with humiliation, matching the mohair blanket that Bianca had thrown around his shoulders. 'Someone must have swapped the barrels. Did you check them?'

They were in Bianca's dressing-room. Sage had made sure the audience had all left, and dealt with the five or six patrons who were demanding refunds.

Bianca took a deep breath. 'Of course I checked them,' she said, her voice patient. 'Twice. Just like we practised.'

'You mustn't have,' said Herb, kicking at the wastepaper basket. 'Someone is *sabotaging* my work!'

'Maybe,' said Bianca, keeping her voice low. 'Maybe Renaldo the Remarkable didn't appreciate your mockery.'

'Don't you *dare*,' Herb spat. 'Don't you *dare* spin your mumbo-jumbo bullshit with me. Not now. Not tonight.' He stormed out of the room, slamming the door behind him.

'Way to thank me for saving your life,' said Bianca to the door. 'You're welcome.'

'What happened?' asked Sage. 'What went wrong?'

Bianca shook her head. 'I don't know,' she said. 'He's been so cagey about his great masterpiece, he hasn't really told me anything about how it works. My guess is there was a second barrel behind the curtain, and Herb got confused when he was moving them around in the dark.'

'Poor Herb.' Sage stood up. 'I'll go and see if he's okay.'

Bianca bit her lip. 'Good idea. But … be careful. He can be kind of vicious when he's angry.'

Sage stopped halfway to the door. 'Vicious?'

'I really shouldn't say anything,' said Bianca. 'It was over a year ago. I'm sure he's grown up a lot since then.'

Sage sat back down. 'Tell me what happened.'

Bianca sighed. 'He's too ambitious by far, is the problem. He's wanted to take over from Armand since he started working here.'

Ambitious enough to dispose of Armand completely? Sage swallowed. 'Go on.'

'Did he ever tell you we used to use three white mice in the act?'

Sage nodded. 'He said they went missing.'

'Is that what he told you?' Bianca nodded slowly. 'That makes sense. We used them in the cups-and-balls routine.

It was a cute finale – Armand lifted up the cups to reveal three white mice, who would run around on the table for a moment until Armand scooped them off into his hat and vanished them. But one day Armand and Herb had a fight. Herb wanted his own spot on the programme, and Armand refused. Herb was only seventeen at the time. He'd never performed to an audience before, except at little kids' birthday parties and a couple of corporate gigs. Herb was furious. When Armand lifted the cups for the last time that night, the three mice underneath were dead.'

Sage felt a chill run through her. 'Herb killed the mice?'

Bianca shrugged. 'I don't know,' she said. 'But I just can't believe it was a coincidence.'

'What did Armand do?'

'Nothing. He just scooped the mice into his hat as usual. He didn't say anything to Herb afterwards. But you could tell he was angry.' Bianca took a deep breath. 'But that's not everything.'

'There's more?'

Tears started to roll down Bianca's cheeks. 'It was my fault,' she whispered. 'You can't blame Herb. He was angry and hurt. And it was all my fault.'

'Why?'

Bianca swallowed and closed her eyes for a moment before continuing. 'W-when Herb asked Armand if he could have the spot, Armand said he'd think about it. Then, after the show, Armand asked me what I thought. I told him that Herb was too green, that he wasn't ready.' She looked over at Sage, her eyes full of sadness. 'I told him not to let Herb have the spot. I crushed Herb's dream.'

Sage went over and put her arms around Bianca. 'Don't be ridiculous,' she said. 'You just gave your honest opinion. That in no way justifies what Herb did to those mice.'

And to Armand, she thought.

'Am I interrupting something?' It was Jason Jones, standing just outside the dressing-room. He carried another gold-wrapped package, but this one was small and thin. *Jewellery*, thought Sage, as Bianca pulled out of her hug. *He's trying too hard.*

'Um,' said Bianca, looking uncomfortable. 'Jason, you remember Sage.'

'Of course.' Jason turned his smile onto Sage, but the magic had totally gone. He just looked like a smarmy con-artist.

'I just have to make a quick phone call,' said Bianca. 'I'll be back in a minute.'

'I hear tonight's show was a bit dramatic,' Jason said mildly to Sage. 'I hope everyone's okay.'

Sage gave him what she hoped was a polite smile. 'I know that for some reason Bianca likes you,' she said, feeling bold.

'I can't imagine why, because you seem completely odious to me. But I just thought I'd let you know that if you hurt her, I'll kill you.'

Jason blinked in surprise, and then smiled a lazy smile. He reminded Sage of a crocodile basking in the sun. She started to head towards the office, but Jason spoke.

'I remember my first solo show,' he said. 'It was a total disaster.'

Sage remembered the newspaper clipping they'd found in Armand's dressing-room. 'Was it?' she said, turning around to face Jason. 'Why?'

Jason shrugged and smiled a self-deprecating smile that Sage almost believed. 'You know,' he said. 'It's hard starting out, when you're so inexperienced.'

'But you had a good teacher, didn't you?' She didn't fall for any of Jason's bullshit. There was something creepy about him, and she was going to get to the bottom of it.

Jason looked genuinely surprised. 'Armand?' he said. 'I thought everyone had forgotten that we used to work together.'

'You mean that you used to be his assistant.'

'I like to think it was an equal partnership.'

Sage snorted. 'Yeah, I bet every assistant would like to think that. Doesn't look that way from where I stand, though.'

Jason's eyes narrowed slightly. 'I'm sure I don't know

what you're referring to,' he said. 'I assure you that any claims Armand has made against me are entirely false.'

Claims? This was interesting. Had Jason stolen from Armand? What if that had a connection to the missing money, and Armand's disappearance?

'Okay, I'm ready.' Bianca was back, rugged up in her red duffel coat and her bag slung over her shoulder.

'Lovely to catch up, Sage,' said Jason. 'Could you do me a favour?' He pulled a white envelope from his bag. 'Could you give this to Herb, next time you see him?'

Sage felt a sudden chill, but the envelope didn't look anything like the creepy notes Bianca had been receiving. 'What is it?'

Jason smiled blandly. 'Just some fan mail,' he said. 'Come along, Bianca. I've made dinner reservations.'

◆◆◆

Sage found Herb sitting at his desk, staring at his notebook and shaking his head.

'This is for you,' she said, and dropped the white envelope on his desk. Herb ignored it.

'I just don't know where it went wrong.' His hair had started to dry, and it stuck out in all directions, making him look young and rather lost.

'I think you should go home,' said Sage. 'Get some sleep. You'll get it right tomorrow.'

Herb shook his head. 'I can't do the show tomorrow,' he said. 'We'll have to cancel again.'

'Okay,' Sage said, trying to sound soothing. 'That's fine. But you should still go home. I'll call the people who have booked.'

'I don't want to go home,' said Herb. 'I want stay here and invent a time machine so I can go back and erase the last few hours from history.' He looked up at her, his eyes plaintive. 'Console me over dinner?'

Sage felt her heart break. 'I–I can't.'

'Come on,' said Herb, leaning in towards her. 'Throw a drowning man a life raft.'

The cinnamon and theatre smell of him almost made her dizzy. She closed her eyes and saw three dead mice, and a spike through Armand's head. 'I'm sorry,' she said, pulling away.

Sage opened the bookings folder and picked up the phone to call the first name on the list. Herb stood there for a moment, watching her, his face a picture of misery. Sage took a deep breath and dialled, keeping her gaze firmly on the folder in front of her. After a moment, Herb sighed and walked away.

Sage spent most of Sunday in her bedroom, looking over the photos she'd taken of Armand. They were beautiful, the balance of light and shadow perfectly capturing the severe drama and mystery of Armand's features.

She was almost certain that Armand hadn't really been called away on an urgent personal matter. His disappearance had to be linked to the other strange things going on at the theatre. Could Herb have done away with him in order to further his own career? And what about Jason Jones?

And where was Armand? Had he been kidnapped?

Could he be ... dead?

Sage shivered, and pulled the ghost photo from her folder. Was there a connection between Armand's disappearance and the ghost? If it really was the ghost of Jasmine, then maybe she wanted a magician to replace her dead husband. That was the kind of thing that ghosts did, wasn't it? Maybe Armand was just one in a series of magicians that Jasmine had lured away to the underworld.

'What's that?' It was Dad, hovering outside her bedroom door.

Sage looked up, startled. 'A photo I took at the theatre.'

'Can I see?'

Dad came into Sage's room and perched on the end of her bed. Sage handed him the ghost photo. Dad peered at it, frowning.

'Is this some kind of arty something-or-other that I'm not supposed to understand?' he said.

Sage shook her head. 'I'm not sure what it is,' she said. 'I think it might be...'

'What?'

'A ghost.' It sounded stupid to say it out loud.

Dad looked at the photo again. 'I suppose it *does* look a bit like a person crouching down,' he said. 'Did you see anything when you took the photo?'

Sage explained about the time-lapse. 'It seems too *solid* to be a trick of the light,' she said. 'It's not light reflecting off a dust particle, or any of the other things that sceptics point to in ghost photos.'

'Spooky,' said Dad. 'Have there been any other ghostly sightings in the theatre?'

'Sort of,' said Sage. She told him about Renaldo the Remarkable and the theatre curse, but didn't mention Armand's disappearance or her strange dream. She didn't want Dad to get too freaked out.

'Maybe a little research is in order,' said Dad. 'See what you can find out about this Renaldo. If he died onstage, then there was bound to be something in the paper about it. Maybe you'll find a clue.'

'That's a good idea,' said Sage, wondering why she hadn't thought of it herself.

Dad hesitated, still looking at the ghost photo. 'Is everything else okay?' he said at last. 'You've seemed pretty happy since you started at the theatre, but today … not so much.'

'I'm fine,' said Sage. 'Just tired, I guess.'

Dad glanced at the calendar on Sage's wall, and the red circle around July 16. 'Nervous about starting school?'

Sage blinked. She'd totally forgotten about the dreaded red circle. After all the drama of the ghost, Herb's betrayal and Armand's disappearance, starting at a new school didn't seem very scary anymore. 'No,' she said slowly. 'I'm not nervous. It'll be good. I'm looking forward to meeting some new people.'

People who didn't work in the magic industry.

Dad smiled and ducked his head in an apologetic nod. 'Moving here has been hard on the whole family, but I think it's been hardest for you,' he said. 'Thanks for being such a good sport about it. You're a pretty awesome kid.'

'Thanks, Dad.'

Dad handed the photo back to Sage. 'Good luck hunting your ghost,' he said, and headed for the door.

'A ghost!' Zacky's head whipped around the doorframe and he bounded into Sage's suddenly crowded bedroom. 'Like Nearly Headless Nick?'

'Sort of,' said Dad, ruffling Zacky's hair.

Zacky peered over Sage's shoulder at the photo and looked disappointed. 'That's not a ghost,' he said firmly. 'It's just a fuzzy blob. You can't see a face, and it isn't see-through or floaty the way ghosts are supposed to be.'

Dad looked at Sage with a twinkle in his eye. 'You're probably right, mate,' he said. 'Come on, I said I'd take you and Roman to the park today.'

Zacky whooped and raced out of the room, waving his arms above his head and making *wooo-oooo* ghost noises.

Sage didn't sleep well that night. She couldn't stop thinking of Herb, damp and humiliated, and how she'd rejected him. Had she done the right thing? Herb had lied to her, and if Bianca was right, he could easily let his temper get away from him.

Sage's bedside clock blinked 3:00 AM at her, and she sighed and rolled over so she couldn't see it.

When she finally fell asleep, she dreamt she was on a fairground-style House of Horrors ride. The car she was strapped into was careening down a hill in a zigzag. Every time it zigged or zagged it jolted sharply sideways, and a shape loomed out at Sage. Armand. Jason Jones. Bianca. Herb. Renaldo. Jasmine.

Even in the dream, Sage's head pounded and her stomach churned from being wrenched from side to side. She hoped the ride would end soon, but it seemed to go for hours and hours.

'Sage.' It was Mum, shaking her awake.

Sage glanced blearily at the clock on her bedside table. It was seven thirty-five on Monday morning. Mum was all dressed up for work, her handbag slung over her shoulder.

'Mngg?' said Sage. The daylight stabbed into her eyes and made her head throb even more.

'I was just heading out the door,' said Mum. 'There's someone here to see you.'

'Whzz?' Sage managed.

Mum raised her eyebrows. 'A young man who claims to work with you,' she said. 'He seems rather anxious.'

Sage tried to clear the fog from her head and wake up properly. 'Whehzacky?'

'I just dropped him next door. I'm running late, so shall I just tell your gentleman caller to wait in the living room?'

'Hnng.'

Mum took this as a yes, and dropped a kiss on Sage's forehead before hurrying out of the room. Sage rubbed her face, trying to keep her eyes open. She'd never been much of a morning person, and the chilly Melbourne mornings made it all the harder to wake up. She could hear muffled voices downstairs, then the sound of high heels on floorboards. Then the front door closed.

Sage sat bolt upright.

Herb. Herb was in her house.

She leapt out of bed and grabbed her dressing-gown, wrapping it tightly over her pyjamas and thick bed socks.

Herb was sitting on the couch, looking painfully uncomfortable. He had his hands folded in his lap, and he was silently mouthing words to himself as if he were practising a speech.

'What are you doing here?' said Sage, pausing on the third step from the bottom.

Herb looked up and jumped to his feet. 'I need to talk to you.' His voice was low and urgent. 'I have no idea what's going on with you, or with us, and right now I don't really care. I just really, really need to talk to you.'

I don't really care. It was like a knife in Sage's heart. But she supposed it would be easier this way.

'How did you know where I live?' asked Sage.

He shot her a puzzled frown. 'We work together,' he said. 'I helped you fill out your employment card. Your address is on file.'

Sage slowly made her way down the last two steps to the floor, but didn't move any closer. If Herb really was behind the terrible things happening at the theatre, was she in danger too? She was completely alone with him. No Bianca. No Mum. No one at all to hear her scream.

'W-what do you want?' she asked, trying to keep her voice steady.

'I was wrong,' said Herb. 'When I said that the bad things happening in the theatre were all coincidences. And you were right about Armand's disappearance being suspicious.'

Sage's blood turned to ice. Was this it? Was Herb really going to confess to her? What then?

'It's Jason Jones,' said Herb. 'I think he's trying to frame me.'

'Oh!' said Sage with a start of relief. 'Really?'

Herb slumped back on the couch, pulling a crumpled envelope from his jacket pocket and tossing it onto the coffee table. It was the same one that Jason Jones had given her to pass on to him. Sage looked at it. Was Herb trying to lure her closer? She tried to remember the moves from the self-defence course she'd taken in Year Eight. Herb was looking at her expectantly. Sage took a deep breath and crossed the room to pick up the envelope. She sat down in an armchair, keeping the coffee table between them, opened the envelope and read the enclosed letter. It was a cease-and-desist from a law firm called Watkins & Tucker, on behalf of Jason Jones.

'I don't understand,' she said, frowning at the legalese.

'He's claiming I stole his effect,' said Herb. 'Houdini's Return. He filed a patent for the mechanism a week ago.'

'But – but this is your trick,' said Sage. 'You've been working on it for ages.'

Herb nodded miserably. 'I don't know how he did it.

I only performed it the day before yesterday!' he said. 'But the paperwork seems to be valid.' He kicked out at the coffee table in anger. 'I've been working on that effect for *years*!'

Sage folded up the letter and put it back in the envelope. 'What went wrong?' she asked. 'On Saturday?'

'I still don't know,' Herb said, rubbing his hand over his head. 'I can't stop thinking about it. I haven't slept.'

'What was supposed to happen at the end?'

'I'm supposed to emerge from the barrel that is now miraculously water and not wine, holding a lit candle.'

Sage knew better than to ask how the effect was achieved. 'It sounds impressive.'

'It is,' he said. 'When it works.' He looked up at her. 'I bet it was him. I bet Jason Jones sabotaged the whole thing, to make sure I couldn't perform it before he stole it from me.'

It was certainly possible. Sage had wondered whether Jason had stolen money from Armand, when he was Armand's assistant. But what if he'd stolen something much more valuable? What if he'd stolen Armand's magic secrets?

Sage swallowed. If Jason Jones was responsible for Armand's disappearance, and was trying to steal Houdini's Return from Herb ... what did that mean for Bianca? Did she know what Jason was up to? Could she possibly be involved?

No, thought Sage. *Bianca is sad and lonely and strange, but she'd never betray us like that. Would she?*

She chewed her bottom lip, frowning. 'So what happens now?'

'I don't do Houdini's Return anymore. I can't.'

Sage desperately wanted to believe him. She wanted to get up and throw her arms around him and kiss the smile back onto his face. But she wasn't sure. What about her dream?

'There's more,' said Herb. 'I got an email this morning from the Magician's League. Jason Jones has reported me. They could take away my membership.'

'You need a membership to be a magician?'

Herb sighed. 'Not exactly,' he said. 'But I couldn't compete in any tournaments. I couldn't register any effects under my name. It's like... being excommunicated. Or kicked out of your own family. Nobody in the magic community will speak to me. There's nobody worse than a magician who steals from another magician. That's why I need your help.'

'My help?' said Sage, feeling even more uncomfortable. 'Why me?'

Herb spread his hands. 'You're all I've got,' he said. 'Bianca hates me, plus she's too busy making up stories about curses. Armand is off dealing with his family crisis

– or maybe that's all fake too. Maybe Jason Jones has done away with him. Who else is going to help me?'

Sage swallowed. 'What kind of help do you need?'

'Come with me. Help me figure out what Jason's up to. We'll follow him. It'll be fun – like we're in a detective show or something.'

Sage thought about long afternoons sitting in cafés, waiting for Jason Jones to appear. She imagined Herb leaning in and kissing her, to hide their faces from view. She imagined them ducking around corners and laughing breathlessly.

Then she remembered seeing Herb's desk in her dream. She remembered the mail spike through the image of Armand's head. She remembered Bianca's look of horror when she mentioned the three dead mice.

'I–I can't,' said Sage. 'Sorry.'

He stared at her for a moment. 'You know,' he said. 'I thought you were different. I thought we had … something. But I guess I was wrong.'

He stood up and left the room. Sage heard the front door close, and burst into tears.

〰〰〰

She decided to head to the photography studio to develop her photos. She needed to be doing *something*, to take her mind off the awfulness of her encounter with Herb.

Learning how to use the developing equipment seemed like a good distraction.

As soon as she entered the studio, Sage felt calmer. The moody red lighting and the wet tang of developing chemicals felt familiar, even though she only had a few hours of previous darkroom experience. There was nobody else in the darkroom. Sage was glad – it meant nobody could judge her inexperience. After thoroughly examining the printout that Yoshi Lear had provided the class, she switched off the lights and hummed along to an old Beatles song on the radio as she wound the film onto a spool. Sage had never been afraid of the dark – it was welcoming, like being wrapped in a blanket. Her fingers seemed to know exactly how to wind the film. She felt as though she'd finally found a home here in the cold, unfamiliar city.

The way she saw it, there were three possibilities. The first was that Herb had somehow done away with Armand. He was definitely ambitious, and if the story about the mice was anything to go by, he could get pretty crazy when he was angry. Maybe Herb had kidnapped Armand (or worse!) and all the rest of it – the creepy letters, the mysterious noises and falling light – was just misdirection, to throw Sage and Bianca off the scent. Bianca was so caught up in her superstitions that she refused to even accept the possibility that Herb might be behind it all.

She clicked the spool into its special tank and screwed on the top before switching on the lights. She poured in developing fluid and set an egg timer for four minutes, lightly tapping the tank on the bench to dislodge any air bubbles.

But that didn't explain her dream. If Sage's dream had been her subconscious mind telling her that Herb was the culprit, why had there been a sprig of jasmine at the end? She hadn't known that Renaldo the Remarkable's wife and assistant was called Jasmine. There had been the incident with the *scent* of jasmine a few days earlier, but she hadn't recognised it, so why would her subconscious include that in her dream?

And why would Herb sabotage his own trick? She remembered how outraged he'd been at Jason Jones's show, when Jason had used an audience member as an instant stooge. Herb's self-righteous indignation couldn't have been faked, could it? He wasn't a cheater. She felt sure of it.

The egg timer ticked away. Sage turned the tank upside down four times at the beginning of every minute. The timer finally chirped, and Sage poured out the developer and replaced it with the stop chemical, slowly turning the tank over and over for thirty seconds before pouring the stop bath back into its container.

So the second possibility had to be that Bianca was right.

The theatre really was haunted by the angry ghost of a dead magician's wife. Sage shivered and thought of the photo sitting in her folder. The dream had felt so *real*, despite the fuzzy edges. And although lots of Bianca's superstitions seemed over the top, sometimes she made a lot of sense. But then, what did the ghost want? Was it angry because they had broken a wand on the stage? Or was it something else? Something else that they'd done? Something that *Armand* had done?

Sage added fixer to the tank and set the timer for three minutes.

Then there was the third possibility. Jason Jones. What if he had stolen Herb's trick? What if he had kidnapped Armand and made it *look* like it was Herb, so he could sneak in and steal all of Herb's tricks while Herb was busy defending his innocence? He'd practically confessed that he'd stolen Armand's ideas all those years ago. Jason was definitely a creep, and seemed to be trying to steal Herb's ideas. But Sage didn't want to believe that he was behind everything. Because if he was, then she had to face the very real possibility that Bianca was in on it too.

It was difficult to think about. Bianca was the only friend that Sage had in Melbourne, except for Herb, and things with Herb were…complicated. She could have forgiven him for standing her up, but after hearing the story of the dead mice, she was pretty sure Herb was not the kind of guy she wanted to get involved with.

More involved with.

But Bianca couldn't possibly know what Jason was up to. She'd been so upset when she'd confessed that she'd ruined Herb's chances at a solo spot before, Sage couldn't believe that she'd do it again. And anyway, Bianca knew that Herb and Sage were close. She'd never risk exposing herself to Sage if she had more to hide.

Pouring out the fixer, Sage turned the tap on to rinse the film. Unscrewing the lid of the tank, she pulled out the spool and held the film up to the light, a tingle of excitement in her stomach. It was something she'd never felt with digital photography. Sage could immediately see how her photos had turned out with her digital camera, which was very useful. But it didn't have the mystery of real film – that moment of excitement when hidden images were finally revealed.

Sage smiled for what felt like the first time in days. There were some good shots. Maybe even some *great* shots. She hoped Yoshi would like them.

She gently blowdried the film, and cut it into strips of six frames. Then she selected six negatives, and loaded the first into the enlarger and focused it using a sheet of scrap paper. Then she turned out the light, placed a sheet of photographic

281

paper under the enlarger and exposed it for twenty seconds before placing it in the chemical bath.

As the image started to take form on the photo paper, Sage felt a kind of aching in her heart. It was Herb, looking directly down the barrel of the camera. It was as if he were there, with her in the darkroom, looking right at her. His goofy smile spread wide across his face, and his eyes were soft and warm. It was the look he got just before he kissed her. It was a look that said *You. I choose you.*

Take a photo that tells a lie.

Sage felt something bitter twist in her stomach. The photo was fully developed now. She resisted the urge to reach out and touch Herb's face. She bit her lip instead, leaving the photo in the chemical bath as the image grew darker and darker. Even if he was telling the truth about Jason Jones stealing his idea, it didn't change the rest of it. He'd still stood her up. He'd still killed those mice.

The photo finally turned black, erasing all traces of Herb's face. Sage lifted it out of the bath and threw it in the bin.

A few hours later, Sage had a stack of about fifteen finished, printed photos that she was happy with. Better than happy. They were brilliant, really. Moody, with dark shadows and feathery outlines. Discarded sequins glittered on Bianca's dressing table. Little pots and bottles of makeup and perfume reflecting themselves in the mirror. A lipstick print around the rim of a water glass. One of Warren loping down the corridor, dragging a silk scarf. One of the storeroom, the light from the grate coming down in dusty shafts.

Sage shivered as she suddenly remembered the feeling of Herb next to her, his hands in her hair, his mouth on hers. She smelled his scent and tasted his skin. She closed her eyes, remembering everything.

'Very nice.'

Sage jumped and spun around to see the black-rimmed glasses of Yoshi Lear. 'Oh!' she said, shaken. 'Um. Thank you.'

'Are these for your assignment?' he asked, picking up a photo of Armand and examining it carefully.

'They were supposed to be,' said Sage. 'But none of them fit the brief. I thought a magic show would be the perfect place to take a photo that was a lie, but it's harder than I imagined.'

'How so?'

Sage chewed her bottom lip, trying to figure out how to explain it. 'A magic trick has two stages,' she said at last. 'The top hat is empty, and now it contains a rabbit. A lady climbs inside a box, now she's gone. If you just took a photo of the rabbit, or the empty box, it doesn't mean anything. It doesn't become magic until you've seen the before *and* the after.'

Yoshi smiled, but said nothing.

'I suppose I could take a double exposure – oh!' Sage clapped a hand to her mouth. 'The fairy photo you showed us – the last one. It was a double exposure, wasn't it? That was why Elsie and Frances both claimed to have taken the photo. Frances took a photo of the flowery grass, and Elsie took another fairy photo using the same glass negative. That's why it looks all misty and translucent.'

Yoshi's smile widened.

'They set out to fool everyone,' said Sage thoughtfully. 'But they ended up fooling themselves.'

'Photography can be tricky like that,' said Yoshi. 'Just because you took the photo doesn't mean that you know its secrets.'

Sage thought about the ghost photo in her folder and wondered if she should show it to Yoshi.

'Do you know if anyone's ever taken a photo of a ghost?' she asked.

Yoshi Lear raised an eyebrow. 'Lots of people have taken photos of what they *claim* are ghosts,' he said. 'Our old friend Arthur Conan Doyle was a big believer in spirit photography.'

'But are any of them genuine?'

Yoshi reached into the satchel slung over his shoulder and pulled out an iPad. He brought up a series of photos and showed them to Sage. One was of a transparent woman on a staircase. Another showed a ghostly figure at a railway crossing. The next photo showed a little girl staring out the window of a burning building.

'Some of these can look convincing,' said Yoshi.

Sage stared at the little girl's face. She was wearing a long white dress, and her expression was solemn. 'What's the explanation?' she asked. 'Is it a double exposure too?'

Yoshi shook his head. 'This one was proven to be a hoax,' he said. 'Someone discovered a postcard with the same photo of the little girl. I suspect the one on the staircase is a double exposure, though. The railway crossing ghost is just a lens flare, or the flash bouncing off dust or moisture in the air.'

Sage remembered Herb saying something similar.

'Look at this one,' said Yoshi, swiping to a new photo.

It was a black-and-white photo of an old building. Steps led up to a series of pillars. Someone had photoshopped a circle next to one of the pillars, showing a shadowy, transparent figure. Sage frowned. The photo was blurry and had obviously been magnified.

'Now unfocus your eyes,' said Yoshi. 'Blur the picture even more.'

Sage did as he instructed, and the blurry figure vanished. She had a sudden flashback to Herb showing her a power plug. 'It's just shadows,' she said. 'Just the way the light happens to fall. We only see a figure there because we're conditioned to make patterns and recognise human shapes. It's called pareidolia.'

Yoshi looked impressed, and Sage felt ridiculously pleased.

'So you don't think anyone has ever taken a real picture of a ghost?'

'No,' said Yoshi. 'Although given I don't believe in ghosts, I may be a little biased.'

Sage raised her eyebrows. 'You don't believe in ghosts, but you still have a whole album of ghost photos on your iPad?'

Yoshi laughed. 'I don't believe in them,' he said. 'But I'm still very *interested*. Especially when it comes to photography.'

Sage hesitated for a moment, then pulled the ghost photo from her folder. 'What do you think of this?'

Yoshi took the photo and examined it carefully. 'Interesting,' he murmured. 'I can see why you think it might be ghostly. Those arms reaching out and up are very emotive. Like a supplicant begging for mercy.'

'Exactly!' said Sage. 'Surely it's too complex a shape to be a lens flare.'

Yoshi nodded. 'It is,' he said. 'And this is clearly a longish exposure, because of the low light. A few seconds?'

'Two,' said Sage.

'So there's something moving in this photo. I can see no evidence of digital manipulation, and I'm pretty good at spotting that kind of thing. I'm confident that you didn't try to fake this image, nor is it some kind of accidental effect caused by the camera's mechanisms.'

Sage swallowed, her heart pounding. 'So you think it's genuine?'

'Oh, it's a genuine photo,' said Yoshi. 'But it's not of a ghost. Look again at those arms. They don't really look like arms at all, do they? They look more like . . .'

The white spectral shape seemed to shift and refocus as Sage looked at it, and her heart sank.

'Ears,' she said. 'They look like ears. It's Warren. He's a rabbit. I can't believe I didn't see it before.'

The image was blurred due to the long exposure, but now that Sage looked at it it was impossible not to see it as Warren, loping across the stage, his ears flopping over his face. Not arms at all. Sage felt like a total idiot.

Yoshi glanced at his watch and put away his iPad. 'I have to go. You're a good photographer,' he said, as he reached for the doorhandle. 'But you need to look harder, with an unbiased eye.'

'I will,' Sage promised.

Yoshi smiled. 'For example, now that you've solved the

mystery of the ghostly rabbit, perhaps turn your attention to the figure standing behind the stage curtain.'

The door banged behind him as Sage looked back at the photo. Yoshi was right. She'd been so busy looking at the Warren-ghost-shape that she'd totally missed it. In the top right-hand corner of the photo, there was a blurred figure. It was difficult to make out, but Sage was almost certain she could see a pale face and long black hair.

It was the ghost from her dream. The ghost of Jasmine, Renaldo's wife.

15. The Sucker Effect:
the spectator is wrongly led to believe they have guessed the secret behind a magic trick.

'Abracadabra!' hollered Zacky, brandishing his wand.

The other patrons on the bus turned and stared. 'How about we play being *quiet* magicians?' Sage suggested.

Zacky gave her a dark look. 'You need to do the pose.'

'What pose?'

'The *assistant* pose. That's what the assistant does. She does the pose after the magician does the trick.' Zacky demonstrated by sticking one hand on his hip, and waving the other in a flamboyant flourish.

Sage frowned. 'She does a lot more than that. Most of the tricks don't work without the assistant.'

Zacky dismissed this comment with a wave of his wand. 'Just do the pose.'

They were nearing their stop. 'How about I be the magician?' suggested Sage. 'And you be the assistant?'

Zacky laughed incredulously. 'Don't be silly,' he said. 'Girls can't be magicians.'

The bus hissed to a stop and Sage bundled Zacky down the steps, apologising to an old lady he accidentally poked with his wand.

'Of course girls can be magicians,' she said once they were on the footpath. 'What about Hermione?'

'Hermione is a *witch*,' said Zacky. 'Girls can be witches. But not wizards or magicians.'

Sage frowned, but decided not to pursue the conversation any further.

The theatre was quiet when they entered – there was no sign of Bianca or Herb. She didn't even know if the show was still on, after the disaster of Houdini's Return. But she hadn't heard otherwise from Bianca or Herb, so she turned up anyway. She looked towards the corner of the stage where the ghost had appeared in her photo, and her skin prickled into goosebumps.

As she led Zacky down the corridor to her office, Bianca emerged from her dressing-room, wearing her sparkly outfit under her cotton robe.

'Hey,' said Sage. 'You're back!'

Bianca grinned, and did a little twirl. 'Yep,' she said.

'Doctor says as long as I'm careful, I should be fine.'

'And those shoes are your definition of careful?'

'Well, it's not like I can wear this outfit with flats,' said Bianca with a shrug. She spotted Zacky and beamed at him. 'This must be Zacky!'

Zacky came over all shy and hid behind Sage, who rolled her eyes at Bianca. 'He's just star-struck,' she said. 'You won't be able to shut him up soon.'

'Really?' Bianca twinkled at Zacky. 'I look forward to that.'

'No Herb?' Sage looked around.

Bianca shook her head. 'He's running late,' she said. 'But I talked to him this morning. We've figured out a new running order. Going for something a little more reserved for the finale. I think he's still really shaken up.'

Sage remembered the stricken expression on Herb's face when he'd turned up at her door that morning. She wondered if he'd told Bianca about Jason Jones.

'W-where is The Great Armand?' asked Zacky, peering out from behind Sage.

Bianca bobbed down so she was at eye-level with Zacky. 'He's on holiday,' she said. 'But Herb is doing an excellent job as the magician.'

She turned her face up to Sage, and they shared a significant look.

Suddenly, one of the elastic straps that held up Bianca's costume snapped with a twang.

'Damn,' said Bianca, grabbing at the strap with one hand and her costume with the other. 'I blame Mr Pham. I've been pigging out all week.'

Zacky's face had gone bright red, and his eyes very round.

'There're some safety pins in my dressing-room,' said Bianca. 'Would you mind...?'

'Of course.' Sage turned to Zacky. 'Don't move,' she said, and hurried off down the corridor.

Sage pulled open a drawer and rifled through the contents. It was mostly junk – little bottles of sparkly nail polish, a sewing kit, an empty bottle of perfume, a pack of tarot cards, an old mobile phone. She found the safety pins in a little plastic case, and slipped them into her pocket. Turning to leave, she noticed a large bunch of red roses on Bianca's dressing table. A white card poked out from the velvety petals. Sage hesitated, then let her curiosity take over, and slipped the card from the flowers.

You are the most beautiful assistant in the world.
Be mine.
JJ

Bianca had said that she'd never work for Jason Jones. But what if she'd changed her mind? Or what if Jason was trying to force her to change her mind? He'd done away with Armand, and now Herb. Could it be possible that he'd faked all of the ghostly coincidences as well? And sent Bianca those creepy letters? All to force her away from the Lyric Theatre and into his arms?

'Sage?' she heard Bianca call. 'Did you find them?'

Sage quickly replaced the white card among the roses. 'Coming,' she said, and hurried back to the stage, where she helped Bianca fix her costume.

'You are, quite simply *the best*, Sage,' said Bianca. 'How did we ever manage without you?'

'How indeed?' said Herb, appearing from the foyer.

Sage swallowed uncomfortably and tried not to meet his gaze. Something felt wrong. There was something she was missing. Was it to do with Jason and the roses?

'Hello,' said Zacky, who had apparently overcome his shyness. He thrust a hand up at Herb. 'I'm Zachary. I'm a magician too.'

'Is that so?' Herb made a visible effort to replace his miserable expression with a smile. 'Can you do any tricks?'

Zacky pulled a coin from his jeans pocket, and clumsily demonstrated the French Drop that Sage had taught him. Herb looked impressed.

'That's pretty good,' he said.

'Now you do one,' Zacky demanded.

Herb pulled an egg from Zacky's ear, then transformed it into a carrot, then into a dollar coin.

'Here,' he said. 'You hang onto that for me.'

Zacky beamed.

Herb glanced over at Sage. 'Can we talk?'

Sage looked at the floor. 'I've got a lot to do,' she mumbled. 'Have to keep an eye on Zacky. Maybe later.'

Bianca looked at Herb, then at Sage, then back at Herb again. 'Hey,' she said in a conspiratorial tone, turning to Zacky. 'Are you staying for the show tonight? We might get you to help out with one of the tricks.'

Sage's uneasy feeling increased. 'Not sure. Maybe I should take you home, Zacky. It's been a long day.'

She could call Mum and tell her that Zacky was sick and she had to come home from work.

Zacky's face crumpled. 'We just got here! And you *promised* I could stay!' His voice rose higher and louder with every word. A fully-fledged tantrum was just moments away.

Sage swallowed. She didn't want Zacky around Herb, not until she knew more about what was going on. Maybe he was right about Jason Jones. Or maybe it was all part of Herb's plan. She didn't know what to think, or who to believe. But what else could she do?

'Okay, okay,' she said. 'Of course you can stay.'

Sage installed Zacky in a front-row seat where she could see him from her position in the wings. He almost burst with pride to be allowed to sit on his own in such a highly coveted position, where he told anyone sitting near him that he knew the magician and that they had exchanged tricks before the show.

She was glad for some time to think, as she went through the progression of lighting cues. There was too much going on in her head – she needed to sort it all out. But before she knew it, she was dimming the lights for the finale. They'd briefly discussed putting Assistant's Revenge back in, now that Bianca's ankle was better, but Herb had wanted to try something different. 'A twist on an old classic,' he'd said.

Herb stood in front of a small table in the centre of the stage. On the table were three metal cups, and one red ball. Bianca stood slightly to his left, smiling gently.

'The cup-and-balls routine,' Herb said to the audience, 'is the oldest piece of magic in the world.' He picked the ball up in his thumb and forefinger and balanced it carefully on top of the middle cup. 'It was performed in Ancient Egypt and Ancient Greece. In Ancient Rome, the effect was known as *acetabula et calculi* – dishes and dice.'

Herb stacked the first and third cup on top of the middle one, then looked at the audience for a moment and grinned. He lifted the stack of cups to reveal the metal ball on the table, as if it had magically passed through the first cup.

'It is the cornerstone of every magician's routine. The great Houdini himself said that no man could call himself a magician until he had mastered the cups-and-balls.'

Herb placed the centre cup over the ball and the other two on either side. He stacked them up and lifted them again, to reveal two balls on the table. Lining the cups up once more, his hands started to move faster and faster in an almost rhythmic dance. The balls appeared and disappeared, truly as if by magic. For a moment, Sage forgot about everything, entranced by the graceful, flowing movements of Herb's hands.

'This routine is also performed by conmen and fraudsters, where it's known as *thimblerig* or the *shell game*. Street hucksters ask passers-by to place bets on where the ball will turn up. If you can turn over the shell or cup that has the ball underneath, you win double your money.' Herb cocked his head to the side and grinned again. 'But you never will.'

He turned all three cups over to reveal that the balls had vanished. He tapped the cups back over and shuffled them around, then lifted the first cup to reveal an orange.

'Orange-ya glad you didn't bet on this one?' he said, and

tapped over the second cup. A lemon rolled out. 'You'd feel like a right lemon.' He lifted the third cup, exposing an egg. 'No matter how much they egg you on, you'll never win.'

The audience started to applaud, but Herb held up a hand.

'Recent versions of this routine have played with the format a little,' he said. 'Some magicians only use one cup. Penn and Teller do a scandalous version using clear plastic cups. But I thought it might be fun to inject a little ... danger into the routine.'

He stacked up the three metal cups and set them aside. One by one, he palmed the metal balls, the lemon, the egg and the orange, making them vanish with casual, almost lazy movements. Then he brought out three white plastic cups – the flimsy kind that the dentist gives you to rinse from. He also produced a metal spike. Sage frowned. It was the mail spike from Herb's desk. The one she had seen penetrating Armand's eye in her dream.

Her blood ran cold. Her eyes sought out Zacky in the dimly lit audience. He looked entranced. Sage's fingernails dug into her palms and her breathing turned shallow.

Jason Jones was sitting directly behind Zacky.

Herb covered the spike with one of the cups, and lined up the other two next to it. He shuffled the cups around. Sage kept her attention on the spike. She knew where it was.

She let her gaze flick over to Bianca, and realised with a start that Bianca was looking right back at her, a broad smile on her face that didn't quite reach her eyes.

'We need a volunteer!' she announced. Herb nodded.

Bianca's smile grew just a little wider. Her eyes were brimming with sadness, and for a moment she looked so beautiful that Sage wanted to cry.

'You, young man!' Bianca said, pointing to the front row of the audience. 'Please join us up here.'

Zacky. He leapt to his feet, and before Sage could process what was happening, he had dashed up the stairs to the stage. She shot a wordless, panicked look at Herb, who gave her a smile that she thought was supposed to comfort her, but only made her feel more anxious. Bianca's arm slipped around Zacky's shoulders, and she winked cheekily at Sage.

Sage glanced back at Jason Jones, whose eyes were locked on Bianca. There was a smug, knowing smirk playing around the corners of his mouth.

Herb was talking, moving the plastic cups around on the table. Sage couldn't hear anything – her ears were full of a fierce buzzing noise. She thought she might faint. Herb took his hands off the cups, and gestured at them. His mouth moved, but all Sage heard was the buzzing.

Zacky didn't look nervous at all. He trusted Herb

completely. He chewed his bottom lip, then pointed at the cup on the right. Herb said something, and Zacky nodded. Herb took Zacky's hand and held it over the cup.

Are you sure? his lips said.

Zacky nodded again. Sage was paralysed.

Herb placed his hand over Zacky's, and pushed sharply downward. The cup crumpled flat. No spike.

Sage thought her heart might leap out of her chest. It was okay, she tried to tell herself. Herb wouldn't hurt Zacky.

Would he?

Zacky's hand was over the cup on the left. Again, Herb put his hand on Zacky's. Sage tried to close her eyes, but found she couldn't. Herb pushed downwards.

No spike.

Herb said something to Zacky, and Zacky lifted up the middle cup, revealing the silver mail spike underneath. Sage's hearing started to return as applause filled the theatre, and she found she could move again.

Bianca ruffled Zacky's hair, and told him to return to his seat. Herb's eyes flicked over to Sage and his eyebrows drew together in a plaintive smile. A smile that said *I'm sorry. Can we start again?*

But she couldn't trust him.

Sage didn't stay to help tidy up after the show. She didn't know what to think, or who to believe. All she

299

knew was that she had to get her little brother away from the theatre before something bad happened. She didn't even bother to say goodbye to Herb and Bianca. She just grabbed Zacky's hand and marched him up the aisle and out through the foyer.

'Sage?' said Zacky. 'Are we going already?'

'Yep,' she told him, squeezing his hand. 'It's time to go home.'

The icy wind cut right through her jacket as she stood on the footpath, taking deep breaths and trying to calm down.

She'd had enough of ghosts and magic. She was done. She would never set foot in the Lyric Theatre again. After all, with Herb kicked out of the Magician's League, and no sign of Armand, Bianca would certainly go and work with Jason Jones. What was the point in staying around to witness the inevitable?

Sage looked at the theatre one last time, tilting her head to take in the whole façade. Above the mostly broken light-bulbs and faded posters, flaking gold paint spelled out the words:

LYRIC CINEMA EST 1936

Sage frowned. She remembered Herb's advice. *To really appreciate anything in this city, you have to look up.*

'Or *down*,' she said to herself.

'What?' said Zacky. 'I'm cold. Can we go now?'

What was it Yoshi Lear had said? *You need to look a bit harder, with an unbiased eye.*

Images zigzagged back and forth through Sage's head. Armand's face when she'd told him about the missing money. The snapped wand. The locked storeroom. Bianca's injury. The creepy letters. Lipstick on Bianca's mirror.

And her dream...the metal spike through Armand's eye. The backwards writing on the typewriter. The ghost, captured blurrily on film.

She thought of the knocking sound she'd been hearing. And the scraping noise that had woken her when she and Herb had been locked in the storeroom. She thought of the sudden strong smell of jasmine. She thought of little pots of makeup and half-used lipsticks. She thought of Zacky, looking for an imaginary basement in their house. She thought of Elsie and Frances, taking dreamy photos of cardboard fairies.

'I have to get into Bianca's dressing-room,' she murmured to herself.

'I thought we were going home,' said Zacky.

Sage tugged him back through the entrance into the foyer. 'Zacky,' she said. 'Can you go backstage and tell Bianca about your Harry Potter trading card collection? Make sure you tell her about every single one. I'll be back in a moment.'

Zacky's eyes brightened, and he trotted through the auditorium to where Bianca was sitting and stretching in the wings of the stage. 'Bianca,' Sage heard him say, 'I have seventy-three Harry Potter cards in a special box.'

Sage slipped down the side aisle and made her way back-stage towards Bianca's dressing-room. As she passed the office, an arm snaked out and grabbed hers. She yelped.

'It's just me,' said Herb. 'Don't freak out.'

Sage tried to conceal the fact that she was, in every conceivable way, totally freaking out.

'We need to talk,' he said.

'I can't,' said Sage. 'Not right now.'

Herb pulled her into the office and shut the door behind her.

'No, it has to be now. What the hell is going on with you? If you don't want to date me, then that's fine. But just *tell* me. There's no need to be such a bitch about it.'

'I'm not being a bitch!' she said, edging towards the door. 'Look, I really have to—'

'What happened?' Herb shook his head, his expression sad and bewildered. 'Everything was great, or at least I thought it was. Then all of a sudden you cancel our date, and you've barely spoken two words to me since. Is it because I asked you to assist me? Is it because I said you looked ridiculous in the red sparkly number? I only meant that you look beautiful just the way you are, you don't need to glitz it up.'

Sage was feeling about a million emotions at once, but didn't have time for any of them. She had to get to Bianca's dressing-room.

'I really can't talk about it now—' she started to say, then stopped. 'Wait. I didn't cancel our date. You stood me up.'

Herb's expression turned indignant. 'I did not! I was just heading out to meet you, but Bianca told me you'd gone home because you were too upset about the letters. You didn't even *tell* me.'

Sage stared at him. 'Did you kill the mice?' she asked, her voice barely more than a whisper.

'What mice?'

'The white mice. Did you kill them?'

Herb looked baffled. 'No. I told you about them. I accidentally left the door to their cage open, and they escaped. They live under the floorboards of the stage. Every now and then you see one sneak out for a bit of popcorn.'

Sage's mind was racing. Herb took a tentative step forwards. 'What's this about?' he asked. 'What's going on?'

'I have to go.' Sage pushed past him, and bolted up the corridor to Bianca's dressing-room.

Nothing had changed. Little jars and pots of makeup still lined the dressing table. A silk scarf was carelessly draped over the chair. The air was thick with the smell of Jason Jones's roses. Sage hurried over and yanked open the drawer.

The old mobile phone.

She picked it up and switched it on, hoping there'd be enough battery. The screen flashed into life, displaying a generic welcome message. Sage willed it to start faster, straining her ears for footsteps in the hall. She should really pocket the phone and go to her own office, but what if Bianca noticed it was missing? This might be her only chance.

With shaking fingers, Sage navigated to the messages screen. The most recent sent message was there, exactly as Sage had dreaded it would be.

NOT COMING IN CANCEL WEEKEND SHOWS.

It was Armand's phone.

Sage reached into the drawer and pulled out the empty bottle of perfume.

'No,' she whispered.

She hurriedly switched off the phone, shoved it back into the drawer and pelted down the corridor to the stage, skidding to a halt just inside the wings.

'And then for Christmas last year I got the Quidditch Cup pack, which had *three* holofoil cards in it.' Zacky was saying.

'Mm-hmm?' Bianca's voice was overly bright, as if she wasn't listening but wanted Zacky to think she was. She glanced up at Sage.

'Are you okay?' she asked. 'You look like you've seen a ghost.'

Sage plastered a smile onto her face. 'I'm fine,' she said. 'Just, you know. Tired.'

Bianca looked at her for a moment, saying nothing. Then she nodded sympathetically. 'It's been an intense few days.'

'Well,' said Sage. 'We'd better go home.' She dragged Zacky to her side. 'You should go too,' she told Bianca, trying to look as friendly as she could. 'I bet you could use a good night's sleep.'

'Great idea,' said Bianca, with a warm smile. 'You read my mind.'

Sage towed Zacky from the theatre out into the cold night air.

'Did you see me during the show?' he said proudly as Sage marched them to the bus stop. 'I helped with the magic trick.'

'I did see!' said Sage brightly. 'I was very proud of you. Were you scared?'

Zacky shook his head. 'Nope,' he said. 'Not a bit. Because I knew it was all pretend anyway, and Herb wouldn't do anything where I might get hurt, would he?'

Sage felt a twist of guilt. 'Of course he wouldn't.'

The bus pulled up with a rumble, the door scraping open. They climbed on board and sat down. Zacky plastered his face against the window, breathing hot fog all over it as he peered out into the night. Sage took a deep breath, and pulled out her phone to text Herb.

You were right. We do need to talk.

16. Escape: the magician or subject is placed in a restraining device, and escapes to safety.

Sage arrived at the theatre on Thursday earlier than usual. The building was deserted and icy cold. She switched on the heating system and set it as high as it would go. She shoved her numb hands into her pockets and tried to convince herself that it was just the cold that was making her teeth chatter.

She stood in the auditorium for a moment and looked at the stage. From here, you didn't notice that the red velvet curtain was faded and worn, or that the scrolled plasterwork around the proscenium was cracked and flaking. It was funny, Sage thought, that people always wanted to sit as close to the stage as possible, when in fact, the further back you were the better it looked.

She took a deep breath and counted to ten, then turned

away from the stage and headed up to the old projection booth where they stored the magic equipment. She'd done some googling the night before, after she and Zacky had arrived home, and learnt that old celluloid film was so flammable it could just burst into flames if it were kept in a warm room. So most old cinemas had built underground cellars to keep the big round canisters of film cool and safe.

Sage squeezed into the booth and examined the floor. There were scrape marks on the wooden boards, leading to the black-and-white lines of the Zigzag cabinet. She took hold of the cabinet and pulled. The cabinet made a squealing noise as she dragged it across the floor. Stepping back, she peered around it.

There was a trapdoor.

Sage felt her heart thump. She remembered it now, from her dream. An unassuming grey square set into the floorboards.

As Sage lifted the trapdoor, she almost expected someone to burst out. The ghost of a dead magician's wife, perhaps. But she knew, deep inside, that there were no ghosts in this theatre.

The dim light from the projection booth showed a narrow, damp set of concrete steps leading down into darkness. A cord hung from one side of the wall. Sage gave it a sharp tug, and fluorescent lights plinked on in the stairwell, one by one. Putting a trembling hand on the steel rail, she made her way down.

The small room at the bottom was exactly as it had been in her dream. An office chair and desk, identical to Herb's, except that instead of the creepy letters and the mail spike, there were four small white envelopes lined up – the kind that magicians used to seal predictions inside.

The fluorescent lights only illuminated the stairs. Down here, a naked bulb swung from a cord, its wattage barely enough to illuminate the room. She looked around. There was another door – a thick steel door with a metal hatch the size of a large film reel.

That's where they used to store the film, thought Sage, and went over.

If Bianca's story had been true, then Jasmine had died on the other side of that door.

But it wasn't true.

Sage's teeth were chattering so loudly that she was afraid her teeth would break. She reached out and put her hand on the doorhandle.

'It's locked,' said a voice behind her, and Sage jumped and spun around.

It was Bianca, holding a plastic bag in one hand, and a takeaway coffee cup in the other. Her handbag was slung over her shoulder.

'I wanted you to leave,' she said, staring past Sage at the locked door. 'I tried to make you leave. I didn't want it to come to this.'

Sage had expected this, but she hadn't realised how gutted she'd feel. She sagged against the steel door, its icy chill seeping through her clothes.

'I've realised why people believe in fairies,' she said, hoping Bianca couldn't hear the tremor in her voice. 'It's because it's easier. Because if two little girls can photograph fairies in the bottom of their garden, then the world is full of beauty and mystery, and people are good. But if those two little girls lied, then the world is tarnished, and people who you thought you trusted turn out to be . . .'

'What?' said Bianca, her voice expressionless. 'Baddies? Villains?'

'Something like that,' said Sage.

Bianca put the plastic bag on the desk, and sat down in the office chair. She picked flakes of varnish off the table. 'Well,' she said. 'You don't always get a choice. Sometimes you're given a role, and you have to play it.'

She indicated to Sage to pull up the plastic chair against the wall. Sage hesitated, then did so, sitting opposite Bianca.

'Have you decided whether or not you're going to keep your promise?' asked Sage.

'Promise?' Bianca still hadn't looked Sage in the eye.

'That you'd never date a magician you worked for.'

'I don't work for Jason,' said Bianca, examining a finger-nail. 'And I never will.'

'I thought,' said Sage slowly, choosing each word care-fully, 'that it might be him. That he was trying to poach you as his assistant, and that's why he got rid of Armand, and tried to get rid of Herb.'

'Oh?' Bianca's expression betrayed nothing.

'But I was wrong.' Sage bit her lip. 'It was you, wasn't it? It was all you.'

Bianca didn't say anything, just looked down at her cof-fee cup.

'Where's Armand?' asked Sage.

'You don't understand,' said Bianca, her voice low. 'I had no choice.'

'You're right, I don't understand,' said Sage. 'I mean, I know your job is kind of demeaning—'

'My job?' Bianca said with a bitter smile. 'My *job*? My job is to wear spangly underwear while men tie me up, handcuff me, blindfold me, gag me, then pretend to throw knives at me, spear me with swords and saw me in half. My job is to be glamorously humiliated, with a smile on my face.'

Sage said nothing, but glanced over to the stairs.

'Let me tell you about my *job*,' said Bianca. 'The most popular magician in Vegas does this sawing-a-girl-in-half

311

trick, where the top half of the girl drags herself offstage. He uses a contortionist and a girl who, due to a congenital disorder, has no legs. That's my *job*.'

'Look,' said Sage. 'I know what you do is very difficult ...'

Bianca dug a vicious nail into the wood of the desk. 'You think you know how *difficult* my job is? The first trick I ever learnt with Armand was the Zigzag Effect, where he shoved me into that tiny cabinet, cut me up and rearranged me. After that was Radium Girl, where he'd stick a whole tube through my stomach and pass objects through. Then there were the constant variations on the sawn-in-half effect. Then there was Origami, where he folded me up into a tiny box and stuck swords into me. Twister and the Wringer, where I get flattened like a pancake or twisted up into a knot. Or the Dagger Head Box, which should be self-explanatory, as should the Guillotine. And my favourite? Impalement. That's where I have to work every freaking muscle in my body to get into this contraption that makes me look like I'm balancing on the tip of a sword. A sword that Armand then pushes me down onto, impaling me through the stomach. I go limp, and everyone thinks I'm dead. Until the Great and Wondrous Armand rescues me – bringing me back to life with a kiss.'

She spoke faster and faster, her voice cracking.

'And the worst one?' Tears began to stream down Bianca's

cheeks, creating rivulets of mascara and eyeliner. 'Worse than getting cut up or stabbed or set on fire or impaled? The worst trick is when he makes me *disappear into nothing*. Well, I know that trick too.'

She took a deep breath and turned her head to the ceiling, trying to stop the tears from flowing.

'But it was you that changed everything,' she said. 'You *listened*. You told me that things could change. And then you ruined everything.'

'It was you who took the money, wasn't it?' said Sage. 'You'd been siphoning funds from Armand for years without him realising.'

'I *deserved* that money,' said Bianca. 'Do you know how many times Armand gave me a raise, in the five years I worked for him? Zero. Zero times. He never would have even noticed if you hadn't pointed it out.'

'He knew it was you, didn't he?'

Bianca nodded. 'I had a plan. I was going to quit. Jason had been after me for months – I was going to give in and be his assistant. Break my own rule. But then Armand told me I had to pay it all back or he'd go to the police. He said I was finished in the magic business. He was going to tell everyone, and I couldn't let him do that.' Bianca's voice started to crack, but she still didn't look up. 'I tried to talk to him, but he wouldn't listen. I just needed some *time* to figure things out. I thought if I could just put him somewhere. Just for a day or two. Then I could sort it all out and fix everything.'

'But it got out of hand.'

Bianca nodded. Her nails raked across the surface of the desk again, and Sage shivered. She looked up at the concrete stairs again and imagined running up them to freedom.

'Looking for your handsome prince?' asked Bianca, her voice suddenly sour. 'He's not coming. I saw you arrive at the theatre this morning, and sent him a message telling him you were in danger. At your house.'

'*Am* I in danger?' Sage wasn't sure she wanted to hear the answer.

Bianca bit her lip. 'I didn't want you to get caught up in this. I tried to make you leave when I realised you were starting to figure it out.'

Sage's heart started to hammer. 'So … what happens now?'

Bianca still hadn't met Sage's eyes. 'Well, it doesn't look like this is a ghost story any more. So I suppose we need a villain. There's no other way.'

'And who's the villain?'

'Well,' said Bianca. 'It could be Jason, so desperate to poach me that he does away with Armand and steals Herb's greatest trick. Or it could be Herb, desperate to claw his way to fame and stardom.' She shook her head with a sad ghost of a smile. 'Or it could even be you.'

'We can't all be the villain,' said Sage.

'No,' said Bianca. 'And I can't choose. So I thought I'd get you to choose for me.'

Sage shrugged. 'I choose you,' she said. 'Or at a pinch, Jason.'

'That's not how it works.' Bianca indicated the four envelopes sitting on the table. 'Did you ever read those Choose Your Own Adventure novels when you were little?'

Sage nodded.

'Well, this is going to be a bit like that.' Bianca pulled out a cigarette lighter.

'Inside each of these envelopes is a possible ending to our story,' she said. 'In the first one I let you go. I release Armand. I make Jason Jones back off from Herb. Everyone lives happily ever after. Except I would almost certainly go to jail, so I'm going to use some of my magic skills to make sure you don't pick that one.'

'So what are the other options?'

'Number two is I go to the police and explain that it was Herb who kidnapped Armand, in order to wrest control of the show. I have an amazing array of evidence. He'll probably go to prison.'

'But wouldn't Armand tell the police it was you?'

Bianca shrugged. 'I doubt you'll pick that envelope either.'

Sage looked down at the four envelopes, then back up at Bianca. Bianca's eyes were red-rimmed and wild, but Sage didn't doubt that she was still completely in control.

'Number three is where I confess that Jason Jones kidnapped Armand in order to steal his greatest magic secrets,' Bianca continued. 'And he forced me to help him. I will of course *rescue* Armand, and be the hero of the story. Armand hates Jason, so he'll be glad to go along with it. Plus he has plenty of evidence that Jason's greatest magic skill is stealing other people's ideas.'

Sage felt a chill wash over her. 'And the fourth envelope?'

Bianca toyed with her coffee cup. 'In the fourth envelope, nobody finds Armand. I have a seat booked on the next flight to London, and thanks to the money Jason gave me for stealing Herb's Houdini effect I can afford to set myself up over there and start my own solo show.'

'So … you just leave Armand to die?'

Bianca's eyes widened. 'Oh, I don't think he'll *die*,' she said. 'Surely someone clever will find him sooner or later. But I'll be long gone.'

Sage swallowed. 'A-and … what about me? What happens to me?'

A crinkle appeared in Bianca's brow. 'I–I don't know,' she said and sighed. 'I suppose I'll just have to make you vanish too.'

Sage wrapped her hands around the seat of her chair to stop them from shaking. She'd never felt so cold in her life.

'So,' said Bianca. 'Time to narrow it down. Pick an envelope.' She moved her hands over the table, mixing the envelopes and then lining them up in a row again.

Sage hesitated, then pointed at the first envelope on her left.

'Interesting choice,' murmured Bianca, picking up the envelope. She held it against her forehead with her eyes closed, as if she were absorbing its contents. Then she held the envelope in front of her and clicked on the cigarette lighter. Flames curled up the envelope, and she dropped it into the metal bucket, where it curled into a glowing husk.

'Second choice?' Bianca's face was wreathed in smoke.

Sage pointed at the next envelope on her left. Bianca's eyebrows raised, and she picked up the envelope and set fire to it in the same manner as the first.

'Last choice.'

Sage pointed at the next envelope in the row.

'Are you sure?' asked Bianca. 'You don't want to change your choice? You can, I don't mind.'

Sage heard Herb's voice in her mind. *If you let people think they have a choice, they're much easier to fool.* She hesitated.

'Go on,' urged Bianca.

Sage pointed to the envelope on the right. Bianca caught

her lip between her teeth. She set the envelope on fire and dropped it into the bucket, then picked up the last envelope and held it for a moment before visibly steeling herself and passing it to Sage.

'I want you to open it,' she said.

Sage took it in her right hand, trying not to tremble. She broke the seal on the back with her thumb and lifted the flap.

'What does it say?'

Sage slid her left hand up her thigh and stuffed into her pocket the other envelope she'd slipped off the table when she'd first sat down. She then unfolded the scrap of paper inside the envelope. 'It says…' She took a deep breath. 'It says *Dear Bianca. Nice try. Love, Armand.*'

Bianca snatched the piece of paper from Sage's hand, stared at it, then screwed it into a ball.

'Seriously,' she said with a hard laugh. 'Do you really think I am so dumb that you, a teenager who only discovered magic two weeks ago, could fool me?'

Sage stood up, feeling more confidant. 'No,' she said. 'I don't. I know I don't have a hope in hell of fooling you.'

Bianca's eyes finally met Sage's, and her face crumpled. She groped in her pocket for a ring of keys.

'But Herb can,' said Sage. 'And so can Armand.'

Bianca scrambled over to the iron door and unlocked

it with shaking hands before wrenching it open. The room was tiny, little more than a cupboard lined with empty metal shelves. A little washbasin and drain took up the back wall. A figure sat on a plastic chair, his back to the door. Next to him there was a dirty mattress and a stack of empty takeaway cartons.

'*No*,' whispered Bianca.

The figure started to clap, slowly. 'Bravo. Very well played.' Herb turned around. 'Hi, Bianca.'

Sage felt an overwhelming surge of relief. She and Herb had worked it all out on the phone the night before, but knowing he was there wasn't the same as actually *seeing* him. Her knees buckled, and she gripped the back of the chair.

'Seriously,' said Herb. 'Really great job. The way you sabotaged my effect while at the same time stealing it for Jason Jones?' He shook his head. 'A masterstroke.'

'Admit it,' said Bianca through clenched teeth. 'I fooled you.'

Herb spread his hands. 'You fooled me.'

'I'm a better magician than you. Say it.'

'Gladly. You're clearly far more skilled than I am. You had me fooled, one hundred per cent. The amount of planning that must have gone into this ...' Herb shook his head. 'It's really quite extraordinary. I take my hat off to you.'

Bianca hesitated for a moment, as though she'd been expecting him to fight back.

'The only thing is,' said Herb. 'Well, you've got one problem. One weakness.'

Bianca narrowed her eyes. 'What, that I'm a *woman*?'

Herb laughed. 'No. If anything, the fact that you're a woman is the best part of your routine. It's the perfect piece of misdirection. Nobody would ever expect you to be the scheming villain.'

'So what?'

Herb shrugged. 'You're clearly absolutely deranged.'

Bianca's eyes flicked around the room. 'Where is he?'

'I'm right here,' said Armand, arriving at the bottom of the stairs behind them. 'Sorry I'm late. I had to shower and change. Thirteen days in the same clothes can make one a little *ripe*.'

Bianca stared at him. 'How did you do it?' she asked. 'You're no Houdini.'

'No,' said Armand with an apologetic grimace. 'I'm not. And I didn't really do anything. It was all Sage.'

He flashed Sage a quick smile, and Sage caught her breath. In that smile she saw a shadow of the charismatic young magician she'd seen in the newspaper clipping.

Bianca's face twisted into something dark and ugly, but she seemed completely lost for words.

Armand gestured at Sage. 'Please,' he said. 'I'd like to hear the whole story from the beginning.'

'Um.' Sage, sat down again to think. 'You've always been unhappy as an assistant,' she said to Bianca. 'You saw how badly your own mother was treated as a magician's assistant. Every night you get cut up and tied up. Every night you have to be a victim. And you were sick of it. So you asked Armand if you could change the act. Become a proper magic duo, not a magician and assistant. Wear some real clothes. Take credit for some of the work you do.'

She glanced at Armand, who nodded. 'And I said no,' he said. 'The last time I let my assistant be more than an assistant, it didn't go so well for me.'

Sage looked back at Bianca. 'That story you told me about Herb asking to do a solo portion,' she said. 'That was true, wasn't it? Except it was *you* who asked Armand for your own spot.'

'Except for the mice,' muttered Bianca. 'I didn't kill the mice.'

'I assume you went to Jason Jones to ask for a partnership as well?' Armand asked.

Bianca's head twitched in a slight nod. 'He only wanted me as an assistant.'

'And when Armand found out about the missing money, you decided to take matters into your own hands.'

Armand nodded. 'She brought me a coffee,' he said. 'The next thing I knew, I was locked in there.' He nodded his head towards the adjoining room. 'She told me to forget about the money, and give her a solo spot in the show. I refused. She told me I wouldn't be released until I agreed.'

'How did you get him down here?' asked Sage, curiously.

Bianca shrugged. 'I'm stronger than I look.'

'Wait,' said Herb, frowning at Armand. 'You were locked down here for thirteen days, and all you had to do to be let free was give her a solo spot in the show?'

'I don't appreciate blackmail.'

'It wasn't like I was starving him,' said Bianca, a touch defensively. 'There's a mattress in there, and I brought him food every day.' She nodded towards the shopping bag on the floor. 'There's even a toilet, so it wasn't like he had to pee in a bucket or anything.'

Armand's mouth narrowed into a thin sliver.

'We were there, weren't we?' asked Sage. 'We came back to the theatre when you were trying to move Armand from his dressing-room to down here. That was why you locked us in the storeroom.'

'I *told* you it was sabotage!' said Herb.

'So the next day you tell us that Armand has gone away on some urgent personal business,' said Sage. 'And suddenly you remember about the theatre curse, which you figure will be a nice distraction. But whenever I suggested that the two things might be linked, you changed the subject. That was when I first started to wonder. And I think it's where you lost control of the whole situation. You love the idea of the supernatural so much, you got carried away with fabricating this ghost story.'

Bianca's expression turned icy.

'Then you let your anger get away with you,' Sage said. 'What was supposed to be a simple piece of blackmail exploded into something much more complicated. First Herb decided to take over from Armand, which made you decide to take him down too. So you stole the secret of Houdini's Return and sold it to Jason Jones. Then you realised that I was getting suspicious, so you amped up the whole Renaldo the Remarkable thing, and directed the curse on yourself – writing that message on your mirror, and faking the accident with your ankle and the stage light.'

Herb shook his head. 'That was a beautiful piece of mis-direction,' he said admiringly.

'You decided I was getting to be too much trouble, so you tried to make me leave. You drove a wedge between me and Herb, and when that didn't work, you pulled off your most remarkable piece of magic – my dream with the ghost.'

She pulled the ghost photo out of her bag.

'I thought that this photo of Warren was a photo of

323

Jasmine,' she said. 'But what I didn't notice was that the real ghost was there all along.' She pointed to the figure behind the curtain. 'This photo was taken at around midnight – after I'd fallen asleep. It's the ghost I saw in my dream. The ghost of Jasmine, Renaldo's wife.'

'Also known as Bianca in a wig,' said Herb. 'It's totally obvious.'

'This photo didn't prove that there was a ghost,' said Sage to Bianca. 'It proved that my dream hadn't been a dream at all. It had been real. You drugged me.'

Bianca shrugged miserably. 'I've never been a great sleeper,' she said. 'I have this nightmare where I'm trapped inside a wooden box and I can't get out. My doctor gave me sleeping pills. Strong ones. I used them on Armand, too.'

'So you set up this room to make it look dreamlike. The things from Herb's desk. The backwards letters. I assume the wig and the white dress came from your costume box.'

Herb frowned. 'Does that mean you faked all the letters?'

Bianca seemed to shrink a little. 'Only the backwards ones,' she said softly. 'All the other letters are real. I've been getting them for years. The one that I left on your desk? I got that after my very first performance, the first time I performed the Zigzag Effect. I was sixteen years old. I hoped it would make you leave.'

Sage felt a surge of sympathy. Bianca's life *had* been

awful. She had always been treated like an object, just a pretty thing that could be cut up and rearranged as needed to distract the audience. But that didn't mean she wasn't still very, very dangerous.

'So what happened next?' asked Armand, who almost looked like he was enjoying himself.

'Bianca made up a bunch of stuff about Herb, to throw the suspicion onto him,' said Sage. 'Then she sabotaged Houdini's Return.' She glanced at Bianca, who shrugged.

'I fiddled with the mechanism on the water barrel,' she said. 'So you couldn't get out.'

Herb's face twisted. 'You could have killed me.'

'I *saved* you!' she replied savagely. 'Remember *I* was the one who pushed the barrel over and let you out.'

'And you want me to be grateful for that?'

Bianca's face returned to its former state of icy blankness.

'So then Jason Jones made the copyright infringement claim against Herb.'

'*He did what?*' Armand's usually expressionless exterior suddenly turned purple with rage.

'Bianca stole my new effect,' said Herb with a scowl. 'She sold it to Jason, who claimed it as his own. He's trying to get me thrown out of the Magician's League.'

'Like *hell* he is,' fumed Armand. 'I will not let that slimy weasel get away with that again.'

'Again?' Herb frowned. 'Jason stole from you?'

'How do you think he got his first big break?' Armand's hands moved instinctively, as if to wring an invisible neck.

Sage nodded. 'He practically bragged about it to me.'

Armand rounded on Bianca. 'How *could* you?' he said. 'Locking me away is one thing, but *this*? A magician's ideas are his *most prized possessions*. To steal them is ... *monstrous*.'

Bianca winced. 'I thought he just wanted to know about the mechanism on the barrel, so he could use it for one of his own tricks. I–I didn't know he'd steal the whole thing and try to destroy Herb.'

Armand's lips drew together in a tight, angry line. 'He's done it before,' he said. 'And he will *never* do it again. I'll make sure of it.'

Bianca seemed to shrink away from him. She looked truly miserable. Sage felt a surge of pity. She was sure Bianca was telling the truth this time. She hadn't meant for Herb to get so hurt.

Armand took a breath and closed his eyes, visibly calming himself. 'So what next?' he said to Sage.

'Well, I had two plausible suspects: Jason, who wanted to get rid of Armand in order to steal Herb's effects and poach Bianca; or Herb, who had got rid of Armand to further his own career. I was ready to throw in the towel – Bianca's campaign to get me to leave nearly worked. But as

I was leaving I stopped to take one last look at the theatre.' She nodded to Herb. 'You told me that to really appreciate Melbourne, you have to look up.'

'So?' said Armand.

'So Bianca told me that Renaldo the Remarkable was a magician who performed in this theatre in the 1920s,' said Sage. 'Except he didn't. The Lyric Theatre wasn't built until 1932, and it was originally the Lyric *Cinema*, not a theatre at all. It was quite a landmark at the time, totally state-of-the-art, with a fancy projection room as well as an underground cellar to safely store the film.'

'So she made up Ron the Raconteur?' Herb snorted. 'Figures.'

'Actually, there *was* a Renaldo the Remarkable,' said Sage. 'I googled him too. He was a real magician, and he did die onstage. In Aberdeen, Scotland. And there was no wife called Jasmine. His wife was called Laura, and she remarried after he died and had five children.'

'I have an active imagination,' said Bianca. 'Nothing wrong with embellishing a story a little.'

'After that I found Armand's phone in your dressing-table drawer,' Sage said to Bianca. 'I realised that you'd lied to me about Herb. And I found the empty bottle of jasmine perfume. So I called Herb, who came back to the theatre after you left last night and released Armand.'

'And here we all are,' said Armand.

'You can't prove any of this,' said Bianca, her eyes flashing. 'I was careful.'

'Not nearly careful enough.' Sage drew her phone from her pocket. 'I've recorded this whole conversation.'

Bianca stared at the phone as if it was an impossible piece of technology. Her eyes closed, and Sage saw a flash of what looked like relief pass over her face. 'So what happens now?' she asked.

Armand shrugged. 'I call the police and you go to jail.'

'No,' said Sage. Armand turned to her in surprise, as did Herb.

Sage bit her lip. 'The thing is, Bianca's right to be angry. Armand, you've treated her like crap. The life of a magician's assistant is a pretty rubbish one. Bianca's made a lot of mistakes, but I can see why it happened.'

Bianca's bottom lip began to tremble, and she looked up at the bare lightbulb, as if to stop herself from crying.

'You were my friend,' said Sage, softly. 'I saw how sad and lonely you were. What you did was wrong, but I don't think you deserve to go to prison.'

Herb nodded slowly. 'Sage is right,' he said. 'The victimisation of female assistants is totally creepy. It's pretty much the one industry in this world that hasn't moved in any way since the beginning of last century. I think I'd go nuts if my whole life was being ritually tied up and dismembered, and my only thanks was a paltry salary and some stalkery fan mail.'

Armand's face clouded over. 'You think I should just let her go?' he said, his voice rising in disbelief.

Herb tilted his head to one side. 'She's just done such a beautiful job of all this,' he said. 'I mean, it's a bit *too* elaborate, messy in parts. But the execution has been utterly brilliant. I'd hate to see that skill waste away in some kind of low-security correctional facility.' He glanced at Armand. 'There must be a better way to do this.'

'I don't see that there is,' said Armand. 'I'm sorry.'

Bianca's eyes brimmed with tears. 'I understand,' she said softly.

'No,' said Sage. 'It isn't fair. She has a ticket to London. You'd never see her again.'

Armand's face was stony cold.

'Please,' said Sage. 'You owe it to her.'

Armand sighed. 'Fine,' he said to Bianca at last. 'Use your ticket. Start your own show in London. Become someone else's assistant. Move to the country and take up chicken farming. I don't care. Just don't ever come back here.'

Bianca's brows lifted in sudden, wild hope. 'What about Jason? What about Houdini's Return?'

Armand scowled. 'I'll take care of Jason,' he said shortly.

'I told you, I'm not letting him get away with this again.'

Bianca drew a deep, shuddering breath. 'Really?' she said. 'You'd just let me go? No trick?'

'You seem to be the expert here,' said Armand. 'It makes sense that you should perform one final trick yourself.'

Bianca swallowed.

'Disappear,' said Armand.

17. Restoration: an item is destroyed, then restored to its original state.

Sage walked slowly around Yoshi Lear's classroom, looking at all the photos pinned to the walls.

A newly married couple holding a chalkboard sign that read *forever*.

Santa Claus standing in a living room, looking dubiously at a fireplace.

A posed diorama of the moon landing.

Sage paused before her own photo. It was a double exposure she'd taken of Warren, superimposed over a photo of Herb posing onstage, brandishing a magic wand. She'd photographed Warren up close, and the double exposure made it look as if he were twice the size of Herb. Herb had an arm stretched out in a *ta-dah* pose, as if he had transformed something into a giant bunny, or produced him from thin

331

air. It had taken her ages to get the exposure settings right on her new camera, scribbling out sums on the back of an envelope to make sure that the image wouldn't end up too bright.

She hoped Yoshi would count a double exposure as an undoctored photograph. She had taken what was in front of the camera – there had been no digital wizardry, nor any manipulation of the negative beyond exposing it twice, superimposing one image over the other. It was, after all, how the girls had accidentally created the final Cottingley Fairies photo.

Yoshi called them all back to their seats, dimmed the lights and clicked the projector on. A black-and-white photo of a woman holding a toddler appeared on the screen. They were both filthy, with sad, exhausted faces. The woman was looking at something behind the cameraman, her mouth slightly open as if she was begging for someone to help her and her child.

'So you have taken a photo that is a lie,' he said. 'But is there any such thing as a photo that *doesn't* lie? Every decision you make as a photographer – the exposure, your choice of colour, the focal point, even the time of day – each of these decisions affects the final photo. Each decision is like a little white lie that *alters reality*. This photo was taken by Dorothea Lange in 1939, and it perfectly captures how we think of the US Great Depression. The despair. The hunger. But it wasn't the only photo Ms Lange took that day.'

He clicked his remote again, and another photo appeared. It was the same woman and toddler, but this time the woman was laughing, and the toddler's head was tilted back, exposing a wide, cheeky grin on a clean face.

'The first photo is a famous one,' said Yoshi. 'It's been used in many books about the Great Depression. But the second one doesn't quite fit. If things were so bad, then why are they laughing? What could they possibly have to laugh about? Ms Lange wrote in her notes that the baby's face was washed for the second photo. Does that make it less truthful?'

Sage opened her folio and pulled out two photos as she listened to Yoshi talk. Both photos were of Bianca. One was Bianca onstage, the stage lights sparkling on her sequins. She was dazzlingly beautiful, her eyes bright and her smile wide. The second photo was Bianca in her dressing-room, the night that she and Sage had slept at the theatre. Her mouth was open in mid sentence, her hands up and active, like she was explaining something. She wore no makeup, and she looked ... real. She remembered what Herb had said when they were locked in the storeroom.

The painting is still beautiful – very beautiful. But it's more of an organic beauty. Like something grew wild and natural,

*and that's why it's beautiful. It's not like the first painting –
that painting took years to prepare. Every brushstroke is perfect.
But my painting isn't perfect. It's real, and real is infinitely
more beautiful.'*

Except Bianca hadn't been relaxed and comfortable when
Sage had taken that photo. The second photo, the one that
was beautiful because it felt *real*, was the one that was a lie.

Yoshi came over to Sage as she was packing up her notes.
'How did you go with your ghost photo?' he asked with a
smile.

'It wasn't a ghost,' said Sage. 'Just someone standing in
the wings.'

'Are you disappointed?'

Sage remembered being snuggled under a blanket
in Bianca's dressing-room, sharing secrets and eating
Vietnamese takeaway. Bianca had been her first Melbourne
friend.

'Yes,' she said.

∿∿∿

Sage strode along the wet streets, filling her lungs with great
breaths of cold air. She didn't mind it so much, now she was
used to it. And it helped that Mum had taken her shopping
and bought her new cashmere gloves, a chevron-patterned
scarf, a cute knitted beret and a stylish wool felt coat. Cold
weather definitely had fashion-related silver linings.

It was to be her last visit to the theatre for a while – school was starting on Monday and she didn't want to have to juggle homework, new friends, new boyfriend, Yoshi Lear's classes *and* her theatre job. Herb had texted her to say that Armand had found a new assistant – an ex-circus performer called Georgia, as well as a part-time usher to replace Sage. Herb had also said that Armand was being much more open and talkative, and had suggested they overhaul the show, getting rid of all the creepy cutting-up-the-assistant tricks and replacing them with brand-new effects.

Sage smelled the steamy hot ginger and garlic even before she turned the corner to Mr Pham's. Her stomach rumbled. She spotted Herb immediately, sitting inside at their usual table. His face split into his usual wide, ridiculous grin when he saw her approaching, and he put his hand up to the window. Sage paused, touching her own hand to the glass and grinning back at him. Then she pushed open the door and went inside.

'You're late,' said Herb, standing up.

'Only five minutes,' said Sage.

He wrapped his arms around her, and she slid into his embrace, feeling extra bulky because of her coat. She rested her head on his chest, and heard his heart beating. Herb stroked her hair, and then dropped a kiss on her head. Sage looked up at him.

'Hi,' she said.

'Hi yourself.'

She reached up on tiptoes, and he bent his head down to kiss her. His mouth was hot and tasted like green tea. Sage sighed happily.

'Get a room!' called Mr Pham from the kitchen. Sage giggled and pulled away.

'How are the photos looking?' asked Herb as Sage sat down.

'Good,' said Sage. 'I'm working on a new assignment.'

Mr Pham came over with a plate of spring rolls. 'Hello, Miss Sage,' he said with a smile. 'Herb tells me you won't work with him anymore. I can't blame you, really.'

'Hey!' said Herb.

'I have to focus on my education,' said Sage with a grin. 'Herb can be pretty distracting.'

Mr Pham raised his eyebrows. 'So I see,' he said, and disappeared back into the kitchen.

'Looking forward to the show tonight?' asked Herb. 'Being an audience member for once, instead of having to do all the work?'

'How's it looking?' asked Sage. 'How is the new assistant?'

Herb tilted his head from side to side. 'Not bad,' he said, grudgingly. 'She can't quite get the timing right on Assistant's Revenge.'

'It's a tricky one,' said Sage. 'Have you made any big changes yet?'

'A few. You'll see tonight.' Herb's smile was mysterious.

It was the first show post-Bianca. Herb had promised that there would be a special surprise.

'I saw in the paper that Jason Jones has cancelled his Arts Centre show,' said Sage, dipping her spring roll in sweet chilli sauce.

Herb smirked. 'He's been kicked out of the Magician's League.'

'How did Armand do it?'

'Apparently he had proof that Jason stole from *him*, back when he was Armand's assistant.'

'So why didn't he use it then?'

Herb chewed thoughtfully. 'I think Jason might have broken his heart a little bit,' he said. 'Armand didn't want to admit that he had been fooled.'

Mr Pham came back with steaming plates of squid and fried chicken. 'Have you told her yet?' he asked Herb.

'Not yet,' said Herb, with a sly glance at Sage.

'Told me what?'

'Get on with it,' said Mr Pham, heading back to the kitchen.

Herb leaned forward, his face shining with excitement. 'I know this guy who owns a nightclub in the city,' he said.

'He's offered me a job, doing my own magic show. Cabaret-style. It'd only be close-up stuff, cards and coins. Nothing too flashy. But it'd be my *own show*.'

'That's awesome!' said Sage. 'I can't wait until I'm eighteen and I can come and see you!'

Herb chuckled. 'I'm sure we can sneak you in before then,' he said. 'As long as you promise to behave.'

'Oh, I promise.'

'I think it'll be really good for me,' said Herb. 'I think it's time I flew solo for a while.'

Sage felt something twist in her stomach. He *was* only talking about magic, right?

Herb noticed her sudden frown, and laughed, leaning in to kiss her quickly. 'I didn't mean *that*,' he grinned at her. 'Definitely not that. On the relationship front, I definitely wish to fly tandem for the foreseeable future.'

He squeezed Sage's hand and ducked his head slightly to meet her eyes. 'Okay?'

She smiled. 'Okay.'

'No, I just meant that I might enjoy working on a solo routine,' Herb went on. 'Like Derren Brown or someone. No assistant.'

Sage nodded.

Herb ducked his head again. 'Unless *you* wanted to—'

'No,' said Sage firmly. 'Absolutely not.'

'I didn't think so.'

'So is this the surprise?' she asked. 'Your most excellent news?'

'Nope,' said Herb with a grin. 'The surprise is yet to come.' He glanced at his watch. 'I've got to be backstage in twenty minutes. You're good at maths. If we finish off all this food, how many kisses can we fit in before the curtain rises?'

Sage laughed. 'Mr Pham?' she called. 'Can we grab the bill?'

'I'd like to invite a friend of mine onto the stage,' said Armand. 'He's a very promising young talent, and I think you'll like what he has to show you.'

Armand left the stage as the curtains swung shut. Sage held her breath.

The curtains reopened to reveal a blackboard, sitting on the left side of the stage, near the wings. In the centre of the stage there was a pot containing a small shrub, completely bare of flowers or foliage. Herb emerged from the wings, walked up to it, and considered it for a moment. Sage felt a grin spread across her face. Herb hadn't *said* that he was working on a new effect, but she'd known he had to be. Herb couldn't stop.

'There are lots of different kinds of magic,' he said to the audience. 'People often ask me, being a magician, whether I can still enjoy watching other people do magic. The answer is yes. Understanding how things work doesn't make them any less extraordinary. Physicists who can grasp the ways in which the universe is put together still find themselves moved to tears when they look at the stars. Psychologists still feel that sense of wonder and endless possibility when they fall in love. And botanists are still filled with joy when what looks like a dead twig suddenly sprouts with life.'

He waved a hand over the bare shrub, and Sage heard gasps as green shoots appeared at the tips of each branch. These shoots curled outwards as the shrub started to grow, branching out and pushing up until it was all green, and taller than Herb.

'Life,' he said, walking around the shrub, which was now a small tree, 'life and love are the most extraordinary feats of magic. I'd like someone to join me up here. Raise your hand if you're in love.'

Sage felt her cheeks grow hot. She started to raise her hand, slowly.

Herb looked out over the audience and pointed at a young woman with curly red hair. 'You, madam. Could you please come up here?'

The woman made her way up onto the stage as the tree continued to spread and grow. Bunches of leaves clustered together in little explosions of green.

'Please,' said Herb, handing the woman a clipboard and pen. 'Write down the name of the person you love, then fold up the paper and put it in your pocket.'

The woman did as instructed, and Georgia appeared to whisk the clipboard away once she'd finished.

'Now,' said Herb, positioning the woman in front of the tree and motioning for her to close her eyes. 'I want you to think about the person you love. Picture their face in your mind. Think about the two of you together, walking in a forest. You're surrounded by rustling leaves. Autumn leaves. I think autumn is the most romantic season, don't you?'

The woman nodded. Herb waved a hand, and the lights in the theatre switched to a golden orange, bathing the stage in warm light. The tree stopped growing.

'Open your eyes,' said Herb.

The woman looked around. Then, one leaf on the tree trembled and fell. Another tumbled after it. A fan was switched on somewhere backstage, and the leaves all started to fall, tumbling and swirling in the air. It looked beautiful.

'They say that you get one happy day for each autumn leaf you catch,' said Herb to the woman. 'I want you to catch one. Just one.'

The leaves danced and spun around them. After a few attempts, the woman caught hold of a leaf.

'Hold it in your hand,' said Herb. 'This is your lucky day.

Look at the leaf you've caught. There's something written on it.'

The woman looked at the leaf, and suddenly went bright red.

'Can you tell us what it says?' said Herb.

The woman stared up at him, astonished. 'It – it says…
Julia.'

Herb smiled. 'And is Julia the name of the person you love?'

The woman nodded, her cheeks flaming red.

The audience burst into applause. Herb turned back to the tree, which had shrunk back to a shrub, surrounded by fallen leaves. There were four flowers sprouting from the tree – a red one, a yellow one, a white one and a pink one. Herb plucked the flowers, and offered them to the woman.

'Choose one,' he said.

The woman bit her lip and selected the pink flower. Herb leaned in conspiratorially. 'Give it to Julia,' he said, and then stepped back. 'Another round of applause, for our wonderful volunteer!'

The audience cheered, and the woman took the pink rose back to her seat.

'Wait!' called Herb. The woman stopped and turned around. 'I'm so sorry! I can't believe I was so rude. I didn't ask you your name.'

'It's Alice,' called the woman.

'Lovely to meet you, Alice,' said Herb. He swung the blackboard over to reveal the other side. Written in white chalk were the words *Alice will give Julia the pink flower.*

Sage felt a smile spread over her face as Herb took his bow, and a glowing, happy warmth spread inside her.

'Don't worry, fair maiden!' cried the wizard, leaping up onto the bed and striking a pose. 'I shall rescue you from that evil monster!'

Sage was tied to the foot of her bed, a pair of what she sincerely hoped were clean socks in her mouth.

'Do not try and fight me, Monster!' said the wizard. 'Your axe may be large, but I am stronger than you! And cleverer!'

He pulled out his magic wand, and pointed it at the wardrobe monster with great enthusiasm. '*Expelliarmus!*'

'Hurrah!' mumbled Sage through the socks. 'The monster is dead!'

The wizard gave her a pitying look. '*Expelliarmus* doesn't *kill* the monster,' he explained laboriously. 'It only *disarms* him.'

After another few minutes of bed-jumping and spell-casting, the wardrobe monster was declared defeated, and Sage was untied.

'Oh, kind sir!' she said, her mouth feeling unpleasantly fluffy. 'How can I ever thank you for your brave deed?'

'And now I claim my reward!' The wizard eyed her hopefully. 'Ice-cream!'

'Nice try,' said Sage. 'But it's way too early for ice-cream.'

'Magicians eat ice-cream for breakfast all the time.'

'Do they really?' Sage stood up and tried to brush an invisible crease from her skirt. 'Well, maybe you should learn a spell to turn Vegemite toast into ice-cream.'

Zacky scowled at her. 'I'm thinking maybe I won't be a magician when I grow up,' he said, with an aloof toss of his head.

'Oh?'

He nodded. 'Maybe I'll be a ghost hunter instead.'

Sage groaned inwardly.

'Or an astronaut.' Zacky started to jump on the bed again. 'Or maybe a fisherman. Because I like boats. Do you like boats, Sage?'

Sage laughed. 'Yes, Zacky. I like boats.'

'But I don't like fish. Do you think I can still be a fisherman if I don't like fish?'

'Sage?' It was Mum, standing in the door to Sage's room. 'Are you ready?'

Zacky leapt off the bed and galloped to his room. Sage swallowed, and glanced at the calendar on her wall. The red circle was still there, around today's date. Her friends were still there too, frozen in the click of the camera. They were having a good time. Maybe there'd be new friends at this school. New photo opportunities.

She tried to remember why she'd been so frightened of the red circle.

'Darling?' Mum took a step into Sage's room. 'Are you ready?'

Sage pulled her new blazer from the back of her desk chair, and shrugged it on.

'Yep,' she said. 'I'm ready.'

Author's note

Most of the magic tricks in this book are real – and all of them are possible. If you'd like to see them in action, there are heaps of great videos online. Check out Penn and Teller's cups-and-balls, and Derren Brown's *Enigma* show. If you look hard enough, you can also find out the secrets to these effects, but make sure you really want to know. Once revealed, a magic trick is never quite the same.

Although Yoshi Lear isn't a real person, the photos he shows Sage are genuine ones. You can see them here: liliwilkinson.com.au/zigzag-photos

Acknowledgements

Thanks first of all to the wonderful Onions – especially Jodie and Hilary, for continuing to be the best publishers and editors a girl could wish for. People always ask whether I resent the editing process – there isn't a NO emphatic enough. An unedited book is like a bunch of raw ingredients before they've been cooked.

Thanks also to my agent Kate Schafer-Testerman, who tirelessly pitches my books and deciphers my contracts.

Thanks as usual to the made-of-awesome Sarah Dollard, whose screenwritery brilliance knows no bounds, and who always finds time to help me nut out thorny plot dilemmas.

Thanks to my mum, who always reads my books before they're published, and my dad, who always reads them afterwards.

And thanks to my wonderful husband Michael, who is ever generous with listening, advice and hugs.

About the author

Lili Wilkinson was first published at age twelve in *Voiceworks* magazine. After studying Creative Arts at Melbourne University and teaching English in Japan, Lili worked on insideadog.com.au (a books website for teen readers), the Inky Awards and the Inkys Creative Reading Prize at the Centre for Youth Literature, State Library of Victoria. She is completing a PhD in Creative Writing and spends most of her time reading and writing books for teenagers. She has written eight books that are published in eight countries.

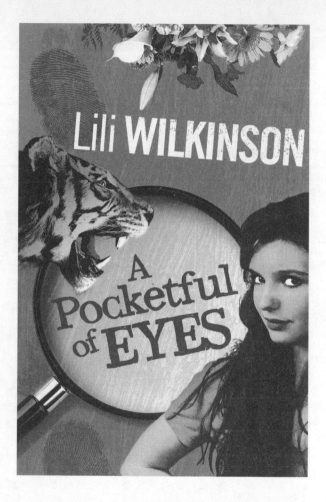

Lili WILKINSON

A Pocketful of EYES

'Wry, sly, funny, smart, and very entertaining.'
JACLYN MORIARTY

'Lili Wilkinson is like a coolgeekgirl Agatha Christie.'
SIMMONE HOWELL

L♥ve-shy

Lili WILKINSON

'Chock-full of sass.'
LEANNE HALL

'Penny Drummond is smart and funny, vulnerable and fierce.'
MELINA MARCHETTA

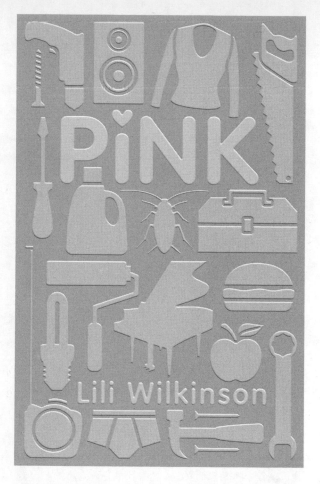

'*Pink* is laugh-out-loud and cringe-in-corners funny.'
SIMMONE HOWELL

'I laughed, I cried and I occasionally burst into song.'
JUSTINE LARBALESTIER

'Fun, razor-sharp and moving, *Pink* – like love –
is a many-splendoured thing.'
JOHN GREEN